Broken

AMI SPENCER

First Edition July 2022
Published by Ami Spencer
Copyright © 2022 Ami Spencer
ISBN: 9798836764388

Cover Design: Melissa Tereze
Editor: Charlie Knight

All rights reserved. This book is for your personal enjoyment only. This book or any portion thereof may not be reproduced or used in any manner without the express permission of the author.

This is a work of fiction. All characters & happenings in this publication are fictitious and any resemblance to real persons (living or dead), locales or events is purely coincidental.

Acknowledgments

There are definitely quite a few people without whom this would not have been possible.

Jourdyn Kelly, for taking the time and offering to read over and work with me when I threw it out there in the abyss of Facebook that it was struggling with a particular chapter. When the time comes that we meet face to face, no doubt I'll fangirl a stupid amount. Forgive me, I'm but a simple lesbian who loves Eve and Lainey Sumptor.

Jayne Finlay-Langley for being the friend I confided in when I thought about having to actually let people who knew me read this book. I apologise that we can never look each other in the eye again, especially after Chapter Twenty-Nine!

TJ Dallas, Skye Kilaen and Monna Herring for being patient and tolerant through my initial, fragmented beta reads, your feedback and advice was invaluable.

Charlie Knight, your advice, encouragement and support never ceases to amaze me. I couldn't have asked for a more understanding, approachable and helpful editor for my first book, and I hope we get the chance to work together again in the future.

Melissa Tereze, I have the honour of knowing you as a friend, not just an author. You have, and continue to be, one of my greatest cheerleaders. Your signature, no nonsense, slap around the face encouragement is what I need on my laziest days. And your gentle, open patient love is what I need on my darkest. Thank you, for being an amazing friend and an inspiration. If some Scouser can do this, then there's hope for us all!

Finally, my gorgeous wife and beautiful children. Every day I strive to be the best I can be, so I can give you all the best I can give. Some days I may fall short, but I know you are all there to carry me the extra distance. I love you all.

Grandad Derrick

We miss you every day. Thank you for giving us the passion to just keep learning something new, however small.
x

Prologue

Twelve years earlier...

Callie stood next to the concrete pillar, half hiding behind its structure, surveying the room. Her eyes darted around, unable to settle in one place for very long. She closed her eyes, telling herself in her head that she was over-reacting.

It's just a bar. You're just here to see a band. Then you can go home.

One hand was clasped around a cold glass, the gin already giving her a confidence boost—enough to keep her from bolting through the door immediately but not enough to stop her panic. She tried to focus on the cool feel of the condensation against her fingers, an attempt to ground her in the moment.

She had heard about the club, and had always wanted to come here, but being so close to home, it was a little daunting. It was a collision of sorts between the life she lived when she was at university and the life she lived at home. It wasn't that her family was disapproving. In fact they had been anything but, going above and beyond to ensure she knew that they loved her and accepted her for who she was. But there was always some element of fear when she was openly out. A feeling like something or someone was waiting around the corner ready to—

No. There's nothing to fear. You're safe here.

In fact, her therapist had encouraged her to come, to combine the life she had lived for the past three years at university with the one she had left behind here.

She closed her eyes briefly and breathed through her nose. The internal dialogue she was having with herself was having somewhat the opposite effect intended and forcing memories she would rather forget to the surface. Instead, she tried running through some of her coping techniques, starting with five things she could see. The stage. The piano. The microphone. Jackie Taylor...*shit.*

Her eyes slammed shut and stayed that way this time, her breathing suddenly speeding up, a lump lodging itself in her throat. What was Jackie Taylor doing here? And Callie could be almost certain Jackie had been looking directly at her.

Another deep breath and Callie cracked open her eyes again, knowing she couldn't stay like this forever. The table where Jackie had been sat was empty; there was no Jackie in sight. Had she imagined it? Maybe this was a bad idea if her mind was playing tricks on her...

"Hey." A soft voice by her shoulder caused her head to whip round, chest tight with panic.

"Oh...I..."

"Hey, I'm sorry. I didn't mean to make you jump."

She hadn't imagined it. Jackie Taylor now stood in front of her, hands held up in a non-confrontational gesture, smiling softly.

"Sorry, I just..." Callie braced her hand against the pillar, trying to steady her legs. The lump in her throat threatened to spew out of her mouth. She licked her lips, suddenly aware of just how dry her mouth was.

"Are you okay?" Jackie's forehead was scrunched up in confusion, and Callie could feel the soft, hesitant touch of Jackie's hand on her upper arm.

"I'm fine. Just..." She tried to take a deep breath in, but the air was warm around her, and it seemed to catch in her throat.

"I really don't think you are. You've gone really pale."

"I'm..." Callie's vision swayed, and she cursed, leaning back against the pillar that was now supporting her as well as the ceiling.

"Tell you what. Come sit down."

"No, I'm..." Callie wasn't even sure what she was planning on saying, any protests clearly a lie considering she couldn't even form a coherent sentence right now. Her head swam and felt thick, every noise muffled yet amplified at the same time.

Callie registered a warm hand wrapping around her arm and leading her away from the relative safety of her hiding spot. She was urged to sit down, and despite knowing she had moved, she wasn't entirely sure of where she was now in the room or how she got there. She looked around, realising she was now at the table Jackie had previously occupied, finding Jackie talking to a young woman, then turning back to her and smiling.

"How are you feeling?"

"Umm..." Callie wasn't sure. It had been a while since she'd had an anxiety attack, and although she thought she had managed to stem this one before it spiralled too much further, it was still having an effect. "Fine. Better, thank you," she managed to croak out.

"Hmm." Jackie seemed unconvinced, and Callie couldn't blame her; she hadn't even managed to convince herself. Jackie looked over her shoulder at another sound, one which barely registered in Callie's consciousness, until the woman from a few moments before reappeared.

"Here," Jackie said, her voice clear in the clamour of the room, holding a glass of water towards Callie. "Drink some of this. It'll help."

"Thanks," Callie muttered, taking the glass and blushing with embarrassment when the clinking of the ice cubes betrayed just how shaky she was. Jackie, to her credit, didn't say anything, just kept her hand hovering beside Callie's reassuringly as she lifted the glass to her lips.

"Do you need me to call anyone?" Jackie asked, watching carefully as Callie slid the glass back onto the table after a sip.

"Oh God, please don't call my dad. This is embarrassing enough," Callie murmured as her head fell in her hands. For the past few minutes, she had forgotten that this was Jackie Taylor, her father's colleague and friend.

"I was thinking more about a friend or a girlfriend maybe…"

"Oh, umm…no. But thanks." She picked at an invisible spot of fluff on her jeans.

An uneasy silence settled over the table, Callie fiddling with her fingers and running hands over her thighs while she felt Jackie study her. She felt every pass of her eyes as they swept over her. She wondered what she was thinking, although she was fairly sure it was probably some contemplation on how someone so small and nervous could be the daughter of someone like her father.

Callie glanced up, and found an easy, soft smile settled on Jackie's lips. The judgement she had expected was missing.

"I wouldn't have had you down as a fan," Jackie said, cocking her head towards the stage.

"Oh erm, yeah. I listen to their stuff quite a lot. A friend introduced me to their stuff. I've always thought she would sound amazing live, but I've never had the chance yet."

"Oh, then you're in for a real treat. You're right; she is amazing live. It's like a whole different experience."

"You've seen her before?"

"Yeah, a few times, actually."

"I'm so jealous right now." Callie laughed softly, her body physically relaxing into the conversation.

"Well hopefully you'll have no more panic attacks, and you'll be able to enjoy the show."

No sooner had they begun to lower, Callie's defences shot up again, instinct kicking in. Jackie must have noticed as her face dropped, watching as Callie stood up, her chair falling to the floor in her scrambled state. She stumbled slightly, knocking the table and spilling the water over.

"Callie?" Jackie asked, the concern and terror clear in her voice to anyone but Callie right now, who just was in survival mode.

"I have to...sorry...I need..."

She didn't even finish her sentence before bolting, bumping into Jackie as she weaved her way, uncoordinated, through the small crowd and out of sight.

Jackie heard the cubicle door slam shut as she entered the toilets, silently uttering a thanks that they were the only ones in there. Stepping up to the closed door, she leant against it, hearing quickened breathing coming from behind it. She wasn't entirely sure she was welcome, but she knew she couldn't just walk away. While she was fairly certain her presence was the cause of Callie's first reaction, this was unequivocally her doing.

"Callie? Callie, I'm sorry that what I said made you panic again. It was insensitive of me. But honey, can you open the door for me?" Jackie listened for any sign of a response; the only thing she could make out was the jumping, hiccupped breaths of someone struggling through their tears. "Please, honey. I'm not leaving you here on your own, so if you let me in, we can work through this."

A moment passed, another hiccuped sob emanating from the cubicle, before Jackie heard shuffling followed by the telltale sound of the lock sliding open. Jackie pushed the door gently to see Callie sitting back on the toilet, feet pulled up, hugging her knees tightly. She rocked with each shaky, jagged breath, and tears streamed down her face. Jackie's heart broke at the sight.

"Oh honey, I'm sorry. Is it okay if I come closer?" After a small, shaky nod from Callie, Jackie stepped forward cautiously, not wanting to spook the younger woman. She crouched down, not caring about her cream trousers which rested on the floor. "What can I do?"

"N-nothing. J-just need to w-work through it," Callie stammered.

"How do you do that? Do you have a technique?" Jackie didn't know much about anxiety, but she knew enough that there was usually something which could help bring a person in.

"I-I need to say f-five t-things I can see," Callie stuttered to Jackie's relief.

"Okay. And what can you see?"

"Umm..." Jackie watched intently as Callie screwed her eyes shut briefly before opening them again. "Toilet, mirror, t-toilet roll, door, you."

"Now what?"

"F-four things I can feel."

"Okay, go on."

"Toilet. Wall. Floor." Jackie reached out her hand and placed it softly on top of Callie's, which was death gripped around her own knee. Callie looked up at her with impossibly dark eyes. "Y-you."

Jackie gave her a small, hopefully reassuring smile. "Next?"

"Three things I can hear. People, music, the air conditioning."

"Great. Keep going." Jackie could sense Callie calming with each step, her breathing evening out, her eyes becoming more focussed, and the hand still under her own loosening and relaxing.

"Two things I can smell. Alcohol and whatever they've cleaned this toilet with."

Jackie chuckled, and a small watery laugh followed from Callie. It was the tiniest of sounds, but it lifted Jackie's heart.

"Last one?" Jackie asked. She'd heard about this strategy before, and by four things Callie could feel, she knew the rest of the pattern. But still, she encouraged Callie to talk her through it, figuring it could help distract her further.

"One thing I can taste." Callie licked her lips. "Gin."

"Good. Well done, honey. How do you feel?" She rubbed her thumb gently over the skin of Callie's hand. Jackie watched as Callie tried to form words, the confusion on her face as she so obviously struggled to put her feelings into a sentence. Her mouth opened and closed, but instead of saying anything after a couple of attempts, she sighed and her eyes closed heavily. "It's okay, sweetie. You don't have to say anything."

Jackie studied Callie's face while she took her time to settle; her eyes were red and puffy from crying, and tear tracks which were starting to dry had ruined her makeup, leaving black smudges where her eyeliner once was painted. Her pallor was pale, almost ashen, and she was blinking so slowly, Jackie wasn't sure she was able to focus on anything. Jackie was seriously concerned that Callie was about to fall asleep here on the toilet as her eyes rolled back with another long blink. The adrenaline had well and truly left her body, and now she was running on the last dregs of fuel.

"Okay, Callie, we're going to give it a few minutes, make sure you're steady enough, and then we'll get out of here. Okay?"

"Mmm."

Jackie didn't know what her plan was, she just knew that Callie wasn't in a fit state to stay here, and she wasn't about to put her in a taxi alone. Whatever she decided, she was going to stay with Callie until she was confident that she would be okay.

She felt Callie's fingers shift underneath her hand, and she loosened her grip slightly, only to be surprised when Callie's fingers slid in between her own. Taking the lead, she turned her hand over, intertwining their digits fully and given them a timid but reassuring squeeze.

"Thank you," Callie muttered, almost so quietly that Jackie missed it.

Chapter One

Present day...

Callie Montgomery reclined in the high-backed leather chair, kicking her shoes off and resting her feet on the large glass-topped conference table in front of her. Crossing her legs at the ankles, she scrolled through the headlines of the news app on her phone, nothing piquing her interest, before dropping it down with a loud clunk in the cavernous room. She looked at her watch—8:40am. Another few minutes of peace and quiet before her day really began.

She had been in the office of Montgomery and Associates since seven o'clock, and in that time, she had managed to start drafting a new tender they'd won a couple of weeks before. Well, kind of. She had started with the intention of designing the new restaurant their client was paying them for, but despite reading and re-reading the specifications, as well as having numerous conversations about what they were envisioning, she just couldn't get started. Something was missing, and it was beginning to frustrate her. Why couldn't she just draw the bloody design like they wanted?

After five attempts, she gave up, threw her tablet on the table, and ran her hands over her face. It had only taken ninety minutes and she was already done with this day. Of course, it didn't help that—

Callie looked up at the sound of the door being pushed open, signalling the beginning of the end for her solitude as her assistant, Beka, arrived.

"Morning," Beka said, decidedly more perky and pleased about the beginning of the workday than Callie was. She was forgiven for her cheerful disposition, however, when she held out one of the two cardboard takeaway cups she was holding, the smell of freshly brewed coffee from the shop across the street assaulting Callie's senses.

"Thank you. And morning," Callie replied, sitting up and taking the cup from her.

"How long have you been here?" Beka asked, eyeing up the empty travel cup beside Callie as she sat down in the chair beside her.

"About an hour or so." Callie shrugged. "Thought I'd get some stuff done while it was quiet."

"How did you get on?"

"Yeah, not bad." Beka didn't need to know she was suffering the designer's equivalent of writer's block. She would only go on about it, and that was the last thing Callie needed.

She took a long sip of her coffee, the deep, chocolatey flavour hitting her taste buds and waking her up. She hummed with the pleasure it brought, a small joy in an otherwise mundane life.

She could feel a pair of eyes on her and looked over to find Beka giving her a look which she couldn't decipher. There was clearly a question she wanted to ask, but Callie had no idea what it was considering it was only Monday morning and the week had barely begun.

"So..." Beka started expectantly, clearly hoping that the one-word prompt would push Callie into telling her something, but she was none the wiser.

"So...what?" Callie asked over the top of her cup.

"So, today's the day we meet the new accounts manager," Beka said excitedly.

"Yeah." Callie looked back at her phone, unsure why this was something Beka thought deserved calling out specifically. Of course, Beka loved a good gossip and always knew the finer details about the people who walked through the office door. This one should be no different.

"Seriously? Come on, you must know something!"

"Nope."

"Someone said she worked here before?"

"Yeah." Callie placed her phone down

"And you can't tell me anything?"

Callie sighed. "It was twelve years ago. I wasn't here then."

"I know that, but you were around sometimes surely since it's your dad's company. Don't you remember anything?"

"I literally know as much as you," Callie mumbled, praying that the uncertainty in her voice could be adequately passed off as disinterest.

"I've heard she's a bit of a ball breaker. Doesn't take any shit," Beka continued, prying the lid off her cup and swirling the liquid.

"Well then I stand corrected. You know more than me. If your water-cooler gossip can be considered a reliable source." Callie reached across Beka and slid her tablet back towards her, hoping to find something to suitably distract her further.

"Aren't you even a little bit interested?"

"No," she answered, tapping at her screen somewhat more forcefully than required.

"But you're a senior partner..."

"As long as she does her job, and she's good at it, then I don't care. The two other senior partners and the Head of HR interviewed her, and I trust their judgement," Callie snapped. She really hoped that her response was short enough that Beka finally took the hint and stopped the questioning.

Truth be told, Callie knew who the new accounts manager

was. She may not have been at the interview, having cited personal involvement with the candidate due to her previous employment entirely under her father, but she had conversed with those who were in the room and agreed with their hiring decision. But she'd excused herself from the actual interview the minute the resume had crossed her desk. She knew before sending the other partners into the interview that the candidate was more than capable of the task ahead of them.

The door was pushed open again, the quiet murmur of early morning chatter drifting in as the room began to fill. Beka quickly vacated her seat and stood behind Callie as was commonplace during the weekly briefings. Another colleague took the empty chair, and Callie nodded a reserved good morning as she straightened up and looked at her tablet.

A nauseous wave rolled through her, and for a moment, she genuinely feared vomiting in front of the entire office. She closed her eyes and breathed slowly, in through her nose and out through her mouth, trying not to draw attention to the fact that she was perilously close to having an anxiety attack. Her thumb pushed the ring around her middle finger, the inner circle of it spinning round its outer counterpart. Callie focused on the feel of the metal underneath her thumb, the slide of one piece against the other. *Five things I can see...fuck.*

There she was. Twelve years later and just as Callie remembered her.

She still remembered the evening she had been introduced to Jackie Taylor. She was twenty-one, fresh from university, and back at home trying to work out her next steps, clouded by a fog of self-doubt and identity issues. Years were spent being her own person and then she was back, unsure as to how to move forward.

Her father, Barrett Montgomery, had spent years building up a highly respected and successful architecture company, designing some of the city's most popular and admired buildings. He had never hidden his desire to have Callie come into the business, ever since she showed a talent for art and design. And once she was back, his arguments had only gotten more insistent. But Callie was still unsure. Everything in her hometown reminded her of darker times, times she was still clawing her way out of, and she wasn't sure if she really wanted to commit to a life there.

Callie and her brothers were used to Barrett bringing home business associates or partners, but Jackie had joined while Callie was at university, and as such, they had never met. Until an evening Callie still thought of often. They had come straight from the office, and Jackie looked absolutely stunning in a tailored grey trouser suit, her cream silk blouse draping perfectly over her curves, enough buttons undone to show just enough skin to tease Callie's immediately piqued attention.

She could still rock a power suit. Today's example was dark grey with a white pin stripe running through it and a crisp pressed white shirt underneath it. She was dressing to make a statement. And boy, what a statement she was making.

Callie watched as Jackie was greeted by Graham, their digital manager, shaking his hand before sliding her hands in her pockets as she listened to whatever he was saying. She'd aged superbly, and from this distance, the only clue of the passing years was the silver flash in the front of her otherwise almost-black-it-was-so-deep-brown hair, which draped over her shoulder.

Callie's breath caught as Jackie scanned the room until her earthy moss green eyes settled on Callie. A soft, almost indistinguishable smile tugged at the corners of her mouth, a silent *hello* between two people for whom this situation seemed overly formal considering past interactions and the last time they saw each other. Callie gave a half, tight-lipped smile back. Her body's instantaneous reaction betrayed her head's uncertainty, a confusing combination of attraction and guilt rolling through her. Yes, she was still beautiful, Callie thought as she furiously spun her ring again, but she was still the woman Callie ran from.

"Hi. Is Miss Montgomery available?" Jackie asked the young woman who sat behind the desk outside Callie's office. She had spent the past fifteen minutes giving herself a pep talk in her own office before walking over here, but the nervous feeling in the pit of her stomach only intensified with each step closer. Callie was briefly introduced at the meeting this morning, but she had quickly made her excuses and left.

Jackie couldn't forget the look of panic that flitted across Callie's face when Jackie first looked at her. She had hoped that the small smile she gave her would do enough to quell Callie's fears about hard feelings between them, but then all Jackie could focus on as the meeting continued was the way Callie had anxiously fiddled with her ring.

"Oh. Yes, she's free. I can get her if—"

"Oh, that's fine. I can knock. Thank you..." She paused, waiting for the young woman's name.

"Beka. Beka Sanderson."

"Thank you, Beka."

"No worries, Miss Taylor." Beka smiled, but something about it sat uneasy with Jackie. It was a little too fake and sickly sweet for her liking. But she pushed the thought to one side, sure that it was just an over eagerness to please and tried not to let her first impression cloud her judgement of the woman.

She turned her attention to the closed door, the silver nameplate pinned to it making her smile to herself. *Callie Montgomery*. Tapping gently so as not to startle her too much, she was greeted with a muffled reply, and then pushed the door open. As she did, Callie looked up from where she was sitting at the drafting table, pencil in hand, the early spring sun shining through the window framing her from behind.

Jackie felt her heart constrict in her chest, all thoughts temporarily erased from her mind except how stunning Callie looked. Twelve years ago, she had this tomboyish vibe, loose ripped jeans and fitted t-shirts showing off her youthful curves. She'd definitely matured into her style; her navy chinos were cut to perfection, sitting perfectly on her hips, a black tailored shirt pinched in to perfectly highlight her waist. Her sleeves were rolled up—a look which Jackie had always appreciated. Her once mousey hair which was usually pulled up into a ponytail was today a rich, deep red and the undercut on one side, contrasted by chin length waves on the other size, sealed her new, rounded androgynous look. It suited Callie in every respect, and Jackie found herself appreciating it more than she should .

Trying to ignore the fact that Callie looked so good after all these years, Jackie instead focussed on her face. "Hi. Is it okay if I come in?"

"Sure," Callie answered with a small, nervous smile. She stood, running her palms down her thighs.

"You, umm, ran off pretty quick after the meeting," Jackie said, slowly walking across the office to where Callie stood. She stopped a few feet in front of her, and tucked her hair behind her ear, nervously repeating the action even though it didn't need doing.

"Yeah..." She swallowed, her eyes darting down to the pencil she was fiddling with in between her fingers.

"I just...I guess I just wanted to have a chance to say hello properly. It all seemed a bit formal in a room full of other people like we don't know each other. And I didn't want you to think that there were any hard feelings or tension between us."

Jackie saw Callie release a breath she had been holding.

"Yeah. Thanks."

"Okay." Jackie looked around, not sure where to focus her gaze and acutely aware of how awkward and nervous Callie looked. "Well, I guess I'll see you later," she said, cutting her losses and starting to back out of the door.

"Jackie," Callie called out as she turned.

"Yeah?"

She watched Callie release a slow, deep breath, not sure if it was for her benefit or Callie's.

"Would you...would you like to stay for a coffee? Maybe?" The anxious fiddling with the pencil between her fingers had ramped up, the wooden stake flipping so quickly it was almost a blur.

"Yeah...yeah that would be nice. Thanks." Jackie wasn't sure that was the answer which Callie was expecting, the pencil coming to a sudden stop and clattering on the floor.

"Oh."

"Is that okay?"

"Yes. Yes! Sorry, just hadn't thought past the actual asking you bit. Wasn't expecting any answer, let alone that one."

Jackie chuckled, pleasantly reminded of just how adorable and enchanting Callie could be when she was flustered. "So...coffee?"

"Yes. Coffee." Callie seemed to try and focus herself, stepping over to the sideboard which sat under the window and firing up the coffee machine. "Take a seat."

Jackie moved to where Callie gestured, the sleek black leather sofa in the corner of the room, but instead of heading towards it, she allowed her curiosity to get the better of her. She strolled over towards the wall besides the door, taking a moment to study the photographs and pictures hanging there: an image of Callie and her mother; a younger, shy, awkward-looking Callie and a man who Jackie instantly recognised as her father, Barrett, shaking hands with another man in a suit, all three of them wearing bright yellow hard hats.

"Was this your Master's?" Jackie asked, turning slightly and pointing to the next photo. In it, Callie was adorned in ceremonial robes, her sash a rich, deep blue and gold. Beside her stood a beaming Barrett, face almost split in two with the grin he had on display.

"Yeah. I'd also just agreed to work at the business for six months, so I think that was the real reason Dad was so ecstatic."

"I'm sure doing so well was enough for him. He's always been proud of you, Callie."

"Thanks," Callie replied, but Jackie sensed her uncertainty.

Callie wandered over to where Jackie stood, passing her a fresh cup of coffee. Jackie sniffed the earthy aroma which wafted from the cup and hummed.

"It's better than that instant crap they have in the staff room," Callie offered, smirking.

"Still a coffee snob then?"

"Life's too short for bad coffee."

Jackie broke into a grin at the familiarity of Callie's attitude. Jackie would always comment on the aroma of coffee which filled Callie's kitchen and had quickly learnt what was classed as good coffee and what Callie felt didn't even deserve the title. It was a lesson and habit which had stuck with her over the past decade or so. While her weekday coffee was often high quality but drunk on the go, her weekend mornings were spent calmly and quietly with a fresh cafetiere of strong Colombian coffee and a good book to ease her soul after a busy week.

Callie grinned, the easy, relaxed expression Jackie remembered, and Jackie wondered if the brief reappearance of their easy banter was the cause. But no sooner had she flashed that beautiful smile then did it disappear again, her head dropping as she looked down at her shoes, reminding Jackie of that small, insecure woman Jackie had met all those years ago.

"Hey...this doesn't have to be weird, you know," she said, dipping her own head to try and catch Callie's eyes.

"I know, and I am...I will try."

"But?" Jackie always knew when Callie wanted to say something more, her struggle to articulate her emotions as endearing as it was frustrating. Pushing her gently to reveal more always used to work, giving her the permission to continue by validating that it was okay to speak, but she wasn't entirely sure it would still be welcome let alone useful.

"Nothing." Callie's dismissal of the opportunity to speak her mind hurt. It was just another sign of the time that had passed.

Jackie's heart cracked. She knew that things would be different, but a small corner of her mind hoped that maybe, just maybe, they would easily fall into old habits, that unspoken, secret language they had for each other.

Resigning herself to the abyss now present between them, she took a sip of her coffee, concentrating on the flavour which danced across her palate as she took another look around Callie's office. She spied the bookshelf on the opposite side of the room and moved to take a closer look at the accolades which adorned it.

"Congratulations. These are some serious awards you've won."

"The company won them. I was just a small cog in the machine."

Jackie frowned, reading one particularly grand looking glass sculpture. "Best Community Space Design, Individual Winner. Doesn't sound like a group effort to me," she commented, turning with a raised eyebrow.

"Hardly the Turner Prize, Jacs. It was a local competition for designers in the area."

"Still something you should be proud of," Jackie answered, biting back her instinct to argue that Callie should take credit where credit was clearly due. Her words didn't hold much weight anymore.

She looked at the name carved into the glass. *Callie Goodman*. How could she have forgotten that Callie had married in the years since they last saw each other? Swallowing down the bitter taste which threatened to rise in her throat, she quietly composed herself.

"I'm sorry to hear about your divorce." Jackie cringed at her own words, the comment sounding hollow and robotic.

"I'm not," Callie replied, her response cold and hard. The sounds of it shocked Jackie, the lack of warmth in her tone something she wasn't used to. The realisation that Callie was still speaking snapped her out of the concern. "So, what does your day look like?"

"Oh." Jackie cleared her throat. "Meetings. Lots of meetings. Only just managed to find time to come see you."

"Aw, thanks. I feel honoured."

"You're welcome." Jackie bumped shoulders with her awkwardly, desperate to thaw the ice which was thickening rapidly between them. She could feel the distance growing already, and it unsettled her. Luckily, the action had the desired effect, and Callie flashed a fond smile. "Don't officially get around to your department until tomorrow though."

"Well, we only draw pretty pictures. Not really that important for a design company," Callie joked.

Jackie frowned, again sensing something else behind her words but not quite knowing what it was. If she didn't know Callie and her love of drawing better, she'd be tempted to say it was indifference. Instead of saying anything, she took a sip of her now cooled coffee, filing her concern at the back of her mind for later time.

"Who's first?"

"Jayne from Finance in..." Jackie tipped her wrist. "Oh shit, two minutes."

"Oh. Starting with a real party there. Well, I wouldn't want you to be late to your first meeting." Callie smirked, sinking down into her plush office chair, her hands cupping her coffee.

"I've not even finished my bloody coffee," Jackie muttered, gulping back another mouthful and annoyed she wasn't able to savour the taste like she wanted to.

"Take it with you. Finance has shit coffee."

"Are you sure?" Jackie asked with a grateful smile.

"What? That their coffee's crap? Yeah. But bring your cup back—otherwise you can't get a free refill." Callie winked playfully. It was probably the only time Jackie had seen her voluntarily relax in the whole conversation.

"Thank you. See you later?" Jackie smiled as she speed-walked towards the door, pausing at the threshold. "It was good to see you again, Cal."

"Yeah. You too, Jacs," Callie replied softly.

As Jackie walked away, towards the office where Jayne from Finance was no doubt waiting for her, she couldn't shift the sense that something wasn't right with Callie Montgomery. And more than anything in the world, that unsettled her an indescribable amount.

Chapter Two

Jackie let her glasses clatter to the desk, sighing as she sat back in her chair. Her first week had passed in a blur, her days filled with meetings and briefings in order to get up to speed with the business. Some of them involved Callie, but outside of those meetings, she hadn't had as many opportunities to see or talk to Callie as she had hoped. But then, she knew this first week would be frantic.

She rubbed her eyes, which were stinging from staring at client statistics for the past two hours, and when they felt clear enough, she glanced at the clock perched on the edge of her desk. When she realised it was nearly six in the evening, the silence which stretched out across the offices suddenly made sense.

She pushed back from the desk, crouching down to grab her handbag before collecting her things from her desk. She was just shutting down her computer when a voice broke through the silence.

"Thought you'd be long gone."

Jackie smiled as she looked up to see Callie leaning against her door frame. She was clearly on her way out, her thick grey peacoat on but still open, her leather messenger bag hanging over her shoulder.

"To be honest, so did I. But I lost track of time. What about you? Thought you'd have better places to be."

"Yes. Me, in my mid-thirties, post-divorce, business-crisis state right now is a total catch. The Friday night lesbians in Leeds are falling over themselves."

"I hope you're not spending too much time here. You need a life outside of this firm," Jackie scolded gently, giving a look which betrayed just how serious she was. She didn't want Callie to be tied to the business. Her dedication to her father's legacy was admirable, but she hoped it wasn't all she had.

"Says the woman leaving at six on a Friday night."

"I feel like this could go on forever. Truce?" Jackie conceded as she approached Callie at the threshold.

"Deal," Callie responded with a grin. "Do you have any plans this evening?"

"Unpacking. To be honest, I've not done a lot, and I'm surrounded by boxes. Don't. Say. Anything." Jackie held a finger up to silence Callie.

Callie smirked. "Wasn't going to say a word."

"Hmm."

Jackie smiled at Callie's non-committal hum. It was a constant bugbear and joke between them, how different they were in their approach to tasks. Jackie hadn't unpacked because there was no real urgency; anything she needed she had already found, and if she discovered that she did need something still in a box, she would just find and open that box. By now, if it were Callie, she would have already had every box unpacked and probably rearranged the shelves three times over. Organisation was key to her coping strategy, and although Jackie mocked Callie for it just as much as Callie mocked her back, she also appreciated how important it was for her.

"So, home then, since we're established you're not off to paint the town."

"No actually. Family dinner."

"Oh." They'd reached the lift and stood together, an awkward silence hanging over them, her change of conversation topic failing miserably. "Will you, umm, say hi to them from me?"

"Yeah. Yeah, sure." Callie answered, not taking her eyes off the lift doors. Jackie imagined she was willing them to open just as much as she was. "Do you not have something booked in with Dad?"

"Oh." Jackie was slightly taken aback by Callie's question. Apart from the brief mention of Barrett on her first day, he hadn't been mentioned since.

"Someone had to bring it up, Jacs. We couldn't just ignore it forever."

"Yeah, I guess. I do have lunch with Barrett next week actually."

"Oh..."

Jackie turned her head, raising her eyebrows at Callie's response. "You asked, Callie," she stated once Callie met her gaze.

"No. I know." Callie turned back around letting out a not-so-subtle sigh of relief as the lift doors opened. Jackie let her step inside first, hovering as she wondered if she was welcome to share the confined space with her ex. The last thing she wanted to do was force Callie into a situation she couldn't escape from.

"It's fine, Callie. I couldn't put it off forever."

"No, I guess not."

"Business I can do, and that'll be what Barrett and I will catch up about mostly." The lift pinged as it reached the ground floor, and the door slid open with a swoosh. Jackie took a step forward, turning when she realised that Callie wasn't moving. "It'll be alright, Callie. Don't worry. Have a good weekend."

Callie let the door close behind her before falling back against the wall with a sigh. She really, really wished her initial plan of just keeping her distance and maybe still feeling some residual yet totally misplaced anger towards Jackie had stuck. But the moment she saw her in that boardroom, Callie realised that idea was futile. Laying eyes on Jackie only served to remind her of all the woman's virtues, and if anything, that only heightened her guilt.

The sound of laughter carried through from the lounge down the hall, and Callie groaned quietly. She didn't feel like socialising, but if she was too distant, her family would worry, and she wasn't prepared to share what was troubling her. She took a deep breath, kicked off her shoes, and pushed off the wall to walk further into the house.

The laughter rippled around the lounge again as Callie walked through the door, her arrival first noted by her oldest brother, Robbie.

"Hey! She's here!"

"Hi, everyone. Sorry I'm a bit late," she offered as she gave a wave to the room.

"No worries, Cal." Robbie wrapped his sister up in one of his signature bear hugs, giving her a kiss on the cheek before letting her go. "Busy day?"

"Yeah. Same old shit, different day, you know. I'm just going to go get a drink." She threw a thumb over her shoulder towards the kitchen.

The room was full of the familiar and loving faces of her family, and it instantly made her well up with guilt at her earlier thoughts. She loved her family, and she loved the group dinner they all made time for every week. Everyone made the effort to clear one evening in their diaries and spend it with each other. And she knew it was for her benefit. Or at least it was when the tradition began.

She carried on through to the kitchen, where the volume died down and she was instead surrounded by the sound of classical music softly playing. Her mother stood at the counter preparing the meal.

"Hey, Mama," Callie said as she came to a stop beside her, pressing a kiss to her cheek. Her mother turned her face, returning the gesture.

"Hello, my darling. How are you?"

"Fine," Callie answered, picking at the salad which Annie was chopping. "Is it okay if I stay here tonight, Mama?"

Annie stopped what she was doing, turning to Callie to look her straight in the eye. "Of course it is, my darling. Is everything okay?"

"Yeah. It's been a long week, and I don't fancy driving back later, that's all."

It wasn't entirely untruthful. Now she was out of the office, she felt exhausted. But mostly she didn't want to go home to an empty house.

"Dinner will be another fifteen minutes. Why don't you pop upstairs and get freshened up? There's clothes in your wardrobe."

"Thanks, Ma."

Callie gave her mother another quick kiss before disappearing out of the kitchen through the back door. There was a second staircase which was added when the family built the extension some years earlier, and it led straight to outside Callie's bedroom at the back of the house. She smiled as she shut the door behind her. Although this was the house they grew up in and they had all moved out years ago, all three of the Montgomery children still had their bedrooms. They had all been redecorated since and were used when guests came to stay, but they all kept a little bit of their owner's personality and childhood keepsakes.

Robbie's room was home to a signed England rugby shirt which hung above the bed. The desk in Jake's room still held his first ever computer, the one he'd started coding on, and the

Rubik's cube which he spent hours solving. Callie's room still had her easel in the corner. But in hers, there were a few extra touches the boys' room didn't have, and they were all down to Annie.

When Callie was a teenager, and she struggled with her anxiety and confidence, it was Annie who encouraged her to create a safe space. Vanilla was the scent which always wrapped around her, making her feel warm and cocooned. Now, Annie always made sure the room smelt of vanilla. In the top drawer of her dresser, she knew she could find a sketch book and some pencils; it was her escape when she was younger, and the avenue into where she was now in her career. On the cabinet by the bed sat a Bluetooth speaker for those nights she stayed over and wanted to listen to music to help her drift off. They seemed like such little things, inconsequential to the casual observer, but each one of them had a reason and a meaning behind them.

Callie stripped her shirt off and dropped it on the end of the bed; walking over to the drawers by the window, she pulled open the second one down, and found a set of neatly folded grey jogging bottoms and a long-sleeved black t-shirt. She smiled to herself; her mother always made sure there was something to wear. When she was a teenager, she remembered asking why Annie kept clothes for her in the house when she didn't live there. Annie had answered that even though she didn't live there all the time, she was part of the family, and was welcome anytime. So, just like the boys, she would always have her own things there.

Pulling the t-shirt over her head, she wished she could just collapse into the pristine bed, but she could hear the laughter and chatter drifting up through the floor and remembered that dinner was almost ready. Her stomach growled in response, reminding her that the sandwich she had hours ago was a distant memory. Quickly swapping her chinos for her joggers, she pulled her feet into the thick socks she found in another drawer and made her way back downstairs.

"There you are," she was greeted by her younger brother who was busy setting the table. Jake, at thirty years old, resembled a perfect mix of Barrett and Annie. His chiselled jawline and soft brown waves matched their father at his age, while his eyes, a shimmering, steely grey, were straight from his mother. When she was younger, Callie wished and prayed on everything she could for those eyes, her deep aqua hues the biggest giveaway that they didn't all share the same lineage. "Thought you'd buggered off to bed."

"Tempting, but no. How's things?"

"Yeah, not bad. How's the office?"

Callie sighed, contemplating her answer. Once, Jake had been a part of the company. He had always wanted to follow in his father's footsteps but never had Barrett's business acumen. She was fairly sure that Barrett had thought he hit the jackpot when Callie agreed to head up the design department and Jake took over the client relations aspect of the business. He retired, leaving his company—the thing he had spent thirty years building up—in capable hands which included two of his three children. However, nine months later, Jake walked away as well, although not quite as freely. Some poor decisions on his part had led to some awkward conversations between the siblings, and their already slightly fractious relationship suffered even more.

Now, when he asked Callie how the office was, he wasn't asking to be polite or courteous; he was usually digging for information to use against Callie in one of his frequent snipes. Clearly, despite the consequences being purely of his own actions, Jake was still holding Callie responsible.

"It's fine, Jake. Busy, but fine."

"I heard you hired someone new."

"We have a new client relations manager, yeah."

"Who?"

Callie exhaled deeply again, fiddling with the place setting in front of her. She could already hear the resentment in his voice as the person who was filling his former position.

"Jackie Taylor. I don't know if you remember her; she worked with Dad when the company was still quite new. Anyway, she's got like, another ten years' worth of contacts now, so hopefully we'll be able to drag in some new clients."

There was pause, just for a split second, when something indescribable flickered over his face before it disappeared.

"Hmm." Jake placed a plate down on the table, firmer than entirely necessary. Callie closed her eyes, sighing with resignation at again having to placate his ego.

"Jake, I didn't mean—"

"Whatever. I'm just going to go see Robbie," he muttered as he walked away. Callie watched as he retreated, still looking like a petulant teenager.

"Thought Jake was setting the table?" Annie asked, breaking her train of thought. Callie hadn't even heard her mother come into the dining room.

"Huh? Oh, I said I'd finish it so he could go speak to Robbie."

"You shouldn't do that, you know."

"What?" Callie asked, finishing laying the last knife.

"Give your brother such an easy ride."

Callie snorted. If only her mother knew just how close to home that statement was.

"I mean it, you know. He always knew how to get you to give a bit more. Let him do his own dirty work. And chores," Annie finished with a pointed glance towards the table. "Besides, you've been at work all day."

"So has he."

"No, he had the day off. Been playing golf with your father." Callie rolled her eyes at the information, only grateful that her back was still towards Annie so she couldn't see. "You should be sitting down with your brother and niece, not him."

"It's fine Mama," Callie replied, not wanting to get into this discussion.

"Hmm. Call the guys in. Dinner will be out in a minute. I've done your favourite, lasagne." Annie walked back into the kitchen. Callie watched as she went before closing her eyes in exhausted resignation. She really couldn't wait to collapse into that bed she knew was waiting upstairs.

Chapter Three

Twelve years earlier...

"So how was your day?"

"Yeah, it wasn't bad," Callie answered as she propped the phone between her shoulder and chin to dump a hefty scoop of coffee grounds into her cafetiere. "Same old stuff, really."

"Your enthusiasm really is contagious," Jackie quipped from the other end of the handset.

"Fuck off."

Callie let out a soft sigh, her inner monologue wondering if she should elaborate on her less than eager response. She decided against it; although she felt comfortable confiding and talking to Jackie, she didn't need to know everything that was running through her mind.

She still felt some residual guilt and embarrassment over their first meeting two weekends prior. Callie couldn't remember much after the toilets, not until she woke up in Jackie's spare bed with a foggy head. Instantly feeling mortified and unwelcome, she went on the hunt for her impromptu host to say a hasty thank you before leaving. Instead, she found Jackie in the kitchen, not a hint of anger or irritation in sight. Callie was met with a fresh cup of coffee, a cooked breakfast, and sympathetic warm eyes which didn't push her to say anything she didn't want to. Jackie even insisted on driving her home. And although her reaction was reassuring, Callie wasn't expecting the text which came through from her that afternoon checking in on her or the conversation which followed and definitely not the three coffee dates, one lunch, and four dinners which had occurred since.

Right now, she was five minutes into their phone call, something which happened on the rare day when they didn't have plans to see each other. A breathy laugh at her last comment brought her back to the present.

"What are you having for dinner?"

"Don't know yet. Probably something from the freezer." Callie was aware she was being short with her answers tonight, but it had been a long day, and while she wasn't aiming to be deliberately obtuse, she was conscious she was bordering on it. She hoped that Jackie wasn't too easily offended.

"I thought you said you could cook?"

"I can! I just...I don't have a lot in right now. I need to go to the supermarket and do a shop." *When I can be bothered*, thought Callie as she slowly pushed the plunger down, satisfied that her coffee had steeped enough. "What about you?"

"I was thinking Italian. There's this little restaurant a couple of streets away from the office which will do takeout portions of everything on the menu. Their lasagne is amazing, and I've been thinking about it ever since we had that conversation at the weekend."

Their Sunday lunch date had developed into a lazy walk by the canal to burn off what they had eaten, and the topic of conversation had been their go-to foods for different occasions. Callie had revealed to Jackie that her ultimate comfort food when she was feeling tired or stressed was lasagne.

"Oh, my God. I could totally eat lasagne right now." The sound of someone pressing her doorbell caught her attention, and she frowned, confused at who it could be. She really hoped it wasn't her parents. She couldn't deal with too much smothering tonight. She wandered over to the door while still talking. "I'm so jealous right now," she declared as she pulled the door open.

"Well, you could always share it with me," Jackie said. Callie stood, slack jawed, as the statement reverberated twice, once through the phone receiver and once directly to her ear. Jackie hung up her phone with one hand while the other held high a brown paper bag, filled with what Callie's nose could determine was fresh Italian food. "Hi."

"What are you doing here?"

"You sounded kind of fed up when you messaged me earlier, so I figured now was the time to share my secret Italian hotspot." Jackie stepped into Callie's flat. She stopped by the still dumbfounded younger woman. "I hope that's okay?" she asked, clearly mistaking her surprise for discomfort.

"Yeah...yeah, of course." Callie beamed, eager to show that Jackie's impromptu arrival was very much welcomed.

"Good." Jackie gave her a soft smile before leaning in and pressing a gentle kiss to her cheek in greeting. "And I kind of missed you."

The blush Callie could feel spread across her cheeks at the unexpected kiss was quickly replaced with a warm feeling in her chest at Jackie's admission. She had been careful throughout the day to not let her own disappointment at not seeing the older woman for a couple of days overtake her thoughts, dismissing it as foolish. But the truth was, when she wasn't with Jackie, she spent a good portion of that time looking forward to their next encounter.

She cleared her throat, realising she had zoned out a little. Jackie was already in her kitchen, slipping her coat off and hanging it on the back of a chair, while Callie still stood with the door open. Quickly closing it, she made her way back into the kitchen and found plates for the pair of them.

"So, how was your day?" Callie asked, trying hard to get the conversation back to where it was on the phone.

"Yeah, okay. I've been in meetings most of the day. There's a client who is putting out their work for tender on a big development project. If we get it, it will set the company out as a real front runner."

"Sounds exciting."

"Mmhmm," Jackie mumbled, licking sauce from her thumb. "Sounds like a lot of work for me. Grab a couple of glasses and then go sit down. I'll be over in a minute."

Callie did as she was told, taking two glasses from beside the sink where they had been left to dry the night before. She made her way to the small dining table which sat against the wall in between the kitchen and living room. She sat down and watched as Jackie finished dishing up their dinner, heaping a healthy portion of fresh, green salad onto their plates. She brought them over and placed one in front of Callie before returning to the kitchen, grabbing the brown paper wrapped package, and producing a bottle of wine from her handbag like a magic trick. Finally sitting down opposite Callie, Jackie smiled as she unwrapped the paper package, revealing a loaf of freshly baked focaccia; Callie's mouth watered at the aroma released.

"Oh wow, this looks amazing."

"Better than something out of the freezer?" Jackie asked with a sly grin.

"Definitely." Callie took a bite of the steaming hot pasta, groaning when the flavours hit her taste buds. "Oh, God. This is heaven."

"Thought you might enjoy it," Jackie said, pouring Callie and then herself a glass of wine before starting on her own meal. Moments passed, both women comfortably enjoying the silence as they ate. Callie looked up as she piled another forkful into her mouth, seeing that Jackie was no longer eating but studying her intently as she sipped her wine.

"What?" she mumbled around her food. She swallowed as quickly as the hot, melted cheese would allow.

"Is everything okay today?"

Callie's fork paused for a split second before she answered with a mumbled, "Sure," finishing off with another mouthful of lasagne. If she had hoped that was enough to put a halt to the conversation, she was mistaken as Jackie continued.

"Really? Because you seem a little off..."

Callie had hoped that she had hidden her missing enthusiasm throughout the day from Jackie, but it seemed that she had failed considering Jackie had turned up uninvited with her favourite comfort food and was now giving her a look which could melt her into confessing everything.

"It's nothing, really," Callie responded, but she was fairly certain Jackie could sense the hesitation in her voice.

Jackie lent forward, placing her wine glass back on the table. "You know you can talk to me, don't you?"

Callie paused again, this time sighing as she placed her fork down. She picked up her napkin and wiped her mouth. Swallowing, she finally allowed her eyes to drift up and meet Jackie's properly.

"It's...really, it's nothing. It's just been a long couple of days."

"You want to talk about it?"

"There's nothing to talk about. I just woke up feeling...I don't know, drained. Apathetic. Unenthusiastic. And I've struggled to get out of my funk all day." She shrugged. "Sometimes it happens. Doesn't it happen to you?"

"Yeah. Of course it does."

"But you're more worried about me because I'm a nut-job who can't even go to a club without having some sort of breakdown, right?" Callie cursed herself immediately. Her exhaustion from not sleeping well the past few nights coupled with her defence mechanism kicking in was starting to show as irritability.

"Do you really think that's my opinion of you?" Jackie asked. Callie could see the flicker of hurt across her face

"No." Callie sighed, slumping back in her chair. "But this is what happens. People want to know what's wrong, I get grumpy and defensive, those people get offended, and then they stop asking. Then that slowly turns into not talking at all. They keep their distance because they don't know what to say. And I end up alone. Again. So it's better to just try and tell them that everything's fine." Callie looked up at Jackie again. "And hope that they don't question it too much."

To Callie's confusion, Jackie pushed her chair back, walked around the table, and crouched low in front of her.

"Again," she asked in a low voice, "does that seem like me?"

"No," Callie admitted quietly. A warm hand covered her own, halting her fingers which she hadn't realised were anxiously picking at the skin around her nails.

"But?" Jackie pushed gently. Callie wasn't even sure she was aware of there being a but to her response, yet somehow Jackie knew.

"But what if I'm wrong, and you leave after a while anyway? And I'm alone again."

Callie's eyes fluttered closed involuntarily as a warm palm cupped her cheek.

"Oh, honey..." Callie felt a thumb swipe across her skin, brushing away a tear which had treacherously escaped. She wasn't sure where this tidal wave of brutally honest emotions was coming from. Swallowing before the floodgates opened, she sensed movement in front of her before another equally soft and gentle hand framed her other cheek.

"Open your eyes, beautiful."

Callie did as she was asked, forehead creased with confusion at the unexpected term of endearment. Focussing on Jackie kneeling in front of her, she couldn't help but smile back when Jackie gave her one of her heart-stopping grins.

"I'm sorry. It's just been a tiring couple of days."

"Don't ever apologise for telling me what you're feeling." A gentle kiss was pressed to her forehead, and for the second time that night, Callie felt her heart flip. As Jackie moved, going to push up off the floor, Callie grabbed her wrist, overtaken by the sudden, inexplicable urge to follow her heart.

"What's wrong?" Jackie asked, worried by Callie halting her.

"Nothing. I..."

Callie felt her senses grow overwhelmed by Jackie, the perfume which had been driving her wild all evening, the soft huff of her exhale against her skin, the sensation of her racing pulse underneath her thumb. Something gave her the final boost of confidence, and Callie closed the tiny distance which separated them. Her touch was tentative, some part of her scared she had read the situation wrong. After the briefest of kisses, the gentlest brush of lips against lips, she pulled back. Jackie's eyes fluttered open, and they bore into Callie, the intensity within them staggering.

"I..." Callie didn't know what she wanted to say, didn't even know if she wanted to say anything, but the silence was suffocating, and she didn't know what else to do. "I'm..." She lent back and let her hand drop, scared she had made a fundamental error in judgement.

"No," Jackie whispered, quickly grasping at Callie's wrist as it fell, holding her in place in a reversal of their position just moments earlier. Callie felt Jackie close the gap again, her nose brushing against her own before soft lips met in an unfamiliar but sure dance. Callie sighed at the contact, her heart pounding for an altogether different reason than the fear that had shot through her just a moment earlier. She was just thinking how this felt so right when soft fingertips caressed her cheek again, and her mind went blank as Jackie deepened their kiss.

Chapter Four

resent day...
    Callie sat at her desk, tapping her pen anxiously against her keyboard. She was reading and re-reading the specifications for the project she was working on. Her first drafts were delivered a week ago, but they were delivered with the caveat that they were rough, early drafts, and the promise that they would have more specific and polished designs within the next two weeks. Now, halfway through that time, she still wasn't sure what she was planning on delivering.

This client was one of their largest and longest standing, hence the fact that Callie herself worked on the account. She threw her pen down, the headache which always seemed to be threatening on the horizon there again. Her attention was suddenly piqued by the low, throaty laugh which she instantly recognised, the sound making her smile subconsciously.

Having Jackie back around the office had not been as awkward as she had anticipated. In fact, they had quickly fallen into an easy working relationship. Callie was grateful for the way Jackie had just come in and taken control, taking some of the pressure off her own shoulders, allowing her to do what she was in the business to do.

Or at least, that was the idea. In reality, there was something still stifling Callie's creativity.

Her train of thought was quickly derailed as a sharp knock to her already open door drew her attention. Any thoughts of Jackie were rapidly dispelled as she saw her father's face, her smile softening as he grinned at her.

"Dad! What are you doing here?"

"What? Can't your old man come and see you?"

"At the office? In the middle of the day? No, not really. What's going on?" She eyed her father suspiciously as she stood from her desk and rounded it to stand in front of him. As soon as she was within reach, Barrett opened his arms and took his daughter into one of his customary hugs. "Hey, Dad."

"Hey, sweetheart." Barrett held Callie at arms length, studying her. "Are you eating enough? You're looking skinny."

"Oh, shut up!" Callie scoffed, pulling out of his grip. "I'm literally being fed by Mum every other day. So come on, spill. To what do I owe this visit?"

"I've just had lunch with Jackie. I walked back with her and thought I would come and say hi."

Callie froze momentarily at the mention of Jackie's name. This used to happen before too, a cold sense of dread slipping down her spine whenever the three of them were in the same vicinity or whenever Barrett would mention Jackie in conversation or if conversely Jackie would let slip she had been in a meeting with Barrett. Callie had forgotten just how debilitating it could be.

Swallowing the feeling back and returning her smile from where it had slipped, she seamlessly carried on their conversation. "Oh, thanks."

"Well, don't sound too pleased!"

Callie cringed. Clearly her facade wasn't entirely perfect, but she could still feign indifference and glide her way through. She'd mastered fooling her father into thinking everything was fine years before.

"Sorry. It's just been a busy morning. While you may be able to go out galivanting for lunch, some of us have to work." Steering the chat back around to the business was a safe bet.

"Everything okay?"

Or so she thought. She'd walked into that one. She should have known her father would have jumped to conclusions.

"Yes!" she affirmed, waving some paper in the air which she'd just grabbed in a vain attempt to look busy and engrossed. "Just a busy morning, I promise. So where's my treat?"

She stood behind her desk as if it was a shield. She hoped an actual physical barrier would make her feel more confident in her own facade.

"I'm sorry?" Barrett asked, eyebrows raised.

"You go to lunch, come here straight after, and don't bring me something? That's just not on."

"Oh. I thought you would have eaten."

"Dad, I'm joking! It's fine," she protested, waving her hands in surrender.

"Have you eaten?"

Now Barrett was back on this.

"Dad..." She walked back around to stand in front of him again, gripping his strong upper arms with her hands. "I'm fine. Work is busy but not so busy that I haven't eaten lunch. And I wasn't really expecting anything, I was just messing with you."

"Okay." Callie heard the hidden words. *Sorry. But I still worry.* "So, do you have time in your busy schedule for half an hour with your dad?"

"Of course. You want a coffee?" she asked, smiling as she walked over to her coffee station.

"Sure."

Callie watched as Barrett walked over to the drafting table, scrutinising what Callie was working on. Trying not to read too much into the way his head tilted or the hum which quietly slipped from his lips, she concentrated instead on choosing a coffee pod, knowing what sort of blend her father liked. The last thing she needed was to project her own dissatisfaction into her father's reaction.

∼

Jackie's footsteps were soft on the carpeted floor as she walked through the bullpen of designers heading towards the open door on the far side of the room. Approaching it, she could hear music drifting out, meaning Callie was busy drawing. As she got closer, she could make out the frantic syncopated notes of Mozart's *Symphony No. 25 in G Minor*. She recognised it as the song she would listen to when she was struggling creatively, a desperate attempt to pump some fire in her through its melody.

Once in the open doorway, she leaned against the doorframe, watching for a second as Callie worked, oblivious to her presence.

It had been nearly a month since she had started at the business, and seeing Callie again was singularly the hardest and easiest part of the whole process. Easy because after an initial spell of awkwardness, they quickly realised they worked well together without any overhanging resentment, hatred, or bitter feelings. Hard because on too many occasions Jackie had found herself staring, wondering what was going through the young woman's mind, worrying about her and having to remind herself it wasn't her place anymore.

As if to make a point, Callie grunted, throwing down her pencil and screwing up the paper in front of her before aimlessly throwing it towards the bin next to the door. She missed, unsurprisingly, and it landed at Jackie's feet instead.

"Woah! Steady on."

Callie's head shot up, surprise painted across her features.

"Shit. Sorry, did I get you?"

"No, not quite. But I'm wondering what the paper ever did to you."

"Urgh, I'm just..." She waved her hands in the air before clenching and unclenching her fists.

"Okay..." Jackie took a step into the office, closing the door behind her. Her previous concerns about not getting involved were rapidly forgotten, knowing that Callie was close to beating herself up. She needed to change focus. "Step away from the table and go sit down. I'll make us a coffee."

She steered Callie by the shoulders to the sofa where she almost pushed her into sitting down before heading to the coffee machine. After setting it off, she turned around and lent against the table, crossing her arms over her chest and pinning Callie with a stare.

"Oh, don't do that. I'm fine," Callie retorted.

"Okay, but that doesn't mean that there's nothing wrong. What's with the frustration?"

Jackie waited patiently, just watching until Callie looked up at her from where she was braced against her knees on her elbows.

"I'm just...going through a bit of a dry spell, that's all. Feeling a bit blocked creatively."

"Hmm okay. Any reason in particular?" Jackie asked, turning to finish their coffees. She left Callie's black but added a splash of milk to her own.

"No, not that I'm aware of."

"It's not..." Jackie paused, watching the milk she had just poured into her cup swirl around. "It's not because I'm back, is it?"

"What?" Callie may have sounded incredulous, but Jackie needed to know it wasn't down to her. If she was responsible for Callie's worrying...

"Look, I know that it's seemingly been okay between us, but what if it's affecting your work? You know, subconsciously."

"Oh, don't be daft!" Callie scoffed, waving her hand towards her coffee and encouraging Jackie to come sit with her. "It's been simmering for months; it's nothing to do with you. It's actually been kind of nice having you around."

"Yeah?"

"Yeah. It's comforting to know there's someone here who gets me. Who sees me for me, not a senior partner or Barrett Montgomery's daughter, you know?" Callie shrugged. "It's been kind of refreshing."

Jackie looked at Callie's face, the raw honesty shining through. She was right, it had been an easy transition to be around Callie again.

"It's been nice being around you again too," Jackie admitted softly, bumping Callie's shoulder lightly. Callie's smile was open and genuine, and Jackie felt her breath hitch at its appearance. "So what's been simmering?"

"Huh? Oh, Dad popped in after your lunch, and him being here always makes me kind of…" She gestured with her hands, some kind of clawing action with tense fingers. That, coupled with the scrunch of her nose made Jackie chuckle.

"I can't believe you still get nervous around him!"

"Not nervous so much as…" She sighed, clearly struggling for the right words still. "I don't know. I always feel under scrutiny when he's in the office. Even when he just pops in. That sounds daft, doesn't it?!"

"A little, yeah. But you look up to him; his approval has always meant a lot to you. So it's kind of understandable."

"Kind of?"

"Well, yeah. You're also thirty-three and now a senior partner of the business which he handed over to you, so I also think you may have gotten his approval."

Callie let her head drop back, eyes closing. She suddenly looked exhausted.

"What if I mess it all up, Jacs?" Callie muttered almost imperceptibly.

"How could you mess it up?"

"I..." Jackie saw something flicker across Callie's face before she sighed and pulled herself back upright. "Nothing. I'm just tired."

Jackie watched as Callie straightened her shoulders, cleared her throat, and rolled her neck. Just like that the mask was back up, a smile plastered on her face, although Jackie could tell it wasn't quite reaching her eyes.

"Callie, is everything okay?"

"Everything's fine," Callie insisted, standing up from the sofa.

"Cal..." Jackie stood as well, her hand instinctively wrapping around Callie's wrist to stop her from moving away. Realising what she had done, she looked down to see Callie's fingers untense and unfurl from where they had obviously been curled into a fist.

"I'm fine, Jacs. Honestly. You don't need to worry about me."

Jackie released her hand slowly, not wanting to sever the unexpected contact but respecting that it wasn't her place anymore. Taking a step back, she headed towards the office door, chest constricting with a heavy uncertainty at what had just transpired. Once at the door, she stopped, turning around to see Callie stood where she had left her. There was a look on her face she couldn't place. An uncertainty to having Jackie in her vicinity, as if she had already revealed too much and was regretting it, despite not saying anything at all.

"I'll always worry about you, Cal. That's never stopped, even though it's not my place anymore," Jackie admitted.

"Jacs..."

"I'll let you get back to work," Jackie murmured, aware that she had probably said too much.

She closed the door behind her, quickly making her way back across the office and praying that no one stopped her on her journey. Once across the threshold of her own office, she closed the door, fell against it, and screwed her eyes shut, fighting back the tears that threatened to flow.

Oh God, where did that come from? It may have been only a few seconds, and it may have only been one small interaction, one gentle touch, and some words, but suddenly... Suddenly it was twelve years ago, and Jackie was overwhelmed by the torrent of emotions which threatened to engulf her.

She always knew that Callie was the one that got away; that's why she'd never really had any other serious relationships in the intervening years. She'd told herself this wouldn't be an issue, that she could work with Callie. But apparently, her heart had other ideas.

Chapter Five

Callie fidgeted with her ring, spinning it around over and over, trying her best to keep her focus in the room. Jayne from Finance was delivering this month's company figures, and Callie struggled to remain interested at the best of times, least of all now when she really was fighting the urge to switch off and bury her head in the sand. She knew the company was struggling; she didn't need reminding on a monthly basis. Her father had put her in charge, had handed her the reins, and so far, she hadn't done a great job at keeping the ship from sinking. *It wasn't your fault,* she told herself, although it really wasn't much of a convincing pep talk.

Looking up from her laptop, she spied Jackie across the table, frantically scribbling something in her notebook while glancing at the screen at the front of the conference room. Putting down her pen, she glanced at whatever she had written one last time, chewing her lip in a sure sign of concentration.

Callie purposefully avoided looking at the action once she noticed what she was doing, remembering vividly just how sexy she used to find it. *What's with the used to? It's still sexy.*

Averting her eyes, she tried to focus again on what Jayne was saying, finding it even harder than before. The sudden shuffle of chairs and movement within the small group signalled the end of the meeting, and Callie realised she must have zoned out for longer than she initially thought.

"Hey."

Jackie stood beside her, confusing Callie further. She wasn't sure when Jackie had walked across the room, so she hurriedly collected her own items from the table, standing in the process.

"Hey," Callie replied with a quick smile.

"Can I walk back with you to your office?"

"Erm, yeah sure," Callie said, gesturing for Jackie to lead the way.

Silence lingered between the pair as they made their way out of the conference room and down the corridor towards Callie's office. Ever since that moment in her office last week, Callie found herself struggling to know what to say to Jackie. It was just beginning to edge into awkwardness when Jackie finally spoke.

"So how much of that did you actually listen to?" she asked, leaning towards Callie's ear slightly as they walked. Callie looked around, a mixture of shock and feigned offence painting her features. "Oh, come on, Callie. I saw you zone out five minutes into that presentation."

"Shh." Callie tilted her head towards her office door as they reached it, ushering Jackie inside. "Did anyone else notice?" she asked, panicking as she closed the door behind them.

Jackie laughed softly. "I don't think so."

"Urgh. I'm sorry. I just really struggle with all the numbers stuff. And Jayne was talking a *lot* of numbers today." Callie grimaced before pushing off from the door and making her way past Jackie.

"Yeah, there was a lot of detail today. And I know it's not your strong point, but Callie, you need to know what's going on. Even just a little bit."

"I know! I know." Callie dropped down into the chair behind her desk. "It's not like I don't know what's going on, Jacs. I do. I know the state we are in, and I know why..."

Callie stopped herself from saying anything else. Why did she nearly say something more? She shook her head, shaking the thought away with it. "My focus is just a little off today. I'll take a look at Jayne's presentation this afternoon, try and re-familiarise myself with what she said."

"I can help if you like?" Jackie said, taking a step closer. "I could go grab us some lunch, and we could go over stuff together. I can highlight the things you really need to know, explain those you don't understand. No judgement, I promise," Jackie reassured, hands up in a diffusing gesture. "And only if you want?"

"Really?" Callie had never had a better offer in this office. Suddenly, all her anxious awkwardness dissolved, and Jackie was like a guardian angel. An angel with the ability to talk finance in plain English.

"Yeah. Of course."

Callie sighed with relief. "That would be amazing."

"Okay, well how about I go grab us something to eat, and I'll meet you back here in half an hour?"

"Sounds like a plan."

"Fab. And I'm going to get Carol to book me out for an hour after lunch, so we're not rushed. Maybe have a word with Beka and get her to do the same?" Jackie suggested as she headed back towards the door.

"Yep, good idea," Callie said as she pushed up from her chair and followed Jackie. "See you in a bit."

"See you soon." Jackie waved over her shoulder as she walked away.

Callie noted Beka watching over the top of her computer screen. She was a good assistant, but she had a need to know everything going on whether it was her business or not. Callie could already sense that she was bristling with not knowing whatever Callie and Jackie were discussing.

"Beka, can you please book me out until one o'clock please?"

"Oh, umm...we were meant to have a meeting at twelve thirty," Beka replied, standing up and brushing down her skirt.

"Oh crap, we were. Umm...can we re-schedule? It's just myself and Miss Taylor..."

"Oh. Miss Taylor. Sure." The bite with which Beka spat out Jackie's name did not go unnoticed by Callie.

"Beka..." Callie tried to bite back the sigh she wanted to release. She'd noticed a certain attitude creeping in with Beka recently, and she needed to speak with her about it. But it was nothing too concerning just yet, and it really hadn't extended much past her own office. If anything, she was worried that something outside of work was affecting her mood. "If I can have these ninety minutes, we'll meet first thing tomorrow."

"You have Carmichael at nine thirty."

"You and I are both in early. I'll bring breakfast, and we can catch up," she said hopefully. Maybe she could work this to her advantage and talk to Beka in a more informal setting. "Please, Beka. I need this meeting with Jackie now. It's important."

"Fine," Beka said sharply, sitting down and tapping on her keyboard. "I'll put you on *do not disturb* until one."

"Thank you."

"I'll have that granola from the coffee shop across the street and an almond milk latte with an extra shot," she replied with an almost smug, definitely insincere smile.

"Consider it done," Callie promised, clasping her hands in front of her. "I've got a few things to sort, so can you just send Jacs in when she gets back with lunch?"

"Of course," Beka answered, not meeting her eyes and not giving her the usual warm smile she offered with her work.

As Callie closed her office door, the tone of Beka's voice

resonated in her head. Why had she sounded so put out when Callie said that Jackie would be coming back? Maybe this was because of whatever was bugging her and affecting her usually chirpy mood. First thing tomorrow, she would address it. But right now, she was very aware that she was about to have lunch with Jackie Taylor.

∽

"Oh my God, why can't Jayne explain it like this?" Callie exclaimed, waving her hands at the laptop screen which was on display on the coffee table in front of them.

"Because I imagine Jayne is used to presenting to groups of fellow number-oriented people and not artistic geniuses such as yourself."

"Ha! Very funny."

Jackie lent back from where she had been sat eating over the table, brushing her fingers on her napkin before crossing her legs. She took a few seconds to look at Callie, who was too busy eating to notice. She couldn't put her finger on why, but this was probably the most relaxed she had seen Callie in the past month. And even then, there was still a tension she carried in her shoulders. Jackie wondered if there was anyone who knew what her burden was or if, like she always had, she was carrying it on her own.

"What?"

Callie's voice broke her out of her train of thought, and she blinked, bringing her focus back to Callie who was now looking at her.

"Huh?"

"What's wrong? You're staring at me."

"Oh. Oh, no. Sorry, I just... I just got lost in my head for a moment."

"Okay..." Callie drew out, not sounding convinced.

"Umm, anyway..." Jackie lent forward and threw her napkin into her takeaway container. "Now that you have a better grasp of what these numbers mean, I do have an idea." Jackie realised she sounded no more confident speaking about this than she did a moment prior.

"An idea?" Callie's face was bright and hopeful, and for a split second, Jackie could see the young, twenty-two-year-old still hidden behind those eyes. She desperately hid the shiver which went through her body at the sight, her breath being stolen by the memory of a youthful, younger Callie. Seeing Callie's questioning gaze kept her in the conversation, but only just.

"Yes, and I want to run it past you before I say anything to the rest of the senior team. See if you think it's worth it before I waste my time preparing a pitch."

"I doubt you'd be wasting your time, but sure, let's hear it."

Jackie grinned at Callie as she kicked off her boots and put her feet up on the coffee table, head on the back of the sofa.

"Comfy?"

"Mmhmm. I'm trying to relax after all that finance talk. Plus, lunch made me sleepy."

"Well, really giving me hope in listening to me, Cal," Jackie playfully scoffed.

"I'm listening! Now come on, what's this idea?" Callie nudged Jackie, and she tried not to read too much into the way her body tingled at the fleeting touch.

Jackie took a final look at Callie, eyes closed and more relaxed than she had seen her for a long while. She was breathing gently, hands resting on her stomach slowly rising up and down in rhythm with her lungs. She turned away and looked back at her laptop. There was no information on it, nothing she needed to tout her idea, but if she looked at Callie much longer, she may never say what she needed to say.

Or maybe you'll say exactly what you need to say? Jackie coughed, clearing her throat and her mind.

"Okay. So has the business ever considered a learning partnership?"

"How do you mean?" Callie mumbled, with her eyes still closed.

"With the local college. I did it at a previous company, and it worked really well. We approach the college and offer them so many work experience placements for students who are pursuing a qualification in any of the areas we work in. Could be design, construction, client services, finance, anything. The students get free experience, we get some help and great exposure, plus potential first pick of the next cycle of talent out there."

A silence settled over the office, and after a moment of no response, Jackie dared to look at Callie. She was greeted with an intense gaze, a slight smile lifting at the corners of her mouth. For a few seconds, they held each other's stare, not daring to move or break the moment. Jackie saw the bob of Callie's throat as she swallowed before she broke the silence by clearing her throat.

"I think it's a great idea," Callie said, her voice quiet but certain as she pushed herself upright.

"You do?" Jackie replied, unconvinced.

"Yeah. I think it's just what we need. The senior team will love it."

"They will?" Jackie still wasn't sold. Even though she knew the merits of what she was suggesting, there was something about suggesting it to Callie which was making her doubt her own idea. *And this was meant to be the easy sell...*

"Yes! I think it's just the new take on things we need. It's brilliant."

Jackie relaxed, Callie's enthusiasm so genuine that she couldn't help but be transfixed and soothed by it. "So you'll help me pitch it?"

Callie spluttered on the mouthful of coffee she had just swallowed, leaning forward to put down her cup on the table in between coughs.

"What? Why do you need my help?"

"Because you know these guys. You know which buttons to press and where to focus."

"I..."

Jackie gave Callie her best pleading look, fluttering her eyelashes. Callie merely scowled in return.

"That's a low blow, Taylor. You know I can't resist that eyelash flutter," she admonished, pointing at Jackie.

"Yes, I know. And yes, it was. But I promise this is going to be good."

"I honestly don't know what you think I'll bring to it, it sounds like you've got it sorted, but anything I can do, I will," Callie resigned, leaning forward to grab her coffee again.

"You need to start giving yourself more credit, Callie Montgomery," Jackie said as she started clearing up their rubbish from their lunch. "You may just draw the *pretty pictures,* as you put it"—she gave Callie a look which said, *yeah, I remember that comment* —"but you are vital to this company."

"Oh God, are you going to start giving me daily pep talks?" Callie retorted as she stood up as well, walking over to the desk with her coffee.

Jackie dropped the rubbish a little more forcefully into the bin than she intended, sighing with frustration. "I'm not joking, Callie."

"No, I know you're not."

"But?"

"But what?" Callie shot back from behind her desk, looking up at Jackie.

Jackie stood with her hands on her hips, staring at Callie from across the room. She was so tempted to say something, to voice the concerns which had been plaguing her for the past few weeks, but she couldn't fathom whether Callie's denial was to do with her burying her head in the sand or her reluctance to speak to Jackie about her life outside work.

"Nothing," she sighed, resigning herself to ending the conversation there. It wasn't her place to make Callie talk. Was it? Isn't that what friends did?

But I'm not sure what I am to her.

Chapter Six

Callie pushed her vegetables around her plate, trying desperately not to let her annoyance show. It had been a long week, her struggle to focus on the finance meeting only the beginning of her troubles, and her lunch date with Jackie the only high point.

Her catch up with Beka on Tuesday morning had been fruitless; the woman had insisted that there was nothing going on outside of work, yet her attitude hadn't changed. In fact, it had gotten worse. Beka was practically scowling when Jackie brought a new client into the office to introduce them to Callie. After her curt and almost rude behaviour, Callie had to take her to one side and have a word, warning Beka that if there was a next time, she would be making a formal report.

Callie wasn't comfortable with confrontation, it made her skin crawl to even think about having to reprimand anyone, and she had been lucky that up until recently, Beka had been exemplary in her behaviour. But the whole affair, however short it was, had put her in a foul mood for the rest of the day. Jackie had called by during lunch and tried to reassure her that she had done the right thing, but even that visit hadn't lightened her mood like they had done of late.

The Carmichael meeting had been productive but frustrating, their new business manager trying to exert his power and make demands now that he had been let loose from under the watchful eye of the company director. Apparently, he thought that a healthy dose of good old-fashioned sexism was the best way to get what he wanted—a fact which didn't go down well with Jackie, Callie, or the female project manager. Callie ended the meeting frustrated and angry, and once again, it was left to Jackie to soothe her, promising that she would speak to not only the project manager to ensure that they were okay but also Carmichael himself about his newest employee's behaviour. Just as she was trying to forget the whole humiliating meeting, Carmichael then rang to apologise. Profusely. And by the time this was all over with, it was only Wednesday.

She had managed to make it through Thursday without any massive dilemmas or issues, however the workload hadn't eased up. She was rushed and in demand from the moment she walked into the office to the moment she left, a full eleven hours later.

Friday had maybe been a little calmer but only marginally, and the rest of the office seemed to think that the last day of the week meant it was acceptable to drop the pace despite none of the deadlines changing. Things were not progressing quickly enough, they seemed to be stacking up on her desk faster than she could remove them, and she could feel herself slowly sinking under the weight of it all.

And now here she was at a family dinner, barely able to keep her eyes open, listening to Jake talk about how great his week was. Whoever this Frank was he kept mentioning, he was clearly charmed by Jake's big talk and even bigger promises.

She reined herself in; that wasn't fair to Jake. Just because he was young and brash when they worked together didn't mean he hadn't matured since working somewhere else. There was every chance he had learnt from his mistakes and was just genuinely doing well. But it seemed modesty wasn't something he had learnt, and whether the story he was spinning was true or not, it was the last thing she needed to hear right now. She really wasn't interested in people self-aggrandizing anyway, but hearing it from her brother after the week she'd had was just too much.

"So, Frank practically confirmed that I'll be getting this quarter's managerial bonus after that," Callie heard Jake proudly proclaim. It was the final straw, and she dropped her fork down on her plate, pushing her chair back with a screech.

"Callie? Is everything okay?" Annie asked, a questioning look on her face.

"Yes. I've just got a headache, and it's killed my appetite," she lied, picking up her plate and walking away.

As she made her way out of the dining room and into the kitchen, she slid her plate onto the countertop, bracing her hands against the marble surface and letting her head hang with a sigh. Her excuse wasn't a complete lie; she'd had the headache which was currently pulsing through her skull for at least forty-eight hours and nothing was seemingly having any effect on it.

"You could at least try to make it a little less obvious," Jake's familiar voice sneered from behind her. Her temples throbbed with the mere thought of having to have a conversation with her brother.

"What are you talking about, Jake?"

"Leaving the table like that," he continued, stepping up behind her and placing his plate on top of hers. The sound of ceramic upon ceramic grated over her nerves.

"I have a headache, Jake. It's been a really tough week."

"Things not picking up with your new recruit?" he asked, almost mocking in his delivery. What did Jackie have to do with this?

"Things are fine. Jackie's working out really well."

"Sure. That's why you look like you've barely slept and you're being evasive when Dad asks questions."

"I'm not...and what do you mean, I look like I've not slept?" Jake did not need to know that was painfully close to the truth.

"You look terrible," Jake continued without caring about just how offensive he was being. "You need a break. Somewhere hot and sunny. I'm thinking of booking two weeks in Spain. Might take Dad. We could find a nice little golf resort. Treat him, you know, with my bonus..."

Oh, there it was. Now this made sense. This was just another opportunity to make a comment on how great things were going for Jake at the moment, sailing through life without a care in the world while Callie was left dealing with the responsibility.

"Are you fucking kidding me?"

"No. I'm telling you, Cal, walking away from the business was the best thing I could have done. Now, I have all the reward and none of the stress of you breathing down my neck." Anger boiled in Callie, but she fought to push it down. Jake lent in closer. "Maybe you should consider it. You know, passing things on and taking on something new. It does seem to be getting a bit much."

"A bit much? It's only a bit much because of you, Jake! We don't all have the opportunity to walk away. Maybe I shouldn't have given it to you either."

"You did me a favour. That company was destined to fail with you at the helm. I just jumped off the ship before it sank."

"You know what, Jake, believe what you want," Callie spat, exhausted and drained. She pushed off from the counter and walked back into the dining room.

"I'm going," she announced, not stopping as she passed through.

"Already? But we've not finished dinner," Barrett said.

"Yeah, well, like I said, I've got a stinking headache and no appetite. I'll call you tomorrow. Night, Rob. Sorry for bailing."

She made her way into the hallway, grabbing her coat and keys.

Just as her hand curled around the door handle, Annie's soft voice stopped her in her tracks.

"Callie..."

Callie sighed and closed her eyes. She struggled with lying to her mother, and she desperately hoped she wasn't going to push this tonight.

"I'm fine, Mama. Good nights' sleep, a lie-in tomorrow, and I'll be good." She turned, giving a weary smile. Something in her look must have conveyed her plea because as Annie opened her mouth to speak, something stopped her, and she snapped it shut.

"If you're sure my darling." She took Callie's face in her hands, kissing her cheek softly. "I love you. Let me know that you get home okay."

"Love you too, Mama."

Chapter Seven

"Hello," Jackie announced her arrival into Callie's office, finding her leaning back on her stool, arms crossed over her chest, a frown marring her soft features.

"Hey." Her response was short and brusque, a sure sign she was in her head about something.

Jackie stepped further into the room, stopping behind Callie and looking over her shoulder at the design which was causing her so much consternation.

"It's a beautiful design," Jackie commented. It really was; Callie always had a certain flair, and it showed in her work. Even the most mundane of designs somehow lifted when Callie put her mark on them.

"It's lines and corners. Windows and doors." Callie shrugged, dropping her arms so her palms slapped against her thighs.

Jackie looked at her profile for a second longer before grasping the back of her stool and swinging it around, bringing Callie face to face with her. Crouching down to be at her level, she studied Callie's face.

"What's going on with you?"

"W-what?"

"Ever since I've got back, there seems to be something... I don't know. Like you're not quite fully engaged. What's wrong?" Callie shrugged again. "Do you not enjoy it anymore? Designing?"

"I... this isn't the place to talk about this," Callie muttered, looking down at her fingers scratching aimlessly at her trousers.

"Tough. Because we're talking about it."

Callie's gaze darted upwards at the harsh tone of Jackie's voice. A second passed before she let out a frustrated huff, pushing up from her stool and effectively forcing Jackie back a step. Jackie straightened up as she watched Callie stomp across the office, clearly contemplating what she wanted to say.

"It's all the same—glass-fronted buildings and big windows. It's client specifications and what's on-trend, and it doesn't excite me anymore." She threw the pencil down on the coffee table before dropping down on the sofa. "I can't remember the last time I drew just for the sake of drawing. Just for me. Picking up a pencil is such an effort these days."

Jackie's heart cracked. For as long as she had known Callie, she had known she was an artist. Drawing was her safe space, the way she came down at the end of the day, the way she channelled her emotions. For her not to be drawing at all scared Jackie.

"Oh, honey. If being here makes you that unhappy, why are you still here?" she asked, tentatively taking a seat next to Callie.

"Because there's no one else. Jake tried and fucked it up. So now I need to stay and make sure that the business survives." Her voice wavered as tears threatened to fall.

"What are you talking about?"

"When Dad retired, I had just agreed to head up the design department, and Jake was in your position. Within a few months, we noticed things weren't really working. Jake was over-promising and under-delivering for a bunch of prospective clients. He undercut excessively on a load of deals in negotiations. To the point he could have put us in danger of litigation. He's why the business has struggled for the past couple of years."

"Does Barrett know?" Jackie asked, fighting down the knee-jerk reaction to tear into Jake. Not only had he jeopardised the business Barrett had spent years creating, but he had also left Callie to clean up his mess. If she focussed too much on that fact, though, Jackie was in danger of saying something she would regret.

"Not the full extent. Jake and I agreed we would say the business and him weren't a proper fit, but we wouldn't tell Dad the details. I didn't want Jake feeling like a disappointment, and I didn't want Dad to feel he had to get involved in the business again." Jackie smiled gently at Callie's selflessness, but Callie shook her head. "I've let him down enough. He's had to pick up the pieces too many times from my messes; I didn't want him to feel he had to do that again."

"Let him down? When?" Jackie asked with a frown. As far as she had been aware, Callie had always been the apple of Barrett's eye.

"Doesn't matter. It was a long time ago. The point is, I told him I could handle this, and I can't." Jackie could start to see the frustration literally radiating from Callie's body. She wasn't sure if it was directed towards Jake, herself, or just at the sheer fact she had been holding this in, but either way, she hated to see it mar Callie's beautiful nature.

"Jake and his decisions are not your responsibility. And I really doubt you've ever let your father down. He worships the ground you walk on."

"Yeah, well, probably not as much as you think. And probably not for much longer."

"I'm sure that's not true, honey—"

"Fuck!" Callie kicked the coffee table across the floor. "Fucking Jake!"

"Woah! Calm down." Jackie held her hands up in surrender. She knew Callie was just venting, but she was concerned about just how wound up she had got herself.

"Sorry. I just... I've made such a mess of everything again."

Jackie really was confused. Callie seemed genuinely convinced that Barrett would be disappointed in Callie, a view which really didn't tally up with what Jackie saw and knew to be true. Unless something serious had happened in the intervening years...*oh*.

A sudden realisation dawned on Jackie. She shifted around in her seat so she could see Callie as best she could. She needed to look her in the eye for this.

"Callie. I need you to know what I'm about to say, your dad told me because he needed a friend to talk to."

"What are you talking about?" Callie asked, frustration subsiding and confusion taking over. "Has he told you something? About the business?"

"No, I...Callie, honey. I...I know what happened."

"Know what?"

"I know what you tried to do..." The words stuck in Jackie's throat, and she could see the panic settle across Callie's features as she realised what she was trying to say. She watched as Callie's body stiffened, preparing to bolt. She grasped her hand out of fear that she was about to run. "I know you..." She looked down at Callie's hand. It was warm and soft and felt so right, even in this situation, within her own. "I know you tried to kill yourself."

She held on tighter to Callie's hand, but she wasn't sure who she was holding on for. Suddenly, Callie's presence felt transient, like it could be ripped away at any moment, and the thought of losing her, in whatever form, was terrifying.

"He called me. It had been a couple of weeks, and you were back home. I knew it was you straight away. I knew something had happened to you. I could feel it, here." She dared to let go of Callie's hand and placed her own over her heart. "He told me what happened, about it all. Or at least the bits he knew." Jackie took a deep breath. "I'm telling you this because you need to know the most important thing in his life is you. He doesn't care about the business if it is making you unhappy. He won't care that you kept this from him; he will understand. You did not let him down then, and you would not be letting him down now."

An uneasy silence settled over the office, Callie staring at Jackie for a few moments before she blinked, regaining her focus.

"You knew?" she asked hoarsely, the emotion clearly lodged in her throat.

"Yes."

"Why didn't you say anything when you got back?"

"Because I didn't feel I needed to. I arrived to see this amazingly beautiful, confident woman with a heart full of love, and you didn't need reminding of a time when that wasn't the case." Jackie wiped away a tear that had rolled down her cheek with the back of her fingers. "Not from me. The Callie I saw standing in that boardroom that first day, I was so proud of her. I still am. And so is your dad."

"Some days, I don't feel deserving of that," Callie said quietly, tears pooling in her eyes.

"I know you don't. But that doesn't change what other people feel or think."

A knock followed swiftly by the opening of her office door broke their moment. Jackie silently cursed the intrusion of Beka as she hastily wiped away any remaining tears and swallowed any residual emotion down.

"Callie, here are these... Oh, sorry. I didn't realise you had company."

Jackie picked up on the terse tone of her voice, which was becoming ever more apparent as the days went on. She wasn't entirely sure what she had done to deserve her attitude, but she couldn't give her a second thought right now.

Callie quickly rose from the sofa, and Jackie watched as she discreetly tried to wipe her face, looking out of the window to hide her tears. She knew that Callie was in no position to say anything, so she decided to take control of the situation. Beka wouldn't like it, but Jackie couldn't care less.

"Can you give Callie a moment, please, Beka?"

"Is everything okay, Callie?"

Jackie bristled as Beka disregarded her completely, trying to get closer to Callie.

"Everything is fine. Callie will be with you in a minute."

"Do you need anything?" Beka peered over Jackie's shoulder, effectively ignoring the fact that she was even there. It was the final straw.

"Beka! Miss Montgomery will be with you in just a moment. Now please leave!" she snapped.

Beka huffed, clearly biting back whatever retort she had on the tip of her tongue and instead turning on her heel and storming out. The sound of the door slamming behind her made Jackie flinch, and she turned to see Callie with her back still to her.

"Thank you," Callie whispered hoarsely.

Jackie walked over, stood beside Callie, and stared out the window alongside her at the murky grey sky, which perfectly reflected what she had no doubt they both felt at this moment.

"No problem." Jackie shot a glance at Callie, her face pale and drawn, tears still silently rolling down her cheeks. She hated seeing Callie like this. Despite Callie's tendencies to hide her emotions from the rest of the world, Callie had always been open around Jackie, and Jackie had known she was hiding something from the first moment she had seen her again. But to see that truth so clearly now, for her to let down those walls and show how much she was hurting, it hurt Jackie as well. "Why don't you go home for the rest of the day?"

"I can't."

"Cal..."

"No, I mean, I can't be alone right now. There's too much going on in here," she waved a hand around her head, "and it'll only spiral."

"Where can you be? Here's not good for you right now."

"Usually, Mum helps. Let's me crash there, but I don't know. I can't go there without being asked questions, and I'm not ready to unpack all of this on them. Not yet anyway."

"Okay. Give me a minute." Jackie walked over to Callie's desk and picked up the phone. "Hi Carol, it's me. Miss Montgomery isn't feeling well and can't drive, so I'm taking her home." Jackie looked up to see Callie staring at her, fighting back another wave of tears. God, did she want to wrap her up in her arms and tell her it would all be okay. Carol's voice on the other end of the phone kept her mind from drifting too far, pulling her back to the conversation at hand. "Can you put me out of office for my emails and calls? I'll get back to everyone tomorrow. And I think I have a meeting at two. Can you reschedule with my apologies? Thanks, Carol."

"Jackie..." Callie started as Jackie put down the phone.

"No arguments. Get your stuff together. I'll be back in ten minutes to get you." Jackie headed towards the door before pausing. "Would you like me to speak to Beka?"

While she wanted to protect Callie from as much additional stress and confrontation as possible, she also wasn't sure how much more she was welcome to interfere. She might have already overstepped, even though she was fairly certain Callie's timid *thank you* earlier was an indication she hadn't.

"Please, if you don't mind," Caille said wearily, already at her desk and packing her laptop away.

"Of course not. I'll be back in a bit."

Jackie paused for a split second as she reached the door. As her hand rested on the handle, she took a moment to breathe. She wanted to collapse, to hide and cry for the woman she once loved. But right now, she needed to be strong for her, a constant in Callie's otherwise chaotic life. And her first challenge was going to be dealing with Beka. She knew that the moment she stepped over the threshold, Beka's questioning eyes would be on her.

As predicted, the door hadn't even had a chance to click shut before Beka was on her feet and striding over. The look on her face was one of pure disdain. This conversation was going to go down like a lead balloon, but that didn't concern Jackie. At this moment, the only thing that mattered was getting Callie home.

"Beka," Jackie held her hand up, stopping the assistant before she had a chance to speak. "Miss Montgomery is going home for the rest of the day. Please see to her schedule as appropriate. I'll be back in ten minutes to pick her up. If you could respect her privacy and not interrupt her during this time, she would be grateful."

Jackie sidestepped Beka and made her way towards her own office. She hadn't gotten further than two steps when Beka spoke.

"I don't know what you've said or done to her, but she's not been the same since you came here."

"Maybe," Jackie replied, turning. "But the difference is, I know which is the right way for her to be."

∼

"I'm fine, you know. You don't need to hang around and babysit me," Callie grumbled as she threw her keys onto the counter, heading into the kitchen and pouring herself a glass of water.

"I know. I just wanted to nosy at your place, and since I haven't had an invite yet..." Jackie stared at her from the kitchen door, a knowing look on her face. Callie just stared back, determined not to be the one to break the stalemate. "Come on, Cal, you really think I'm going to leave you? You said it yourself; you didn't want to be alone right now."

"Why are you here?" Callie asked, leaning back against the counter.

"What?"

"Why are you here? What do you want? Is it to get back at me for leaving?" She scrutinised Jackie, looking for some sort of clue as if she was just going to let her motives slip in front of her.

"Get back... do you really think I would do that? I don't want anything, Callie. Why would I want anything?"

Callie tried to ignore the look of hurt which flashed across Jackie's face at her insinuation.

"Because I can't think of any other reason why you would be doing this."

"Doing what?"

"This! I don't get it! Okay, I don't get it. After everything I put you through, after everything I did, why are you here? Why did you come back? Why have you been nice to me? Why the fuck have you come *here* this afternoon?" Callie's chest heaved with her outburst, months of pent-up confusion coming spilling out in one long tirade. There was no relief with her release. Instead, her shoulders were more tense and knotted than they had been in weeks. She clenched her hands by her side, feeling the blood pump through the veins in her neck as her jaw clenched. She watched intently as Jackie took a step towards her.

"Because none of that was your fault," Jackie said calmly. "Yes, I was angry at you for a while. I didn't know why you'd pushed me away, and that feeling stayed for years. But when Barrett called me... All I want is for you to be happy and healthy, Callie."

Callie suddenly started to feel suffocated under the weight of Jackie's kindness. "Sorry." She turned her back and let her head hang between her shoulders. "I'm sorry, I shouldn't have said that." She let out a deep breath, trying to calm herself, but it shook and trembled as she did so. She could feel her heart beating against her ribs, shame at how she spoke to Jackie rising in her throat. It was as if the emotion had come and cut her strings, all the fight and strength leaving her body in one giant wave. "This is why I shouldn't be alone when I'm like this. Too much stuff, not enough reason. Everything gets jumbled up."

"Apology accepted. Come sit down, and I'll make us a cuppa, yeah?"

"Okay." Callie took a step forward as Jackie moved towards the kitchen, their paths crossing. As they came level with one another,

Callie paused, her fingers gently resting on Jackie's arm to get her attention. "I really am sorry, Jacs."

"I know. Go on, I'll be in a minute."

Callie continued through to the living room, dropping down onto the sofa with a loud sigh. Letting her head fall into her hands, she ran her fingers through her hair and screwed her eyes shut at the dull throb which reverberated through her skull. Today had turned out to be a lot. There was still so much that needed to be said before everything was out in the open, but it already felt as though so much had been revealed. Jackie had always had the ability to see through her facade, to get her to open up, but she had so much she wasn't sure she wanted to share, or that she thought Jackie wouldn't want to hear, that she had tried even harder than usual to hide it all. But hadn't she always tried to do that with Jackie? And hadn't it always failed? That woman's perceptiveness was a blessing and a curse.

But really, wasn't this the opportunity she had been waiting for? For so many years, she had missed the presence of someone who would listen without judgement. Always wishing for someone like Jackie to come along and fill the void which had been left when Callie walked away all those years ago. Why was she fighting against admitting it was still there? Why was she still yearning for a replacement when the original was in front of her, and more importantly, offering to listen again?

The clunk of ceramic on wood and the dip of the sofa beside her brought her out of her musings, and she turned to see Jackie's soft, comforting smile radiating through her face and out from her eyes. God, those eyes would always melt her heart.

"It was Darla," Callie blurted out, shocked at her own abrupt start to the conversation.

"What?"

Callie closed her eyes, preparing herself for this conversation. Even those three words were hard for her to say; she wasn't sure how she was going to get through the rest.

"It...it was Darla."

"Your birth mother? That Darla?"

Callie nodded, already uncertain that her voice would hold out for the whole story.

"What was her? What did she do?" Callie could hear concern with a touch of anger in Jackie's voice. To say Jackie wasn't a fan of her mother would be an understatement. She'd never met the woman, and for that Callie was grateful. She wasn't sure Darla would survive if Jackie ever saw her.

"She came to visit me."

"When?" Jackie's voice suddenly took on a steely tone that shocked Callie.

"Umm...it was a couple of weeks before I...before I left you." She heard the sharp intake of breath beside her, the fact that after twelve years, Jackie might just be getting the answers she had been missing.

"What happened?"

"She must have been waiting for me. She was drunk and high as usual. Said I'd ruined her life. She couldn't get a job since being released and that was my fault, so I owed her. For that and all the money she'd wasted on me when I was growing up considering what a mistake I was." Callie sensed Jackie stiffen. "When I told her I didn't have anything and to leave me alone, she just started yelling at me about how I ruined everyone's lives, ruined everything I touched. How I was disgusting and no one wanted me anyway. And I wanted to run. I wanted to run away and ignore it all but..." Callie sobbed, tears flowing down her face. "But my legs wouldn't work, and I just stood there crying, letting her say these things. And then when she was done, she just looked at me like I was nothing, like I was dirt, spat at me, and walked away."

"Callie..." Callie barely registered that Jackie had said anything, she was so in her own memories.

"I couldn't stop hearing what she said. It just kept playing over and over in my head, reinforcing everything I'd ever thought about myself. Until I convinced myself that everyone would be better off if I wasn't around. I convinced myself that maybe if I wasn't here, so close to everyone and everything, it would be easier. For me and them. I knew things would go wrong between us sooner or later when you realised just how messed up I was. So I thought, if I just left, moved away to somewhere new, it would be better."

Callie paused, taking a deep breath as she tried to get her emotions under control. The tears were still coming, though, years of hidden truths coming out for the first time. She felt a hand cover her own and squeeze gently.

"Do you need to work through it?" Jackie asked softly. Even now, when she recalled how she ran away, scared and confused from the woman she loved, that woman was sitting here, Callie's concern paramount, offering to talk through her coping techniques. Jackie deserved so much better than what Callie had afforded her the past twelve years. Callie shook her head. She needed to finish this.

"I met Jen not long after I moved there, and she didn't ask too many questions or want to know too many details, and that was fine. It was good. It was what I thought I needed. Except it wasn't because everything was still there, just colliding in my brain and making less and less sense. The depression and feeling of worthlessness never lifted, just sat there, hiding in plain sight, festering away. And then I found out that Jen had been cheating on me. Another failure to add to my list. And she blamed me, so another life I'd messed with, right? So I started to think, maybe just moving away wasn't enough."

Callie looked at Jackie, whose face was also stained with tears, mascara making her eyes smudged and black. Her hand was still settled over Callie's, and Callie felt stronger, braver for it being there. A strange sense of contentment settled in her chest.

"It's weird because, for three years, I'd lived in a haze. Nothing seems clear when I look back on it. But that night..." She breathed deeply, closing her eyes as if she was right back at that moment.

"That night I remember perfectly. I remember taking my tablets from the cupboard, and there were only two missing because it was a new prescription. I remember finding Jen's diazepam in the cabinet, which she had for when she flew abroad. I remember picking a really nice bottle of white wine. I crushed them all up and stirred them into a glass of water. I tried to drink it but it took me a couple of tries because it hadn't all dissolved. Then I sat on the sofa with my glass of wine and just waited." Callie wiped a tear from her jawline where it threatened to fall. "After that, there's nothing until I woke up in the hospital."

"I'm so sorry, Callie. I don't—"

"It's fine. No one knows what to say," Callie interrupted with a shrug, wiping her face with the back of her hand.

"Does Barrett know? About Darla?"

"No," Callie whispered. "How could I tell him? I remember the look of rage from when I was a kid. If he found out she had come back and said those things...I was scared what he would do." She looked at Jackie, knowing what she was about to say. "Don't worry, though. I told my therapist. I've not been keeping it to myself entirely. But apart from her, you're the only other person I've told. Sorry, that's a lot to drop on someone," Callie added with a watery laugh.

"It's fine. Really, it's fine. I'm glad you told me," Jackie reassured her with another squeeze of her hand. Callie closed her eyes at the touch, her pulse calming momentarily.

"I'm sorry. About you finding out the way you did. I never thought Dad would ring you."

"It's—"

"Please, don't say it's fine. It's not." Callie looked at her thumbnail, picking at the skin along the edge. "I can't imagine how I'd have felt if it was the other way around."

"Honestly?" Jackie asked. Callie looked at her, nodding. She had been brutally honest with Jackie; the least she could do was let Jackie off-load back. "I was devastated. I cried for days. I didn't sleep properly for months, and I was distracted at work. Barrett was vague with the details, and I was grateful for that. But it was also horrific to know so little. My imagination filled in all the gaps, and it played out in my head every night when I tried to sleep. I kept thinking back to when I saw you last, how I knew that something was wrong, and I wish I had pushed harder to find out what it was. I ended up seeing someone as well, a therapist, because I couldn't stop thinking about it."

"Did it help?"

"Yeah, a bit. They taught me I wasn't responsible for you and your actions. That I couldn't blame myself for missing something, and even if I had said something, there is no guarantee it would have stopped you."

"Is that why you didn't get in touch? Because you didn't care anymore?" Callie asked quietly, her chest constricting.

Jackie shuffled across the sofa, closing the gap between them so their knees were touching. Callie watched as she lifted her hand, lacing her fingers through her own and gripping firmly. Jackie kept her head bowed, focussing on their joined hands.

"No, honey. There's a difference between not feeling responsible and not caring. I still cared very much." She lifted her eyes and met Callie's gaze. "I still do."

"So why didn't you? Get in touch, I mean?"

"Because you needed to heal on your own. As much as I wanted to be there with you, I knew this was something *you* needed to do. You needed to learn how to be that person who you had the potential to be and exist and be happy with yourself. But trust me when I say there's not been a day when I didn't think about you or how you were doing. All I ever wanted for you was happiness and peace."

"Thank you."

"For what?"

"Doing what was best for me, even when I had hurt you. Even

now, you're still looking after me. I don't deserve you in my life, let alone like this."

"I'm glad I'm back in it."

"Really?"

"Yeah, really," Jackie smiled. Callie swallowed thickly, the admission hanging heavy in the air. As if sensing the shift, Jackie spoke again. "Now, did you have any lunch?"

"No," sighed Callie, the weight of their previous conversation suddenly hitting her as a wave of exhaustion passed over her body.

"Well, how about I find us something to eat, and then you can get to bed?"

"Mmm sounds good," replied Callie, voice already starting to slur, her eyelids heavy.

"Okay. Lasagne coming right up."

Chapter Eight

Callie: Just arrived at Mum and Dads now. x
Jackie: You'll be fine. Just be honest. x
Callie: Easier said than done. I just know Dad is going to go crazy at Jake. x
Jackie: And if he does, then that's on Jake. This was his mess to sort, and it's time he did that. x

Callie blew out a breath, taking a moment to look up from her phone and through her car windscreen to the front door of her parent's home. Callie and Jackie had talked about what had happened with the business, and Jake, at great length over the past couple of days, with Jackie even taking the time to look at the finances and upcoming projections so Callie could argue in cold hard numbers if she needed to. But it hadn't all been business, Jackie offering more than just financial support, slipping seamlessly into an emotional sounding board when she sensed that Callie's thoughts were going awry. Now, she had conceded that she was as prepared as she was ever going to be for this conversation.

. . .

Callie: Thank you. Don't know what I would have done without you these past few days. x
  Jackie: Anytime. x

Callie wasn't sure what that meant. The past few days—few weeks, if she was being entirely honest—had thrown up a lot of long-buried feelings. Having Jackie as a confidante, someone she could trust and talk to, felt so natural and right, she wasn't sure how she had coped without her for over a decade. Being around her instantly provided Callie a sense of calm, her very presence acting as a comfort blanket. She found herself thinking of the woman more and more, conversations no longer just business-based and often going late into the night. At times, she thought that Jackie felt the same, but then Callie convinced herself that she was imagining it. What would Jackie see in Callie, the woman who broke her heart and literally ran away without explanation? Surely she couldn't develop feelings for such a person again, especially after so long apart.

Her radio silence didn't go unnoticed, another message popping up and breaking her from her reverie.

Jackie: Let me know when you're done. You can come over and unload if you need to. x

With a final, supposedly settling breath, she locked her phone, slid out of her car, and walked into the house. Dropping her keys onto the table in the hallway, she looked around for any signs of life, unsurprisingly hearing something from the kitchen.

"Hey, Mama," she called as she walked through.

Annie spun on the spot, wiping her hands on her apron and

stepping away from the cake batter she appeared to be in the middle of mixing.

"Callie! What a surprise! Why aren't you at work?" She lent in, pressing a kiss to her daughter's cheek as Callie came nearer.

Callie dipped her finger in the bowl, taking a swipe of the uncooked batter. "I took the day off," she mumbled as she licked her finger clean.

She could feel Annie study her for a second, and she looked around expectantly. Callie knew that such a flippant response wouldn't be enough for her mother.

"Everything okay?"

Callie lent against the counter, picking at the chocolate chips which were also sitting there waiting to be used in whatever Annie was baking, "Everything's fine. I've just had a headache for a couple of days." It wasn't a complete lie—the headache which had flared two days previously was only just subsiding.

"Oh, sweetie—"

"I'm fine," Callie stopped her before Annie could administer any more sympathy. She didn't think she could go through with the reason she was here if she had her mother fussing over her. "I've been sleeping it off. Is Dad here?"

"Yes, he's in his office."

"Okay." Callie breathed out, palms suddenly clammy with nerves. "I need to speak to you both about something."

"Callie? What's going on?"

Callie could hear the panic in her mother's voice, and it instantly made her stomach turn. Intent on getting this discussion started sooner rather than later, she started out of the kitchen and towards her father's office. "Everything's okay, Ma, I promise. But please come with me so I can talk to you and Dad together?" She tried to steady her voice as much as possible, her mother's concern only exacerbating her already skyrocketing anxiety.

As she pushed open her father's office door, he looked up, and she gave him a small, nervous smile.

"Hello, love. Didn't expect to see you today."

"Barrett, Callie needs to speak to us," Annie spoke before Callie could respond, and the worry present in her voice was overwhelming. Callie cursed herself, and her brother. She hated being the cause of that emotion in anyone, least of all her mother.

"Callie?" Her father's own concern jumped into the mix, albeit somewhat more stoic and measured than Annie's.

"Please, stop worrying. I'm fine." Callie had lost count of how many times she had said that since walking into the house ten minutes ago. "But there is something I need to talk to you about. Something I've not been entirely truthful about." She took a deep breath, an action she realised too late wasn't helping her parents keep calm. Now all she could think to do was spit out the words as fast as possible. "Jake didn't leave the company voluntarily."

There was a moment of eerie quiet in the room as the words sank in. Callie realised it was a strange thing to shout out, there was no explanation or build up, but she just wanted to stop Annie looking at her with *that* look on her face. Callie swallowed, hoping sooner or later someone would say something. Even if it was for her to repeat herself, at least it would be better than this silence.

"What do you mean?" Annie asked.

"She means he was fired," Barrett said, his voice low.

"Fired?" Annie stepped backwards and sank into the armchair which sat in the corner of the room. "Callie, is this true? Was Jake fired?" she questioned.

Callie nodded at her mother, before her vision focussed on her father. She could already sense the seeping anger that he was so desperately trying to hold in, his hands clenched against the arms of his desk chair, and this was before she'd told him any details.

"It was politely suggested that he leave before things got any more formal, but essentially, it was a consensus amongst the senior partners that he should go. I'm sorry I didn't tell you sooner, but I didn't want to upset Jake, so I told him I would keep quiet."

"What did he do?" Barrett asked bluntly.

"He messed up a load of contracts. Said we'd do them cheaper or quicker than we could."

"And this is why we saw that dip in the business a couple of years ago?"

"Yes." Callie swallowed. For some inexplicable reason, she felt more nervous now than before she had told her father. He was uncharacteristically calm and quiet compared to how she thought he would be reacting.

"I'm going to kill him."

"Dad..."

"Barrett..." Annie warned, at the same time.

"I'm not even mad about his stupid decisions. I'm more mad he made you lie to cover up his mistakes."

"I didn't lie, and he didn't make me." Although it was Jake who got her into this situation, Callie wanted to minimise any more comeback. Besides, she had had plenty of opportunities to come clean and had decided against it.

"No. I'm sure you suggested withholding this information from me, but I'm sure as hell he didn't fight you to change your mind!" Barrett finally lost his temper, rising from his chair with a screech as it pushed back across the floor.

"Is this why you've been so distracted?" Annie asked, trying to diffuse the situation and turning slightly to stand between Callie and her father. Callie just looked over her shoulder to where Barrett was now pacing back and forth behind his desk.

"Yes. Kind of. I'm struggling at the minute anyway. Having this on my mind as well was just too much."

Barrett's eyes shot to his daughter, rage suddenly replaced with worry. "What do you mean, you're struggling?"

"Not like..." Callie took a breath, knowing that her father's words only came from a place of love, however frustrating they could be. She hated how he always automatically meant a bad day meant she was relapsing in some way. It was the one of the reasons she hid how she felt from him. Putting on a mask was easier than defending her mental health every other week. "I'm just... My focus isn't there at the moment. I'm sure it's only temporary, but I also know that dealing with Jake isn't helping."

"Dealing with Jake? Callie, darling, is there something else going on?" Annie asked, picking up on Callie's poor choice of words.

"No! I just..." She dropped down into the chair which sat on the corner of Barrett's office, resting her forearms on her knees. "I'm sorry, I'm not explaining this very well, and the last thing I wanted to do was worry you."

"It's okay, sweetheart." Annie rested on the arm of the chair beside her, stroking a hand across her hair in a move reminiscent of when she was younger. Callie caught her giving Barrett a look across the room, silently telling him to sit down and listen. "Why don't you start with Jake? When did this happen?"

"Six months or so before he left. I don't know what happened; it was like he was trying to be more decisive or assertive or something. He started making decisions without discussing them with the senior team. Started getting pushy with deadlines or asking to squeeze budgets on projects. He was pulled into a meeting and told he needed to come back into line, but he just kept doing it. I don't know what he was trying to prove or to who. He tried to argue he knew what he was doing and that it would all work out in the end, but then he blew the Carmichael account—"

"That was him?" Barrett scoffed incredulously.

"We told him that at least two senior members needed to sign off on things, but he moved a meeting so he could sign off on it without anyone's knowledge." Callie spun her ring around her finger, using the repetitive motion to calm her mind so she could explain everything properly. "Carmichael rang me afterwards, said he had some concerns. Jake had cut the budget so much, he didn't actually know how we were going to hit all the essential requirements within the limit. When I looked, he was dangerously close to signing off without all the necessary checks."

"He was cutting corners?" Barrett asked quietly, seething behind his desk.

"No." Callie was quick to defend Jake even with everything he had done; she couldn't help it. "I honestly believe this was the worst case. We were lucky Carmichael knows us and the business well enough that he knew it wasn't right. Anyone else, I'm not sure they would have phoned me."

"What about the clients who left us? Was that him?"

"After we found out what had happened with Carmichael, we put a hold on all his accounts, and the senior partners reviewed them all. Those which we felt were unobtainable, we contacted and revised our proposal. Some pulled out, some we had to promise that we would cover the additional costs."

"And Jake?"

"Jake was pulled into a meeting with the senior team. We didn't fire him, but it was made very clear that he no longer had a position at the company."

"And you suggested keeping it quiet?"

"I didn't do it to be secretive. I suggested that maybe it would be beneficial for everyone if it was said that Jake left. The other partners agreed that it wouldn't benefit anyone if it came to light."

"And two years later, you're still dealing with it?" Annie asked.

"These things last for years, Annie. Even without the safety concerns out there, people will talk about how we promised one thing and then went back on our word. It'll get out that we're an unreliable company to deal with." Barrett fell back into his chair, rubbing his hand over his face.

"Business is improving, Dad. We've kept afloat for the past two years, and now we're starting to see an upturn. You've seen the numbers; you know we are. Jackie has pulled in a load of new projects and has started talking to some of our old clients again."

Callie couldn't help but feel a swell of pride when she mentioned Jackie and what she had brought to the business in these first couple of months.

"Stop defending him, Callie. He should never have put you in a position where you had to rebuild. And more importantly, he should never have put you in a position to lie to us." Barrett's finger jabbed the table in a move reminiscent of when he used to be in the boardroom.

"I'm not defending him. I'm defending the business and what we have done to keep it going. But while we're on it...I just don't want this to ruin the family."

"I don't want him putting you under this pressure!" Barrett shouted, shooting up from his chair again.

"I'm not made of glass, Dad! I can handle pressure!" Callie snapped back, standing and staring at her father. "The fact I'm here telling you now is surely a sign I'm dealing with this better!"

"Okay. Calm down, both of you." Annie stood between the two of them. "Yes, Barrett, Jake should never have done this and got Callie to lie. But Callie is right. Ten years ago, she wouldn't have told us, but she's grown since then, and you know it." Annie turned to Callie. "We worry about you, darling. You know we do. But you did the right thing in telling us. Thank you." She lent in and placed a gentle kiss on her cheek, whispering into her ear, "I'm proud of you."

"I'm sorry, Callie, love," Barrett conceded, also coming to sweep his daughter into a hug. "I just worry about you."

"Well, there's really not as much need these days, Dad. I'm good."

"I know," Barrett tried to say, not particularly convincing. Callie pulled back and gave him a look. "Really! I really do."

"Okay. But please, Dad, when you speak to Jake, tread carefully. I know he's in the wrong, but you're not going to get anywhere if you go in all guns blazing."

"I promise I'll try to keep calm. But Callie, I will need to know exactly what has happened."

"Okay," she sighed, but despite Barrett's reassurance, she knew it wouldn't all be as simple as that.

"At least it's out in the open now. You don't have to worry about it on your own anymore," Jackie said as she placed a glass of wine in front of Callie.

Callie looked up, a look on her face she couldn't quite place. She had turned up at Jackie's house an hour ago after having what she described as a horrendous conversation, in which she had to detail every transgression Jake had been involved in. Having the figures Jackie prepared had helped, apparently. Barrett dealt best with hard facts; numbers and statistics were how he saw the world, and Jackie knew that was the way to convince him that the business was flourishing again under Callie's guidance and leadership. Before turning up on Jackie's doorstep, however, Callie admitted she had spent a little time driving around, needing some quiet to settle her head.

"Really? Because Jake doesn't seem to think that way."

"He's been in touch already?" Jackie sat down next to her, eyebrows raised in partial surprise.

"Yep," Callie confirmed, reaching for her glass and taking a big gulp.

"Wow. Barrett really didn't waste any time," Jackie murmured into her glass. She took a sip of her wine as well, the taste cool and crisp on her tongue. They had shared a bottle of this wine earlier in the week, and they had both commented on how much they had enjoyed it. She wondered if Callie realised it was the same one and that it must have meant Jackie had been to get another bottle. Was she trying too hard? *Trying what,* she asked herself. *To be her friend? Or something else?*

"What did you expect? I've been gone"—Callie lent over to look at Jackie's watch— "an hour and a half. He probably rang him as soon as the door shut behind me. And knowing Dad, I imagine he summoned him to the house like some sort of business meeting."

Jackie could see the tension in Callie's shoulders, her forehead creased with thought.

"What did Jake say?"

Callie swiped open her phone, thumbing until she reached the message she wanted to read to Jackie. "I thought you said you would keep quiet! Now they'll think I'm a liar and incompetent! While precious little Callie comes out on top again!"

"He said that?" Jackie was already angry at Jake, but she'd managed to conceal it for the past few days, concentrating on what Callie needed. But the message was a true final slap in the face. If she ever saw Jake Montgomery, he was going to hear what she had to say.

"He's always had this thing about me being the favourite child. To him, I just turned up and moved in when he was a kid and took away the attention of his mother and father."

"But—"

"He doesn't know all the details, Jacs."

"Oh." Jackie looked down into her glass. She had always assumed that the whole family knew Callie's history. She'd never considered that maybe it was still a secret to some within the house.

"He was too young at the time; Mum and Dad thought it best if he didn't know. Huh, guess that's where I got it from. How ironic." She took a sip of wine, rolling her eyes.

"I think that one was definitely best for all involved," Jackie said softly, placing a reassuring hand on Callie's leg without thinking about it. She was about to retreat, panicked at having overstepped the mark, but when Callie didn't react, she let her hand linger a little longer.

"Mmm." Callie took another drink, clearly starting to relax. "Anyway, how was the office today? Did I miss anything?"

"Everything was fine."

"That's it?"

"You really want to talk about work? Surely there's something else you would prefer to think about?" Jackie was starting to resent the fact that the only bond which tied her and Callie together these days was the office. She had enjoyed spending time with her this week, but she wanted a reason other than company finances to be around her.

"Says the woman whose dining table is covered with account summaries... I'm not blind, Jackie. When was the last time you did something outside of work?"

"I—"

"And coming round to mine this week doesn't count, considering we were talking about work." Callie interrupted her with a knowing look and pointed finger.

"Fine!" Jackie huffed in defeat, falling back against the sofa with her drink. "I've just been so busy concentrating on settling in that I haven't had time to really go out much, that's all."

"Settling in? Jacs, you worked at the company before. You were literally hired prior to interviewing. You know all the clients and their accounts. And even if you didn't, it's been nearly two months. I don't think you need to spend any more time settling in."

"Hmm," Jackie hummed, looking into her glass as she swirled the wine around.

"Jacs?"

She sighed. For every look, noise, and action Callie made that she knew like the back of her hand, Callie knew hers back. She should have known that her non-committed answer wouldn't wash with her.

"What's going on? This isn't the Jackie I know. The Jackie I remember was confident and vivacious, wouldn't need time to settle in, would just go in there and own it. Where's this doubt coming from?"

"It's not doubt, so much as...I'm feeling a lot of pressure this time around."

"From who?" Jackie couldn't help but smile as Callie sat

upright, her defensive nature kicking in. This was a new side to Callie, something that had clearly developed as she had grown and matured, but it wasn't unwelcome or entirely surprising. Callie had always been selfless and caring; it would only make sense that as she got older and more confident within herself, she would develop a protective streak.

"Calm down. It's from no one. Or at least no one in the office." She sighed. "It's me. I'm putting myself under more pressure," she admitted.

"What? Why?"

"Because..." She cleared her throat, knowing that what she was about to say next would be met with shock and resistance. "Because I want to do things right. This company means a lot to me."

"Because of Dad?"

"Because of you." Her final statement was said with a level of softness. Admitting that Callie was important to her in any respect was new territory for this time around, and she wasn't sure how it would be taken. Jackie looked up, unsure what to expect when she finally looked at Callie's face. Her silence wasn't particularly forthcoming in helping her judge the situation. What she wasn't expecting was to look up to see tears glistening in her eyes. "Callie..." Her voice broke, cracking with emotion.

"No." Callie stood up, Jackie respecting her need for space, shuffling to the edge of the sofa but not following any further. "You're doing this all for me?"

"In a way, I guess. Although that sounds far too black and white when you say it like that."

"Then what is it? Explain it to me."

Jackie patted the sofa beside her, beckoning Callie back over. Once she was next to her again, Jackie lent forward, placed her wine glass on the table, and braced her arms on her knees.

"When I first heard there was a position at the company, I

wasn't going to go for it. I knew you had taken over in a senior position, and I thought it would be a mistake to come back. But then I got the call from the senior team, and I know you would have had to be part of that decision. So I came for the interview, not promising myself anything one way or another. I could see that the business was in need of a boost. I mean, I didn't see it as failing, it wasn't like it was in dire straits, but I could see somewhere I could help. And I wanted to help. I wanted to bring it back to where I knew it could be with you at the helm. I didn't want you to regret me being back."

"I haven't regretted a single second of you being back."

Jackie looked up, heart constricting at the sight of Callie with tears streaming down her face. The statement was soft and timid in the emotionally charged air which had filled the room, and Jackie almost couldn't believe what she was hearing.

"Really?"

"Really. I was nervous about you returning. At best, I expected to be civil with each other. I wasn't expecting to find it so easy to talk to you. I..." Jackie watched as Callie grappled with what she wanted to say next. "I wasn't expecting to find my best friend again. I'm sorry if that's too much..."

"No! No, it's not." Jackie leaned forward, brushing a tear from Callie's cheek with her thumb. The act was overly intimate for a couple who were still only just rebuilding their friendship, but Jackie could never bear to see Callie cry, and the urge to have contact with the woman in any way was overwhelming. Her breath hitched as she saw Callie's eyes involuntarily flutter closed at her touch. "I'll always be here for you, Callie."

A soft smile played at the corners of Callie's mouth before it was rudely and suddenly overtaken by a yawn. Callie pulled back, covering her mouth, leaving Jackie's hand now cupping nothing but empty space. Jackie let her hand drop reluctantly.

"Sorry."

"No, it's fine. You've had a stressful couple of days," Jackie said, trying to hide the disappointment in her voice. "You should get an early night."

"I still feel a little on edge," Callie answered, rolling her head on her shoulders.

"Then," Jackie continued, taking the chance while it presented itself, "How about you stay for dinner? I'll cook."

"You cooked last night," Callie said, letting her head drop back on the sofa cushions. They'd easily fallen into a routine the past few nights, taking turns to make dinner.

"I'll let you off this one time, and you can cook next time. Maybe you could find a film for us to watch while I do if you can stay awake long enough." Jackie stood and walked towards the door.

"No thanks," Callie said, herself half-rolling off the sofa to a chuckle from Jackie. "Rather come keep you company."

Chapter Nine

Jackie pushed the shopping trolley across the car park, fighting with it slightly as its wheel hit a stone and suddenly veered off course. Pulling it back in, she heard her phone ring, and she paused, lifting it from where it sat on the top of her handbag, which in turn sat in the trolley. She smiled at seeing Callie's name flash on her screen; Callie was meant to be coming over again for dinner in what was fast becoming a regular occurrence.

Since their heart to heart after Callie's conversation with her parents a few weeks ago, they had subconsciously (or maybe not) fallen into an easy routine; three or four times a week, they would have dinner together, usually leaving the office within minutes of each other only to meet again outside one of their front doors. Tonight, Jackie was cooking, but she had left the office not long after lunchtime to attend a business meeting with a potential new client and, as such, was stopping for ingredients on the way home.

She swiped to answer the call, unable and unwilling to wipe the smile off her face.

"Hello, you."

"Hey. Where are you?"

"Just at the supermarket picking up some bits for tonight. What about you?" Jackie asked, pushing the trolley the final short distance one-handed until she was at her car.

"I'm at the office, but was about to call it a day, so I thought I'd call and see where you're at. How did the meeting go?"

"It went fine. I'll give feedback to the senior partners in the meeting tomorrow morning."

"What, no sneak peeks?"

"No, no sneak peeks. Not that they would be very exciting anyway. Plus, you know the deal."

Once they had acknowledged just how much time they were spending together, they agreed that they needed to keep their office lives and personal lives as separate as possible. No work talk was allowed outside the office, barring initial rants if they had had a rough day. Although it wasn't a rule which they needed to enforce very often, the conversation between them never really faltered, and even if they didn't speak, the silence was never awkward.

"Yeah, yeah, fair enough. So what time do you think you will be back?"

"I'm just about to leave, so should be home in around half an hour," Jackie said, lifting the shopping bag into the boot.

"Brilliant. I was going to ask if you need me to pick anything up, but I guess you've got that covered."

"Yep. Thought I would try that new pasta recipe we found at the weekend."

"The one with the chilli oil and roasted garlic?"

Jackie chuckled at the little spark of excitement in Callie's voice. Carbs had always been her biggest food weakness. "Yeah, that one. And that white wine we love is on offer, so I stocked up on a couple of bottles."

"You're incorrigible, Miss Taylor."

"You love it," Jackie replied, met with a chuckle down the phone. "Right, I'm going to get off then. I'll see you in about thirty minutes?"

"Okay. See you soon."

Jackie hung up the phone as she slid into the driver's seat, clipping it into the hands-free holster on the dashboard. Still smiling, she started up the engine and edged her way out of the parking space and towards the exit of the car park. Her meeting, while relatively straightforward, had been bothering her. But she couldn't put her finger on what it was. Actually, something about the appointment had been bothering her all day.

You know exactly what. It wasn't the meeting; it was the fact that it was out of the office, and away from Callie.

Shaking the nagging feeling of her own conscience talking, she concentrated on the road, spying an upcoming gap in the traffic and pulling out. She'd barely got half her car out when there was an almighty crunch, and both Jackie and her car were shunted sideways. Jackie sat, stunned. After a moment of eerie quiet, a cacophony of noise erupted into her consciousness.

∽

Callie burst through automatic doors, barely giving them time to open far enough to let her through, stumbling over her own feet as she reached the reception desk.

"Hi, I'm looking for a patient who was brought in by ambulance. She was in a car accident," she blurted to the woman there, short of breath from her sprint across the car park.

"Okay, love, what's her name?"

"Jackie. Jacqueline Taylor."

The receptionist clicked away on her keyboard, the few passing seconds it took for her to find Jackie's name still too long in Callie's opinion.

"Yep, she's in Assessment Cubicle Four. Go through this door. It's down there and to the left."

Callie barely listened to the directions, instead taking off down the corridor the receptionist had gestured towards and frantically searching the curtained area which held Jackie. Head snapping side to side with each bed passed, she almost shot past when she spotted Jackie. Suddenly grinding to halt, she stood, fixed by shock at the sight which greeted her.

"Oh, fuck."

Jackie lifted her head from where it had been resting back against the pillow when she heard the muttered curse, a small lift appearing at the edge of her mouth when she saw Callie. It was positive but not enough to be called a smile in Callie's opinion.

Callie took a step up to the bed, hands hovering over Jackie's body, unsure where she could settle them which wouldn't hurt. One of her arms was immobilized in a luminous orange foam cage along the side of her body while her face was caked with dried blood, her nose covered with white surgical tape and cotton wool. Callie's fingers flexed, anxious to touch but not to inflict pain, and she sniffed back the tears forming.

"Hey," Jackie croaked. "This hand's still good," she offered, lifting up her left arm. She hummed and sighed with relief when Callie looped her fingers around it, kissing the back of her hand.

"How are you feeling? Are you in pain? Shall I get the doctor? Or some drugs?" Callie rambled.

"I'm fine. Well, I'm not, but all I need is you here."

Callie wasn't sure if it was the pain, the medication, or the situation, but something was making Jackie brutally honest. It didn't matter, though. Even if Jackie hadn't said it, there was nowhere else that Callie was going to be at this moment. She lent forward, pressing a kiss to Jackie's forehead in response, her own inhibitions lowering.

"I'll fucking kill the bastard," she murmured against her skin.

"I hear his airbag did a pretty good job of exacting some revenge."

Callie sat down on the edge of the bed, careful not to jostle Jackie too much, winding her fingers fully through Jackie's and resting their joined hands on her lap.

"Still, the little shit. What the fuck was he doing, driving at that speed down that road?"

"Don't be angry, please. It's not you," Jackie pleaded, exhaustion dripping from every word.

Callie sighed. Jackie needed her, and she could seethe in private at the moron who had hurt her. "Can you tell me what the doctors said?"

"I need to go up to X-ray. They think I've got a broken wrist and a broken nose."

"Does it hurt a lot?"

"I don't know. These drugs are pretty good," Jackie murmured, eyes closing yet again.

"Yeah?"

"Yeah. Making everything fuzzy. Hey." Her eyes snapped open again, surprising Callie. "I want to see what my face looks like. Can you find me a mirror?. I should have one in my bag." Jackie shifted slightly in bed, almost as if she was trying to sit up herself.

"Why don't you wait until I've cleaned you up a bit? You're still covered in blood," Callie replied, gently coaxing her back down on the bed with a sure but gentle hand on her good shoulder.

"Hmm bet that's a good look. Bashed up nose and blood everywhere."

"It's a beautiful nose."

"You're beautiful."

Callie swallowed and looked down at Jackie. Big, blown pupils stared back at her. "Jacs..."

"Thank you for being here," Jackie said softly.

"Wouldn't be anywhere else," Callie answered, brushing back the loose strands of hair which had fallen from Jackie's now dishevelled ponytail. She smiled as Jackie's eyes fluttered shut again, this time not opening but instead partnered with a soft, contented hum.

"I should have fought harder for you. Loved you so much."

Callie watched as Jackie blinked a final, long, heavy blink, before her eyelids remained closed. "Still do," she mumbled to a sharp inhale from a shocked Callie.

And with that, Jackie drifted off into a drug-hazed slumber, leaving Callie to sit alone with the revelation she'd just uttered.

∼

Jackie moved down the stairs, slower than she was used to, hand gripping the bannister to steady her wobbly gait. Despite her injuries, she slept surprisingly well—a combination, she suspected, of the painkillers and general exhaustion of being thrown about inside her car. However, now she was stiff and sore, and placing one foot in front of the other was proving more difficult than she first anticipated. But she needed to move, and she needed some more pain medication.

As she hobbled slowly into the lounge, her heart ached and breath hitched with the sight that greeted her. Curled up on the sofa underneath the fleecy blanket Jackie had spent so many evenings wrapped up in herself slept Callie. She should have known she wouldn't have left.

"Cal," she quietly called, tentatively leaning over to shake her shoulder. She winced when even that small action sent a shooting pain through her abdomen.

"What?" Callie mumbled almost incoherently before focusing bleary eyes on Jackie. "Shit, what's wrong? Are you okay?"

Rolling off the sofa in haste, Callie got her foot caught and stumbled, ending up on her knees before straightening out and standing up. The clumsy show of concern made Jackie chuckle even through the pain.

"I'm fine," she tried to assure Callie, who was now standing in front of her, eyes sweeping over her in a search for any obvious injuries. Despite her physical discomfort, the action stirred something inside of Jackie. Gentle hands resting on her shoulders brought her attention back to Callie, and the inquisitive look on her face. "Really, I'm fine honey. I just woke up and wanted a cup of tea."

"You should have shouted for me," Callie said, tossing the blanket to one side and guiding Jackie to the sofa.

"Not sure you would have heard me, *Sleeping Beauty*. Besides I didn't even know you were still here."

Callie scoffed. "Where else would I be?"

"Home. In your own bed. Not curled up uncomfortably on my sofa."

"Firstly, it's a very comfortable sofa. And secondly, as if I'm going to leave you. You can barely walk."

"I'd have managed," Jackie insisted.

"Yeah, well you don't have to. Now...tea?"

"Yes please." Jackie sighed, a combination of exhaustion and resignation. She had to admit, just getting from her bedroom to the living room had been harder and more draining than she was prepared for.

Callie moved across into the kitchen, flicking the kettle on and gathering the mugs and tea bags as if it was her own home. *She does look at home here.* The thought shocked Jackie, but not because she hadn't thought it before. Because the idea of this happening on a regular basis filled her with a sense of contentment.

She allowed herself to entertain the idea some more. Callie had already started spending more and more time at her place. What if she hadn't woken to find her on the sofa but instead in her bed? Her body betrayed and shocked her, a flare of arousal shooting through her, even breaking momentarily through the pain. She hadn't even elaborated on how she was in her bed, just the thought of lying next to her was enough to apparently make her body react.

God, what if there was more...

Her train of thought was abruptly cut off by the sound of Callie's phone ringing in the kitchen, and she couldn't help but overhear the conversation.

"Hi, Carol. Yeah, thanks for ringing me back. She's fine. Cuts and bruises and a broken arm, but I reckon she's going to be fairly stiff and sore for the next few days. Thanks, Carol. To be honest, I think it'll probably be next week when she's back in the office. Yeah, I'll pass it on. Do you know if Beka is in yet? Can you put me through to her?"

She paused, pouring water into two mugs while she clearly waited for Beka to pick up. "Beka, I'll be working from home today. Miss Taylor may not be in today either, but that's not your concern. You are my assistant, Miss Sanderson." The use of Beka's formal name surprised Jackie, and she pushed herself up from the sofa, tentatively making her way across to the kitchen. She could sense the frustration in Callie's voice and see the tension in her body. "If there are any issues, I will be available on my mobile. I will see you tomorrow."

Jackie watched as Callie dropped the phone on the counter, shoulders hunched and tense. Oh, how she wanted to ease that tension...

Before her mind could wander any further again, she spoke. "Problem?"

Callie shot around, clearly surprised at Jackie's voice being so close. "What are you doing up? You should be resting. Go sit down."

"You were on the phone to the office?" she asked, ignoring the order.

"Yes. Just sorting out today for us both."

"Us? You don't have to stay. I'm a big girl; I'm sure I can manage. I would have done if you weren't around."

"Well, I am, so we don't have to worry about that," she snapped. Jackie could visibly see the regret suddenly clouding her features, before they softened again. "Sorry. I want to be here." Callie smiled at Jackie, uncharacteristically nervous about her presence compared to the past few weeks. She cleared her throat before continuing, "I'd rather be here and make sure you're okay. If that's alright with you?"

"Okay." Jackie didn't have the energy to argue too much. "Don't you have meetings, though?"

"Nothing that can't be rearranged," Callie said quickly, stirring milk into Jackie's tea.

"Don't *I* have meetings?" Jackie tentatively slid up onto one of the stools by the counter, her back starting to throb at standing for too long. She managed to hide the grimace of pain while Callie's back was still turned.

"Again, can be rearranged."

"That's not what Beka seemed to think…"

Callie turned, giving Jackie a look she couldn't quite decipher. "How much did you hear?"

"Enough to know she's not happy."

Jackie watched as Callie moved back towards her, stopping just in front of her and placing the freshly made tea beside her. Jackie's heart raced with her proximity.

"Beka seems to think she has the monopoly on knowing my whereabouts and what I'm doing lately. She's annoyed she's out of the loop, but that's not her job or any of her business."

"I think the biggest problem is the fact it involves me."

"Probably. But I don't care. Again, it's none of her business."

"I don't want to cause you stress…"

Callie softly cupped Jackie's face with her hand, and Jackie instinctively lent into the contact.

"I'm where I need and want to be."

Callie pulled away, leaving cool air where her body once stood, and Jackie instantly felt it. Within seconds she was back, gesturing for Jackie's hand. When she lifted it, Callie dropped two white capsules into her palm.

"I imagine you've got a stinking headache this morning, not to mention a sore body. These should help."

"Thank you. I feel like I've been trampled by a herd of elephants."

"Hmm. Sorry, but you look like it as well."

"Charming."

"Don't worry. You somehow make black eyes look attractive," Callie responded casually as she walked away. Jackie tried to not focus too much on the comment, but it only added to her emotions at the fact Callie was in her home, caring for her, and how right it felt.

Jackie threw the tablets back into her mouth and swallowed them dry, before taking a scalding sip of tea. She hummed as her taste buds were hit with the taste of a cup made just how she liked it. Callie always had the ability to make her tea perfectly, and it seemed she had not lost her knack.

Callie's voice pulled her from her thoughts. "You want some breakfast? I can do you something small, even just to line your stomach for those pills."

"Yeah, that would be nice."

She watched for a moment while Callie went about making what appeared to be a bowl of porridge, pouring the oats and milk into a pan and placing it on the hob. After a minute, though, she rested her head in her hands, yawning with the residual tiredness that was only increasing with constant waves of exhausting pain rolling through her. She sighed as she felt a warm palm run up and down in between her shoulder blades, soothing some of the tension that sat there.

"Did you get much sleep?" a soft voice uttered by her ear.

"Yeah actually, I got more than I thought I would. Think the painkillers had a lot to do with it."

"Hmm, you fell asleep on the way home. I had to practically carry you upstairs."

"Sorry," Jackie offered, sitting up slightly.

"No need to apologise. Just glad you're okay."

Jackie let herself lean into Callie, burying her nose in her hoodie and catching her scent. She felt Callie's warm arms envelope her around her shoulders, tentative so not to hurt her but firmly and safely, and for a moment, Jackie couldn't actually imagine being anywhere else.

"Thank you," she murmured.

"For what?"

"Everything. Coming to the hospital. Staying with me. Looking after me."

"Wouldn't want to be anywhere else, babe." Callie pressed a kiss onto her forehead, holding her face there for a moment. Jackie smiled at the term of endearment, suddenly realising how much she had missed it after all those years.

Chapter Ten

Callie watched as Jackie walked slowly but determinedly across the car park. She'd made her argument, more than once, that she thought Jackie should stay at home longer, but Jackie was adamant that she was ready to be back in the office. But bending to get in and out of Callie's car, not to mention the thirty-minute drive, had left Jackie sore, and Callie could tell in the way she was holding herself. But she kept her mouth shut, fairly sure that if she protested one more time, Jackie would smack her with her handbag. So she kept a few steps behind, walking at Jackie's agonisingly slow pace, firmly biting her tongue.

"I can feel you staring."

"I'm not staring," Callie argued swiftly.

"Well, I can hear what you're thinking."

"That's clever of you."

Jackie stopped, huffing as she did so. Spinning on her heel, albeit slowly, she looked up at Callie. Callie could make out the faint outline of the black eyes which had developed, not completely masked by her makeup. The swelling around her nose had gone down, but there was still a cut across its bridge from where it had collided with the steering wheel.

"I just mean...I can feel you being so careful around me. Like I'm fragile and made of glass."

Callie averted her eyes, looking down at her feet and fidgeting on them. She'd avoided having to mention this so far, how much the phone call from the hospital had scared her, but now she felt she was rapidly hurtling towards having to disclose some of those feelings. And if she was honest, she wasn't anywhere near working them out for herself yet, let alone talking about them with Jackie. For the time being, she would try and keep them hidden. Or at least try and do a better job of it until she knew how to fully articulate what she was feeling.

"I'm sorry. I'm still a bit...I'm just worried it's too soon."

Jackie sighed. "Look at me. Callie, look at me please." Callie brought her eyes up, locking stares with Jackie. "I love how much you worry and how much you've looked after me this past week. But I cannot stay in that house any longer. It's driving me crazy."

Jackie's whiplash had kept her at home for nearly a week, her back suffering the most. On a couple of occasions early on, it had seized completely. In one particularly embarrassing incident, Jackie had been in the middle of running a bath. Luckily—or unluckily—depending on how you viewed it, Callie was in the house. She came into the bathroom to find Jackie bent over the bathtub, wrapped in nothing but a towel, unable to move. After recovering from the initial sight (and truth be told, she wasn't entirely sure she still had), Callie managed to help Jackie sit on the toilet and ease her back muscles into releasing.

But physical discomfort aside, Jackie had never been very good at sitting inside four walls for very long. Callie shouldn't have been surprised when she announced last night she was going back to work. But the insurance company was being slow in processing the claim, and so she was still without a car. Callie hadn't even thought about it when she offered her a lift until it was sorted, especially since Jackie wasn't ready to drive herself yet anyway.

"I know. I know you hate being cooped up inside."

"I do. But I hate seeing you so worried even more."

"I just..." The words got stuck in Callie's throat again, torn between letting themselves free, releasing the weight she felt on her shoulders, and the fear of saying too much. She closed her eyes, trying to work out what she wanted more.

The shuffle of Jackie's shoes against the concrete of the car park floor was an odd sound since she was so used to the click of those heels, but her back wasn't quite up to it yet. She immediately sensed the closeness between them.

"I get it. That dull ache in your chest when someone you care about is hurting. I remember it from when..."

Callie heard her sigh, the silence enough to finish the end of the sentence for them both. The gentle but solid pressure of Jackie's forehead resting on her own grounded her, erasing all her doubts about her feelings for Jackie and making her feel wanted. She really hoped she wasn't interpreting this all wrong; she wasn't sure she could cope with the rejection if she dared make that decision.

The sound of a car entering the car park echoed around the bare walls reminded them of their very public location. They pulled away from each other. Callie afforded herself one more glance at Jackie and found impossibly deep eyes looking back at her.

"We should get into work," she said, taking a step to the side, only to be stopped by Jackie's hand on her arm.

"I promise to look after myself. And call you if I need you," Jackie said softly.

"Thank you."

∼

Callie left Jackie at her office door, Carol instantly taking over mothering duties as soon as she clocked the cast on her arm and the slight limp to her walk. Making her way to her own door, she breathed a sigh of relief and said a silent prayer that Beka's desk was unattended. While Callie hadn't spent all the time Jackie had been off working from home, she had done more remote work than usual and it had not gone unnoticed, or uncommented on, by Beka. Recently she had gone from being efficient to over-attentive and nosy, and it had long since gone past the point of being irritating for Callie. And Jackie was right in her observation, that her return to the company and their burgeoning friendship, if that's how she was willing to define it right now, seemed to be the catalyst in her change of behaviour.

That irritation quickly spiked when she crossed the threshold to find Beka in her office, straightening out some papers behind her desk. Her head shot up as if she had been caught doing something wrong before her smile slipped perfectly in place. Callie scrutinised her, something feeling off about the situation.

"Everything okay?"

"Yes, everything's fine. Just dropping off that stuff you forwarded over for printing on Friday. You know, while you were working from home."

There was a definite snipe in the way that Beka emphasised the words *working from home*, but Callie didn't have the energy to respond to it.

"Thank you."

"No problem. Can I get you anything?"

"No. Are the agendas ready for this morning's senior meeting?"

"Yes. Do I need to organise to send one on to Miss Taylor?"

Callie rolled her eyes. It literally took four sentences before Beka mentioned Jackie. "No," she said sharply. "Miss Taylor shall be attending."

"Oh. She's back then?"

"I just said she was attending, didn't I?" Her emotions were all over the place, and she snapped firmer than she had intended.

However, she refused to be apologetic when it was Beka who was digging where she wasn't welcome.

"Yes, sorry. Well, if you need anything..."

"Put me on *do not disturb* until the meeting at nine," she said, not looking up and instead pulling her chair out and dropping down into it.

"Yes, of course, Miss Montgomery."

She heard the door click and dropped her head into her hands. She could feel a headache coming on, which was the absolute final straw, and it was only coming up to eight o'clock. She needed to get her head straight, otherwise she was going to be no good to anyone.

It was the same cycle of thoughts she'd had every evening for days, ever since Jackie's drug induced confession. It hadn't been spoken about since, she wasn't even sure if Jackie was aware or remembered saying it, but either way, it kept playing on repeat in her head. *Loved you so much. Still do.* But love was such a complicated emotion, so full of technicalities and descriptions, and Callie had already admitted to Jackie that she saw her as a best friend returning. Is that what Jackie meant? Did she love her as a best friend? All Callie knew is that every evening, she resolved to herself that she would keep a distance until she worked it out, to protect herself, and every morning when she saw Jackie, her resolve went out the window. Maybe now, with the confines of her office and focus of work right there in front of her, and with Jackie busy as well, she would find it easier. Maybe.

Chapter Eleven

Five weeks later...

"Hey!" Jackie practically skipped into Callie's office.

"Hey. You're happy this morning."

"I am! The insurers have finally released the pay-out. I can get a new car." Jackie grinned. She was almost back to full health, a twinge in her back now and again, and the cast on her arm the only reminders of her car accident just over six weeks ago. And in a few days, the cast would be gone and then she could finally be rid of the last of them.

"Oh...that's great," Callie replied.

"You sure? You don't sound very happy."

Callie watched as Jackie crinkled her forehead in confusion. She knew the moment the words came out of her mouth she hadn't feigned her excitement very well. If at all. Jackie could see through the best of her facades; there was no way that one was going to wash.

"Sorry. I am. Happy, I mean." She smiled, but she knew it was weak.

Jackie came closer, bypassing the chair on the opposite side of the desk to perch against the desktop itself beside Callie. Callie desperately tried to ignore how her hips, perfectly accentuated in her black high-waisted trousers, were directly in her eye-line. "What's wrong?"

"Nothing."

"Cal..."

"I guess...it'll be weird, coming in separately, that's all." She could feel tears well up in her eyes and hear the waver in her voice. She knew she couldn't lie to Jackie, but she hadn't expected to be quite so emotional. She'd been working hard on keeping her feelings in check around the older woman. Apparently badly.

"Oh, honey."

"Don't mind me. I'm just tired, and it's making me soft."

"Tell me what's going on."

"It's nothing."

"Just because I'll have a new car doesn't mean we have to stop coming in together. We can just share the driving."

Callie waved her hands at the suggestion, shaking her head and turning back to face her computer. "It's fine. You don't have to—"

Jackie lent forward and gently grasped Callie's chin in her fingers, stopping her rambling and turning her head to face her.

"I really love our time together too," she whispered softly before leaning forward and planting a gentle kiss on her cheek.

Callie let her eyes flutter closed at the soft feeling. When she opened them, the air felt thick and charged, like a corner had been turned. As if Jackie had just given her an answer to the unspoken question she had been stressing over for weeks.

Her body tingled with a need to have Jackie touch her again, anywhere, and the feeling only intensified when she caught sight of Jackie's eyes, dark with a desire she hadn't seen in years.

A forced cough sharply brought her back into reality.

"Apologies for interrupting, but I have your presentation package for this afternoon pitch meeting *we're* attending."

It was obvious from Beka's tone and body language she was not sorry for interrupting, and the way she had emphasised that they were both attending this afternoon's meeting hadn't gone unnoticed by Callie or, most likely, Jackie.

Jackie straightened up, smoothing down her shirt. "I've got a meeting. This weekend, *we'll* go car shopping, yeah?"

"Yeah. See you later." Callie struggled to hide the smirk at Jackie's retaliatory comment. God, she was hot when she was being righteous.

Callie watched as Jackie sauntered past Beka, acknowledging her with a single nod and mutter of her name before closing the door behind her. The sound of Beka scoffing not so subtly broke the momentary silence and refocussed Callie's attention. She held out her hand for the paperwork, greeted by a blank look from Beka.

"The presentation, Beka." She reminded her.

"Oh, yes. Your talking points are all in there, highlighted as you like." She handed over the folder.

"Thank you."

"And I'm just confirming details for the charity gala at the end of the month. Is it still just you going?"

"And the other senior partners, yes," Callie responded absent-mindedly, her focus on the presentation which Beka had just handed her.

"But you're not taking a guest?"

"No."

"And...Miss Taylor?"

Callie sighed at the comment, knowing what Beka was trying to fish for. She was growing tired of her attitude towards Jackie. She looked up, pinning Beka with a stare she rarely used but was becoming more frequent. "Miss Taylor will be attending as she is a senior partner, as I have just said. Carol will no doubt be in touch with you regarding her transport and guest needs if any are required."

"Yes, Miss Montgomery," Beka responded, suitably admonished for the time being.

"Now, if you don't mind, I need to do a final run through of this before our meeting."

"Yes. Thank you, Miss Montgomery."

"Thank you, Beka."

Callie waited for the sound of the door clicking shut again before she allowed her composure to slump and dropped back into her chair. She really wished that Beka hadn't mentioned the charity gala, not today and not including Jackie in the conversation. She hated this time of year, and dreaded it every single time. She wasn't the most comfortable or natural at socialising as it was, least of all at formal occasions, but she always managed. But this event was different.

The annual Greenacres Charity Gala had been going on for nearly thirty years—a group of local businesses who got together, drank too much wine, ate fancy food and donated to local charities, either through the auction or through donations collected on the night. It was also the location where, nine years ago, Callie had discovered her wife was sleeping with her secretary.

Callie shivered at the thought. Jen wasn't remorseful in the slightest when Callie had caught her in a side room with her hands very much up her secretary's dress. Her clear disrespect and disregard for Callie only continued as the next few months went by, resulting in a final blow which still hurt Callie when she thought about it too much.

Consciously pushing it to one side, she blinked and tried to refocus on the papers in front of her. Maybe this year would be different. To begin with, Jackie would be there, and Jackie was good at distracting her in any situation.

⁓

"What about this one?" Jackie asked, pointing to the white Audi. Truth be told it was a little flashy for her taste. She wanted something a bit toned down.

"Hmm? Yeah, that's nice," Callie answered half-heartedly, before yawning.

Jackie noticed the action and non-committed answer. Something had been off with Callie all week, and it was starting to worry her. "I could always ditch the car idea and just splash out on a motorcycle. I know you'd appreciate the leather…"

"Mmhmm, yeah," Callie muttered, staring at a car. "Wait! Leather?"

"Oh hello! I did wonder if you were with me!" Jackie smirked.

"I zoned out again, didn't I?"

"You've been zoned out for days. Everything okay?"

"Yeah. Tired." Jackie knew that wasn't the whole truth, but she wasn't about to push Callie for any more in the middle of a car dealership, so she left it there and changed the subject.

"Are you all sorted for next weekend?" Jackie instantly noted the small hold of breath and frown on Callie's forehead. "Callie?"

"Hmm, yeah. I'm all set." Callie had tried to recover but it was too slow and quite frankly too poor an attempt to escape Jackie's attention.

"Okay. Out with it." Jackie stood in front of Callie, stopping her from wandering onto the next car. Her reluctance just moments before at discussing whatever Callie's problem was here and now had quickly been squashed by the small flicker of distress and what she thought was fear over Callie's face.

"What?"

"You've been distant for days. Like something is on your mind. And a minute ago, I told myself I wasn't going to ask here, but when I just mentioned the gala, you had that little look on your face like…I don't know. Like you were scared of something."

"I'm not scared. I mean it's just a party."

"So it *is* something about the gala?"

"No."

Jackie noted the stubbornness in the sharp response, a sure sign that Callie wasn't saying everything. "Is it because it's such a big group of people? I thought you rarely struggled with crowds anymore."

"I don't. I'm fine."

"Then what's going on?" Jackie pushed gently.

"I...I just don't particularly like *this* gala," sighed Callie

"Why, what's special about this one?"

"I..." Callie flicked her thumb over and over, spinning the ring on her finger as fast as she could. Jackie halted the action with a soft hand over hers. Callie took a deep breath, clearly preparing herself to say something.

"I think Jen might be there."

"Jen, your ex-wife?" Jackie felt herself bristle at the mere mention of the woman. She still didn't know what happened to end Callie's marriage, but she couldn't understand who would marry Callie Montgomery and then let her go. Let alone cheat on her as Jen had.

"Yeah. In fact, it's more than likely she will be there. I've heard she's moved to a company just out of the city centre who attends."

"Oh. Yeah, I can see how that would be awkward." Jackie felt herself deflate a little. She was looking forward to spending time with Callie without someone judging them, and she thought she was going to get that since Beka wouldn't be attending. "And that's what's worrying you? Seeing her?"

"Yeah. A bit. I just... The person Jen cheated on me with was my old secretary." Jackie looked up as Callie continued her explanation. "I found out by walking in on them at the charity gala."

Now her hesitance at attending the gala made perfect sense. In fact, Jackie wondered why Callie went for the past few years at all if that was the case.

"I'm sorry. I didn't know."

"Yeah well, I don't exactly advertise it. Plus, it's the beginning of a whole other messy story. Things weren't particularly civil as it was, and then I...ended up in hospital. But even that didn't stop her from doing what she wanted to do." Jackie frowned and waited for an explanation. "She started divorce proceedings while I was still in recovery."

"What?" The anger she felt bubbling up inside her was unprecedented. She'd rarely felt such rage directed to another person before. The only other person to evoke this response in her was Darla.

"It was about two months after; I was still attending weekly recovery therapy sessions, I wasn't working yet, and I'd moved back home. I mean, it wasn't like we were together, and I was under no illusion that my marriage wasn't over, but still. I really didn't think she was in such a rush to make it official that she would serve me divorce papers while I was still...but apparently she couldn't wait to be rid of me."

Callie cleared her throat, and Jackie could see the emotion threatening to take over. "Anyway, sometimes being back at the gala makes me nervous, takes me back to that person I was then, you know. It comes around every year, so I should be fine by now, but this year she's also back so..."

"We don't have to go."

"Yeah, we do."

"No, we don't. Your health is far more important than some opportunity to network with a load of old blokes who are rapidly edging towards retirement."

"That's sweet, but she's not kept me away so far, and she won't start now," Callie stated, plastering on a not so convincing front of confidence.

"Hey." Jackie took Callie's face in her hands, cradling it softly and bringing her eyes up to hers. "You are so much more than who you were then. And if you do have a wobble, I'll be at your side all night."

The air in between them was charged with something palpable, and Jackie couldn't help but take in every feature of Callie's face. Suddenly, she seemed so breath-takingly beautiful, more so than she had ever really appreciated—and she had appreciated it a lot recently.

"Excuse me, miss...would you like to test drive the Audi?"

The sound of the salesman's voice interrupted them harshly and Jackie mentally cursed him...and then the fact that she had forgotten they were having this monumental conversation in a car showroom.

Before she could answer, Callie spoke. "No. The Audi's not right. She suits something more understated."

Chapter Twelve

"Hi."

Callie turned around at the gentle voice in her ear, her breath instantly hitching at the sight which greeted her. Jackie stood in front of her, wearing an aqua ball gown that shimmered slightly under the lights of the bar. One shoulder was bare as it cut across her chest at an angle, perfectly teasing her collarbone, her long dark hair styled perfectly in loose waves which draped over her exposed shoulder. The material clung and flowed over her curves, reaching down until it just brushed the floor, and judging by the slight height advantage Jackie had right now, a killer pair of heels were hidden from sight. Callie swallowed, momentarily struggling to form words.

"Hey."

"You look amazing."

"Nothing compared to you," she murmured, blushing slightly when she realised she had said it out loud.

Jackie chuckled, a low, husky sound deep from her throat, which had Callie's heart racing even more. "Oh, I don't know. This looks *very* dashing."

Only then did Callie realise that Jackie's eyes were roaming over her own outfit, taking in each cut and curve of her suit. She'd, rather unusually, bought something new this year, a dark grey three-piece suit. She'd foregone the jacket, though, instead just wearing the waistcoat and trousers, pairing it with a black shirt with the top two buttons left undone to show a flash of a silver chain. Her sleeves were rolled up to show off the chunky watch on her wrist.

"Thanks," she managed to choke out, feeling the blush creep up her cheeks.

Jackie looped her arm through Callie's and turned her back around, leading her the few steps towards the bar.

"I'd forgotten how cute flustered Callie was until I came back and saw her again first hand." Callie felt her cheeks heat even more, although she wasn't sure it was possible. "Come on. I'll get you a drink before you cringe any harder."

Callie stood as Jackie ordered them both a drink, eyes flitting around the room. She hated that she was spending her time on the lookout instead of being fully present with Jackie, but with every flash of blonde hair, every hollow laugh, she thought she had found her ex.

"Stop looking for her," Jackie said quietly in her ear.

"Sorry, I—"

"No. We're not apologising for it. I just want you to stop worrying. If we see her, we see her. But I'm not going to let her ruin our night."

"Yeah. You're right." Callie breathed out, shaking her shoulders into relaxing at the same time.

"Now," Jackie said, handing a tumbler of ice-cold liquid to Callie, "I recognise about three people here, and they all look ready to drop dead, they're so old. Fancy being my chaperone for the evening and showing me around?"

Callie smiled before offering her arm for Jackie to link her own through again. "Absolutely."

. . .

"Oh my God," Jackie whispered into Callie's ear, the noise of the chatter making it a little harder to hear one another but mainly so she wasn't overheard by anyone else. "I forgot how mind numbingly dull these events are."

They had been doing the rounds for well over an hour, Callie introducing Jackie to the new generation of business folk, although new was probably a generous term for a lot of them. The average age was still well past the mid-century mark, most were just unfamiliar to Jackie and Callie. To be honest, the range of businesses was vast, and Callie had trouble socialising within the office some days let alone in the wider world of local commerce. But it was made bearable with Jackie by her side, the whispered flirtatious comments and soft touches serving to tease and entertain her.

"It's definitely not exactly the social event of the year. Well, unless you're—"

"Watch how you finish that sentence!" Jackie gave Callie a stern but jovial look, bumping shoulders with her.

"I was going to say, unless you're over sixty."

"Hmm good save. But even that will be soon enough."

"You're not even fifty yet!"

"Not for much longer," Jackie commented, tipping back her wine glass and emptying the last of it. Callie found herself transfixed by the way her lips pressed against the glass.

"Well, I think you'll make a gorgeous fifty-year-old." She dipped her head, breathing directly into Jackie's ear, feeling bold in response to Jackie's uncharacteristic dip in self-confidence, "And an even sexier sixty." She saw Jackie's eyes flutter shut at her words, leaning in imperceptibly. "Jackie..."

"Mmhmm," Jackie managed, swallowing. Callie saw the bob of her throat and the overwhelming urge to pepper the skin there with soft, gentle kisses overtook her. Blue eyes bored into her as she went quiet, not for fear or disregard but from pure emotion.

"Have dinner with me," Callie blurted out.

"I—"

"Hello, Callie."

Callie tensed instantly at the greeting, and she knew Jackie felt the shift, a comforting hand quickly coming to rest at the small of her back and a questioning look taking over in her eyes. Callie took a second to compose herself before she turned.

"Hi, Jen."

"Aren't you going to introduce me?" she asked, gesturing towards Jackie.

"Jen, this is Jackie Taylor, our new senior client relations manager. Jackie, this is Jen Goodman. My ex-wife."

"Hello, Jackie," Jen greeted, a sickly-sweet smile on her face and a hand outstretched. Jackie ignored both.

"Here you are, babe," a familiar voice interrupted them, and Callie cocked her head at the unexpected company before her, watching as Jen took the glass from the woman who had joined them.

"Thank you," Jen said with a kiss to the woman's cheek. "Callie, I believe you are familiar with my date."

"Yes. Good evening, Beka."

"Callie." Beka had the good grace to look slightly awkward, although the fact that she didn't immediately question how the two knew each other told Callie Beka already knew.

"Hello, Beka," Jackie greeted the woman politely. Even with all the attitude which Beka gave her on a daily basis, the woman still had the class to make the first step in the conversation.

"Miss Taylor," Beka replied coolly.

"What are you doing here?" Callie turned her attention back to Jen. Even though she had her suspicions she would turn up, she still knew there had to be an angle to it. Jen never did anything without an ulterior motive, and since she was here with Beka, she was almost certain of it.

"I'm in the business too, Callie, remember? Your family

doesn't control everything. In fact, from what I hear, your precious little family business may be somewhat floundering."

Callie's eyes flitted to Beka, who suddenly looked incredibly nervous. A memory of Beka being in Callie's office, behind her desk and looking incredibly suspicious, flashed through her mind. *The sneaky cow.* Callie kept her composure.

"I have no idea what you're talking about. Montgomery and Associates are doing brilliantly at the moment. Plenty of new clients coming through the door. Plenty of old ones returning."

"Is that so?" Jen still thought she had the upper hand, while Beka was wilting with each passing comment.

"Not sure where you're getting your information from, Jen, but I'd make sure it was a reliable source before saying too much." Callie fixed Beka with a stare which left no room for interpretation. *I know you've been talking.*

"I heard Barrett himself came in last week. I imagine he usually doesn't do that unless there's a crisis these days."

"Couldn't be further from the truth. Barrett comes in quite a lot; he's still friends with a lot of the staff. He was actually there last week to see us sign off on a massive partnership deal we're about to announce."

Callie saw the annoyance seep into Jen's stance. She hated being outsmarted, and Callie guessed her entire piece was based on information Beka had fed her mixed with her own illusions.

Callie, emboldened by the chink in Jen's armour, and by the presence of Jackie beside her, stepped forward and leaned into Jen's space. She wasn't sure how long this sudden bout of confidence was going to last, but she was going to ride the wave while she could. "Don't try to intimidate me, Jen."

"Please." Jen scoffed. "You may think you're doing well, but you forget I know all your dirty little secrets."

Even though she knew there was nothing Jen could realistically use against her, her mouth grew dry at the threat. She hated that Jen could still elicit such a response. "You know nothing."

"Really? I mean, Beka here says you've been acting strangely recently. Not your usual self. Hiding away, doing things secretly. That along with recent, bad decisions for the company and your history of poor judgement...just a few suggestive comments, and your state of mind could be called into question."

"How dare you!" Callie felt Jackie step forward, rage radiating off her body. She stopped her with an arm out to her side.

"You really have reached a new low, Jen. I thought your dump-and-run act was bad enough, but this? Dating my assistant to get half-baked rumours which you can twist to your own liking? This is a whole new level."

"Don't underestimate me, Callie."

"Trust me. I won't *ever* make that mistake again."

Jen scoffed, turning on her heel with an air of faux superiority as she disappeared into the crowd. There was a tense silence left where she once stood, only broken by a small voice.

"Callie..."

"No, Beka," Callie said calmly yet firmly, still in shock at the betrayal. "We'll discuss this Monday morning."

"Yes."

Once she too had gone from view, Callie allowed herself to release the breath she had been holding. The soft grip on her arm, which was still held out rigidly in front of Jackie, loosened and dropped, and at the loss of contact, Callie turned to face Jackie.

"I'm sorry—"

"I just have to go—"

They both spoke at once, Callie quickly registering and frowning in confusion at Jackie going anywhere.

"I just need the loo. I'll be right back," Jackie finished, barely ending her sentence before stepping away.

Callie watched her hurriedly weave her way through the crowd, silently cursing Jen and Beka for overstepping the mark so monumentally and herself for reacting. Following Jackie's path, she pushed through the toilet door seconds after her. She found Jackie hunched over the sink in the empty bathroom.

"Jacs?"

"Sorry. I'll be back out in a minute."

Callie couldn't be sure, but it sounded like Jackie may be close to tears. "No, I should be sorry. I shouldn't have reacted to what she was saying. I'm sorry I upset you."

Jackie turned, blinking back unshed tears in a futile attempt to save her makeup. "You have *nothing* to apologise for."

"But you're upset..."

"At her! I'm angry at her! How dare she speak to you like that, make you feel guilty and, and *less than*? And Beka! God, I've always disliked her, but now..."

"Hey," Callie stepped into Jackie's space, grabbing her hands which had closed into fists. "Hey, it's okay."

"No, Cal, it's not okay. It's so far from okay. She has no right to speak to you like that, to act like that. You deserve to be treated so much better. You are so much more than *that*."

Callie let go of Jackie's hands, instead gently holding her face, thumbs brushing away the stubborn tears which had rolled down Jackie's cheeks.

"Listen to me. She doesn't have any power over me anymore. Don't let her have any over you either."

"I'd never treat you like that." Jackie sniffed, the gentle touch of Callie's fingers washing away her rage instantly.

"I know you wouldn't."

In their confrontation, they had drifted closer together, Callie still cupping Jackie's cheeks softly, their faces now so close she could feel the still slightly uneven rhythm of Jackie's breathing as it washed over her skin.

"I'd treat you like a queen. Like you deserve to be treated," Jackie whispered, the air in the room shifting subtly.

Callie watched as Jackie's eyes flickered from her own eyes, down and across her features, before pausing on her mouth. She felt Jackie's thumb feather over her bottom lip, and Callie's eyes fluttered closed.

"Jacs..."

"Come home with me. Right now. Just...come home with me. Please."

Chapter Thirteen

The taxi ride back to Jackie's house was quiet. Neither really knew what else to say or if anything even needed to be said. The feel of Jackie's fingers entwined between her own settled Callie, the rhythmic brush of her thumb across the back of her hand soothing her otherwise thrumming body. She had been craving this since Jackie had first walked back into her life, and Jackie had apparently been feeling the same. Now, standing in Jackie's hallway, the atmosphere between them was palpable, and butterflies erupted throughout Callie's body. Jackie reached forward, clasping Callie's other hand, running her thumb over her knuckles.

"We don't have to do anything," she whispered into the dark.

Callie's body was calling for Jackie to be closer, pushed up against her until you couldn't tell where one ended and the other began. She needed to feel her, to show her that she meant what she said.

Despite her bravado and Jackie's earlier words, Jen's voice lingered in the back of her mind. She needed to know that what she still felt for Jackie was reciprocated. What she didn't know was how to tell that to the woman standing in front of her.

"Kiss me," Callie said, unable to articulate her need in any other way.

Jackie's mouth turned up into a soft smile as her hand came to brush back Callie's hair from where it had fallen across her eyes, her fingers lingering on her cheek. Callie sighed as she finally felt the familiar touch of Jackie's lips on hers, and Jackie apparently recognised it as a sign to deepen the kiss, hand coming round to thread through her hair. Callie's hands rested on Jackie's hips, fingers gently squeezing as she felt Jackie's tongue swipe across her bottom lip, asking for permission. Callie tightened her grip at the action, opening her mouth wider, tongue flicking out to meet Jackie's as she pulled her closer.

She took a step back, trapping herself between the wall and Jackie's body, and Jackie took the hint, pushing herself up against Callie, clearly just as desperate to be as close as possible. Jackie broke off the kiss, moving down across Callie's jaw and towards her neck, sucking gently on her pulse point. She was rewarded with a low, throaty moan which only served to stoke the fire within her.

"God, I've missed that sound. I missed you," Jackie muttered into the skin of Callie's throat with a scrape of her teeth.

"Fuck," Callie exclaimed as her hips jolted at the sensation. "Jacs...I need you."

"I've got you, baby."

Jackie pulled back, Callie instantly mourning the loss of her solid weight against her, the warmth of her body, but not before a hand wrapped around hers and led her up the stairs. She followed, watching every step Jackie took, her hips swaying in that dress she had spent all night admiring, fingers now itching to push up the hem and explore the skin underneath. Jackie led them into the bedroom, and before she had a chance to do anything, Callie spun them both around, so she had Jackie pinned against the wall. Her hand instantly found the soft skin of Jackie's thigh, and she dragged her nails up the slit in her dress until it was cupping her backside while her mouth trailed kisses up her neck. Jackie groaned, her own hands bunching in the lapels of Callie's waistcoat before fumbling with its buttons.

"Fuck, Callie, I need you out of these clothes."

Between them, they managed to discard Callie's waistcoat and shirt, Jackie's fingers now focusing on unbuttoning her trousers, those quickly joining the rest of her clothes on the floor. Jackie held out Callie at arm's length, taking in the sight of her in only her black girl boxers and skin-tight white vest. Callie shivered as Jackie ran her finger along the top of it, teasing against her cleavage, before clasping the material in between her fingertips.

"Can I?" she murmured softly.

"I...can I...I'm sorry...I just..." Callie faltered, hating herself for her hesitation and the sudden bout of anxiety.

"You want to keep it on?"

"Does it bother you?" Callie asked, a wave of uncertainty rolling through her.

Jackie looked up sharply, her eyes locking onto Callie's. "Never," she stated. "I love your body, I think you're the most beautiful woman alive, but I never have and never will make you do anything which makes you uncomfortable. Including taking this off," she added, laying an outstretched palm across Callie's covered stomach.

"Thank you." Callie closed her eyes, breathing a sigh of relief as she felt Jackie's fingers feather up her abdomen.

Jackie stepped back into Callie's space, and the feel of fabric against her bare legs reminded her that Jackie was wearing significantly more clothes than she was.

"Turn around," she asked softly, guiding Jackie by her shoulders.

She dragged the zipper of her dress down, the frantic nature of a few moments before calming to something far more sensual and slow, her lips caressing Jackie's neck and back with each inch of freshly exposed skin. The dress pooled to the floor, Callie's hands sweeping round to feel across her stomach, goosebumps being left in their wake. As they crept upwards, Jackie halted their journey with her own, much to Callie's disappointment.

"As amazing as that feels," her breath hitched as Callie ran a finger across the underneath of her bra, "I need you on that bed."

Jackie spun back into the room, taking the few steps to the bed and pulling Callie with her, their bodies colliding together, hands freely roaming across each other, reacquainting themselves with each other's bodies, as their lips met in a heated kiss. Jackie pushed Callie down into the bed, laying down on top of her, her forehead resting on Callie's.

"Is this too fast?"

"No. Please, Jacs." Callie gripped Jackie's hand and ran it down her stomach and into her boxers. Jackie moaned when she was instantly met with slick, wet heat.

"Fuck, Cal. You're so wet," Jackie gasped, kissing Callie firmly.

"You've been driving me crazy all night," Callie admitted, catching her lip in her teeth as she felt Jackie's fingers stroke her. Her fingers dug into Jackie's shoulders, and she trembled at the teasing touches. "Please, Jacs, just fuck me."

"My pleasure," Jackie mumbled from Callie's neck, where she was busy painting the skin crimson with her mouth. Pushing off her, Callie instantly missed the feel of Jackie on top of her, but for her to soon forget it as she felt her boxers be dragged down her legs, and gentle but sure fingertips trail back up them to her aching centre.

"God, you are so fucking beautiful." Fingers swiped through her again, her hips rising off the bed. "Is this all for me?"

"Jacs, please." Callie could hear the desperation in her own trembling voice, and she brought her legs up, digging her heels into the bed beneath her, inviting Jackie to take her.

Within a second, Jackie was back in her vision again, filling it with her beautiful face, pupils blown with arousal, mouth slightly slack as she swirled her fingers around Callie's clit, coating them with her arousal before sinking two fingers deep inside her. As she did, Callie's eyes slammed shut, her mouth open with a gasp and a moan, and she felt herself clench around them.

"Fuck. Callie..."

Callie opened her eyes at the sound of Jackie's shaking declaration, overcome with emotion at the sheer volume of love that she saw in her eyes. Pulling her in, she kissed her hard, tongue swiping against Jackie's, her fingers tangling through her hair, holding her close. She groaned into her mouth as Jackie started to rock her hips, pushing in and out, each brush against her walls edging her closer and closer. She'd been turned on all night, the sight of Jackie's slight curves, the way her dress hung over them, kicking her arousal into gear the moment she walked into the gala. And if she was honest with herself, it didn't take much, each moment with Jackie over the past few weeks breaking down her walls and heightening her senses whenever she was around. All it took was the faintest sniff of her perfume, and she could sense the hairs on the back of her neck stand to attention. Jackie dropped her head to her shoulder, her mouth beside Callie's ear, and she could hear and feel each laboured breath coming from her, the sensation turning her on even more.

"Oh...you feel so good. God, I've missed you," Jackie muttered, punctuating her comment with a swipe of her tongue across the top of her ear. A combination of Jackie's fingers, her breath, her words, everything she was and was giving Callie in this moment made Callie pulse, and Jackie must have felt it, them both groaning in unison.

"Oh fuck..." Callie moaned, dangerously close to the precipice.

"You're so close, baby. I can feel you. Let go..."

With a strangled cry, Callie's whole body tensed underneath Jackie, hips bucking into her hand, draining every last drop of pleasure from the mind-blowing orgasm she was experiencing before slumping down into the mattress. She lay there, eyes closed and chest heaving for a second, as her senses started to return to her body.

"Fuck, you are so beautiful," Jackie whispered.

She opened her eyes to find Jackie looking down at her, the most open and adoring look crossing her face, which made her heart clench with emotion. Suddenly, the overwhelming need to feel this woman come against her flooded her body. She reached up, grasping Jackie's face with both hands, bringing her down for a searing kiss which had them both moaning into each other's mouths. Callie shifted her body, bringing her leg up in between Jackie's, forcing her to grind down onto it. Jackie broke the kiss to groan at the sensation, her hips involuntarily rolling into the action again. She gasped as she felt Callie's hands cup her backside, forcing her to push harder against her.

"You look amazing like this..." Callie said, knowing that it would have an effect on Jackie. It had taken her a while to get used to saying what she wanted or how she was feeling in bed, but with Jackie's encouragement and the obvious effect it had on her, she quickly learnt to get over her embarrassment. "Did you think of this while we were apart? Did you think of me making you come?"

She watched as each word made Jackie shake and stutter, her movements becoming clumsy and uncoordinated as she neared her peak, clearly not far off after making Callie come only moments before. The speed at which she was unravelling in front of her only served to boost Callie's confidence as she guided Jackie's hips faster and harder.

"Fuck! Callie!" Jackie screamed as she came, her body collapsing on top of Callie.

Callie wrapped her arms around Jackie, holding her close, waiting contentedly as she came back around, feeling her bury her nose into her neck and take a deep inhale, the warm press of a kiss over her pulse making her shiver. A comfortable quiet settled over the room as if it was cocooning the two of them in a world of their own. The only noise which broke through was the faint sound of a car passing by outside, and in that moment, Callie knew she'd never felt happier.

"I did, you know," Jackie spoke into the silence a few minutes later.

"Hmm?" Callie asked, body and mind still blissed out in a post-orgasm haze.

"Think about you. Not like this. Well, maybe a few times..." Callie shook with silent laughter, jostling Jackie on top of her. "But about other things."

"I thought about you too," Callie admitted.

Jackie shifted, pushing herself up and off of Callie, staring down at her. She missed the solid weight of Jackie's body on top of hers, the way she could feel her heartbeat underneath her hand, the softness of her skin under her fingertips. As Callie studied her, she noticed goosebumps break out across her body. "You're cold." She sat up as well, guiding Jackie up the bed before dragging back the covers and clambering under them, pulling Jackie into her as soon as they were settled. "Jacs?"

"Yeah?" Jackie asked from where she had settled against Callie's chest, lazily drawing patterns up and down Callie's bare arm with her fingertip.

"I know I hurt you," Callie started, a tremble in her voice.

"Stop. Stop right there." Jackie propped herself up on her elbow, her hand coming to rest against Callie's breastbone, right over her still thumping heart. "I know there's going to be a lot to talk about, but can we just have the rest of tonight without worrying about anything?"

Callie smiled, blinking back inexplicable tears which threatened to fall, grateful for the respite from the heaviness of her emotions.

"Yeah, of course." She beamed, still overtaken with emotion. Callie yawned, the endorphins dropping in her bloodstream and the late hour finally making itself known.

"Tired?"

"A little. All I want to do is fall asleep with you for the first time in forever," Callie replied, shuffling in closer to Jackie, pulling her into her body as their legs entwined underneath the covers.

"Really?" Jackie lent over Callie, propping herself up with her elbow. "That's *all* you want to do?" she asked, tilting her head to whisper against Callie's ear as her hand slid in between her legs again, finding the slick arousal which had already started to pool there again, her touch sending a soft gasp from Callie into the room.

"I could be persuaded into other things as well," Callie moaned, rolling over to capture Jackie's lips.

Chapter Fourteen

Jackie woke to the sun creeping through the curtains, her mind filled with memories of the night before. For a moment, she wondered if she had dreamt it all, but then she became aware of the weight of the arm which was draped across her waist and the heat from the body which lay behind her. She rolled over, and her body ached in a way it hadn't done in a long time. She was greeted by the divine sight of Callie, asleep, her face peaceful and free of worry. She studied her; she was obviously older than the last time they had laid like this, but she was just as beautiful, if not more so. Gentle lines graced her face, she hoped through years of laughter, but she feared more through stress and unhappiness. There was a small scar across her forehead, which hadn't been there when she was younger, her cheekbones were more pronounced, and there was just an air of something different she couldn't put her finger on but came with maturity.

"I can feel you staring at me," Callie mumbled from where her face was pushed into the pillow.

Jackie smiled and brushed a strand of hair that had fallen forward out of her face. Callie sighed and smiled softly at the action, eyes still closed. Jackie ran her fingers through her hair, scratching gently at her scalp, eliciting a hum from the slumbering body.

"Just admiring how beautiful you are now."

"You mean to say I wasn't beautiful before?" She cracked one eye open and quirked an eyebrow.

"You were always beautiful." Jackie leaned down and pressed a kiss to her lips.

"Good save," Callie said as she closed her eye again.

Jackie lay there, her head propped up on her arm, fingers combing through Callie's hair, savouring the quiet moment. The sense of calm which lay between them was new; there was always something simmering in the background when they were together before, a fear of what would happen when people found out about them. But for some reason, that wasn't present this time. Maybe now that they—Callie especially—were older, people wouldn't worry so much about the age gap. Maybe it wouldn't be such a big deal that they worked together either. Her fingers trailed down Callie's shoulder, catching on the fabric of the vest she wore.

Callie lay back in Jackie's arms and sighed. The sound of the television was playing quietly in the background, but Jackie knew she wasn't watching it. Something had been plaguing her girlfriend's mind for a while now, and although she longed to know what it was, she wasn't about to push her to tell her. She hoped that in providing her a safe and comforting environment, gently supporting her silently, she would open up when she was ready. She had the feeling that Callie was close, and she just needed to keep waiting patiently. She wrapped her arms around Callie's shoulders and squeezed her gently before dropping a kiss on the top of her head, smiling when she heard the absentminded hum of contentment from in front of her. This thing between them had been progressing slowly for the past few weeks, and Callie made Jackie happy in every way. She could only hope the same could be said for Callie, and while she was fairly certain, she couldn't help but worry about her. As if she had some sixth sense, she felt Callie stiffen slightly in her hold, her shoulders tightening and her body retreating into itself.

"Hey," Jackie murmured. "Where did you just go?" She hoped that her soft tone soothed whatever thoughts had just caused Callie to flinch.

"Oh...I'm sorry. I'm here, I j-just..." Callie stammered, something akin to shame or embarrassment lacing her words.

"You don't need to apologise. I just need to know you're okay. You went all tense there for a minute," she explained softly. Jackie couldn't help but smile when she noticed Callie shiver as her lips brushed her ear. It was a beautiful thing to witness the effect she had on Callie, but she wished that she wasn't so consumed with her thoughts that it was a fleeting occurrence. She held herself there for a moment taking in the subtle scent and feel of Callie and grounding herself in it.

"I-I didn't realise," Callie admitted quietly.

"Your body is so expressive sometimes. It gives a lot away." She bent her head, pressing a kiss to below Callie's ear. "At least, to me, anyway. I think you've spent so long pushing down and hiding yourself, you don't even realise what your tells are anymore."

"I love that you know me so well already." Callie leaned back into her embrace, pushing herself into her body, and Jackie gave herself over to the woman trying to seek strength from her.

"But?"

"But there's so much you don't know, so much I don't let anyone know. And I want to tell you, but I'm so scared to."

"Hey." Jackie's voice was still quiet but had taken on a strong, steely tone which she hoped conveyed just how serious she was. "I never want you to be scared about talking to me. Whatever it is, I will be here to carry it with you. I'll be here to listen, and I'll never judge. But I also only want you to tell me when you are ready to. It doesn't have to be now."

"Thank you. But I know, if we're to go anywhere...I just don't want this hanging over us. And if I don't tell you now, I'm scared I never will."

"Then I'm listening." Jackie tightened her arms momentarily, a silent sign of support to say, she hoped, take your time, I'm here.

"You know Annie, isn't my real mum, right?" Callie began.

"Yes."

"My real mother is called Darla Connor. Dad left her before he knew she was pregnant, but she still decided to have me. She thought keeping the baby—me—would bring him back." Callie sighed. Jackie could tell this was exhausting her already, and she'd only just started telling the tale. "But she was wrong. And instead, she was just pissed off that she was stuck with me. She hated me for it, and as I got older, and Dad had Robbie and Jake, it only got worse."

Jackie felt Callie shift, shuffling around and burrowing her face into the sleeve of her jumper as if seeking refuge there. She ran her fingers through Callie's hair, scratching lightly at her scalp in a way she knew calmed her.

"I used to visit Dad at the weekend, and I begged him to let me stay longer. He would tell me that it wasn't his choice. Mum wouldn't let me live with him because I was the only link she had to him still. I couldn't tell him how bad things were because she told me Social Services would take me, and then I wouldn't see him at all."

Jackie's heart cracked, and she absentmindedly kissed the top of Callie's head.

"How bad was it?" she whispered, not wanting to break the intimacy of the moment.

"She drank. A lot. I had to look after myself most of the time. She was either out drinking or passed out from it, and that was fine by me."

Jackie bit back her anger. How could a mother—and she used the term loosely—be so cold-hearted and cruel that her child would prefer her to be missing in action than at home. Unless...

"Callie. Did she...did she hurt you?" Jackie guessed, choking the words past the lump that lodged in her throat. She hoped to God she *was wrong, but the renewed tension which crept through Callie's body confirmed her worst fears.*

"The only time she was guaranteed to be home was when Dad dropped me off," Callie answered, seemingly avoiding Jackie's question. "She'd stay sober enough on those days to keep up appearances. But mainly, it was so she could ask me about Dad. What did we do? Where did we go? Did he and Annie fight? Did he ask about her? If I didn't give her the answers, she wanted..."

Callie's voice drifted off, but Jackie didn't need her to finish. Her stomach turned at the thought of anyone laying a finger on Callie, a white rage burning in her chest directed at a woman she'd never even met. She pushed a kiss to Callie's temple, holding her face there and taking in everything she was in this moment. The scent of her shampoo, the feel of her jumper in her clenched fingertips, the perfect stillness of a body that had detached itself from the soul Callie laid bare. Jackie let the tears roll down her face silently, crying for the young girl who'd had her childhood tarnished by the person who was supposed to be her constant.

"One day, I came home from school, and she was there..."

Cold dread ran through Jackie's veins at the stony tone of Callie's voice. She rubbed her hand up and down Callie's arm, trying to fight off the chill which had settled over them both.

"She was at the table, the belt she used ready next to her. And she had my diary. I wrote everything in that book. How I wanted to live with Dad. How I hated Darla. How I wished Annie was my mum and I could be with Robbie and Jake all the time. And how I had a crush on this girl at school...apparently, that was the final straw. Not only was I a waste of space, but now I was sick and disgusting as well."

Jackie felt Callie squeeze her fingers where she had entwined her own earlier in the story. She let her hold them as tight as she needed, not caring about the fact it was starting to hurt. She felt Callie's breathing quicken to short, shallow breaths, which gave away the fact she was slipping.

"It's okay, baby. You're here with me now."   Jackie guessed that Callie was struggling to stay out of her memory, and she hoped that her reassurance would keep her with her. "You don't have to say anymore."

Something about her words caused the dam inside Callie to break as she let out an anguished sob, tears finally cascading down her face as she released what Jackie assumed was years of built-up shame and guilt. Jackie sat there, cradling her in her arms. She had never seen Callie so small and vulnerable than she was now, but she clearly needed the release, and so she held her until she was all cried out.

"W-when Dad came round a few days later, he found me in my bedroom. By that time, the cuts had become infected...God, I was in so much pain." Jackie's stomach churned with the image her mind had created. "I-I don't even remember going to the hospital. Annie said that between the swelling, and the infection, I-I couldn't lie or sit still for very long. They had to sedate me just so I could rest. The one across my ribs where she used the buckle instead..." Callie's words hiccupped with the sobs which racked her body, Jackie sharing her pain and tears.

"Shh, sweetheart..." Jackie breathed, voice thick with emotion. How anyone could hurt such a beautiful and caring soul like Callie was beyond her. Untracked time passed as the two just lay together, wrapped up in their own cocoon of emotions. Jackie wished she could take it all away, all the hurt and pain that Darla had inflicted. Instead, all she could offer was her unconditional presence.

"They left marks, s-scars, and I..." Callie whispered, choking on her own words.

I feel ugly. *Jackie could hear the unspoken words loud and clear in the stillness of the room.*

"Listen to me. That doesn't matter. Not to me. You are the most beautiful woman I have ever met, inside and out. And whatever shadows that woman left over you, we work through together. Okay?"

Callie cleared her throat, taking a shaky breath. "There's always a part of me which thinks she's going to find me. This is home, I should feel safe, and she destroyed that for me."

"You're safe here," Jackie spoke into her skin, the warmth of her breath brushing over her temple. She could feel her try even harder to pull her close, hold her tighter as if the grip she already had on her wasn't enough.

"I feel it. You make me feel it."

"Why do you hide yourself again?" Jackie asked softly, playing with the strap of Callie's vest. It was her armour, and Jackie still remembered just how honoured and overwhelmed she felt when Callie first removed it. Callie stilled further if that was at all possible, considering she was resting in bed, but Jackie noticed the way her shoulders tensed under her fingers and how her chest stopped moving as she held her breath for a split second. "I'm sorry, I shouldn't have—"

"She didn't like to see them," Callie murmured quietly.

"Who... Are you fucking kidding me?" Jackie hissed as the realisation dawned on her.

Callie shook her head, just barely, but enough for Jackie to see, before burying her face into her pillow slightly.

"If I ever see that fucking bitch again..." Jackie pulled away, shaking with rage. Feeling the anger rise within her, she got up from the bed, pulled an oversized t-shirt over her body, and started to pace the room. "How fucking dare she? Does she even realise what they mean? Does she know how much it takes for you to even talk about it, let alone show someone? And she makes you feel ashamed, like you have to hide them. It's just..." She turned and saw Callie had sat up in bed, her knees pulled up under her chin, arms wrapped tight around herself, with tears streaming down her face. She ran over, crawling onto the bed beside her, pulling her into her arms, smoothing her hair down with her hand. "Oh, baby, I'm so sorry. I'm sorry. I didn't mean to get so angry."

Callie sobbed into her shoulder, her body shaking with each one. She wasn't sure whether it was her outburst, the fact she had asked, or just bad memories causing the tears, but she didn't really care. All she cared about was the fact that she needed to stop them. Long moments passed when all Jackie did was hold Callie until the crying started to slow, and Callie shakily pushed herself away to sit up. Jackie lent over, grabbing a tissue to wipe her tear-stained cheeks, lingering a little as Callie looked up at her.

"I wish I could take it all away. All the hurt and pain she caused you. I wish I'd fought harder and stuck around. Then maybe you wouldn't have even met her, and none of this would have happened. You did so well, and then she just comes along and makes you feel like this..."

"I'm sorry if I disappointed you."

"No! No, baby, you have not disappointed me! You are not to blame for this."

"She would tell me she couldn't...she didn't feel...if she saw them. That the only way she could ever...was if I kept them covered. And when I found out about her affair, I thought maybe that it was because of them. If I didn't have these stupid scars..."

Jackie felt the anger in how Callie's body tensed and her fists clenched into her vest, tugging it with every furious word. Stilling her hands with her own, she held them tight.

"Listen to me. None of what she did to you is your fault. She is a horrible excuse for a human being." Jackie cupped Callie's face, pulling it up so they made eye contact. "And I will spend every second making sure you know I don't care about them. That I think you're beautiful no matter what. Working until you know that they are nothing to be ashamed of. And if we never get to that point again, I'll still think you're beautiful, and I'll still lo—I'll still want to be with you."

Jackie internally chastised herself for nearly letting slip the extent of her feelings for Callie. Yes, they'd said it before, a long time ago, but so many years had passed, and with their reconnection literally hours old, this most definitely was not the time.

Callie dropped her head and rested it on her own, foreheads pressed together in a silent prayer for strength.

"What is this, Jacs?" Callie asked quietly, voice hoarse from crying. "We've been dancing around each other for weeks, and now this. What does this mean for us? Is there even an us?"

"I hope so," Jackie answered honestly.

"Can you really forgive me for running away? Friends is one thing, but to trust me like this again…"

"There's nothing to forgive anymore, baby. That's all in the past. And you are in such a better place this time. I saw it the day I first walked into that office."

Callie finally lifted her head at Jackie's admission, her gaze shifting over her face as if she was trying to take in every detail and minutiae, eyes lingering over the shape of her mouth, before coming to settle and remain locked on her own eyes. Jackie got lost in the stormy marine shades which were swirling before her.

"When you told me about Dad calling you, the fact you knew," Callie paused, lifting a hand to Jackie's cheek, and she felt her run her thumb across under her eye, wiping away a tear she didn't even know had fallen. Jackie involuntarily lent into the touch, cherishing the feel. "I couldn't be mad at you for that. Because as much as it hurt to know you knew and didn't reach out to me, I knew you were doing it to protect me."

"I'd do anything for you."

"Just promise me it won't be staying away again."

Jackie lent forward, capturing Callie's lips in a tender kiss. "Not calling, not hearing your voice and knowing for myself…it killed me those first few months. And ever since I've been back, those feelings I had have only grown every day. I tried to tell myself that I needed to get this under control, that there was no way you'd still have feelings for me, but I couldn't help it. And when I saw you last night… God, you looked amazing."

"I need time, Jacs. There's more than ten years of stuff to unpack. But if we're doing this, I want to be completely honest with you. I need you to be patient with me. I will tell you, just…in my own time."

"I've waited this long, baby. I can wait as long as you need me for everything else." She sealed the promise with another kiss.

Chapter Fifteen

Callie had never seen Beka Sanderson quite as sheepish as she was that morning. Walking into the conference room, Beka sloped past Callie, all her swagger and bravado gone, and took a seat at the table she was directed to. Callie studied her as she sat herself, watching as her hands fidgeted in her lap, and she looked anywhere but at her.

"Beka, this is Frances Beecham from HR. She's here to witness this conversation to prevent any issues from arising in the future. Is that okay?"

Beka's line of sight shot up to take in the other woman in the room, and Callie could see the regret in her face. It was almost enough to change her mind on what she was about to do. But it wasn't just her decision. The other senior partners had agreed when she debriefed them first thing this morning.

"Y-yes."

"Okay, Beka. Your behaviour recently has been below expectations. You've been spoken to or reprimanded about your rude and dismissive attitude, including in particular the way you address and speak to Miss Taylor. You were already on a warning, when, at the function on Friday night, it was suggested you have been passing on confidential information to outside parties."

"I'm sorry, Miss Montgomery. If I knew—"

Callie stopped Beka with a raised hand. "I believe you knew exactly who you were talking to and the effect that those actions could have. Did you?"

Beka nodded and answered quietly, "Yes."

Frances scribbled on her notepad at Beka's admittance.

"You were aware that Miss Goodman is not only my ex-wife but also an employee of a competing company?"

"Yes."

"And did you pass on confidential information pertaining to this business to Miss Goodman?"

Beka nodded, and Callie sighed. "But it was only things like meetings and who was here. I never gave her anything like numbers or accounts!" she pleaded.

Callie looked to Frances who gave her a nod.

"You've left me no choice. Effective immediately I'm terminating your contract with Montgomery and Associates."

"No..." Beka looked back and forth between the two women opposite her.

"You broke the company confidentiality clause which you signed when you started. The consequence is immediate dismissal. Frances will go through all the exit paperwork with you and help you collect your things."

Callie stood up, pointedly ignoring Beka as she started to cry, and walked out of the conference room and across the hallway to her office. Dropping heavily into her chair, she threw her pen onto the desk and closed her eyes. She had never fired anyone before, and despite the circumstances, it didn't feel good. Beka may have fed Jen information, and it didn't matter that it was incomplete or inaccurate; the fact was she was still stupid enough to do it in the first place.

A sound outside her office door alerted her to Beka's return, and she walked over, watching Beka load her things into a cardboard box.

"Why did you do it, Beka?" she asked quietly.

Beka looked up at the unexpected question, eyes red from crying and full of remorse.

"I don't know. Because Jackie just walked in and all of a sudden it was like I didn't exist. And I hated that. I hated that you relied on someone else."

"But Beka, I never relied on you for my personal affairs. That's not the relationship we had."

"I know, but I liked to think that maybe you would. You're so kind and generous, I always admired you, but it became something more than that. And when Jackie—*Miss Taylor*—arrived, I became jealous of what you and her have. I got drunk one weekend and started talking to this woman in a bar who said she understood how I felt."

"Jen?"

"Yeah. After a while she started asking questions, and I happily answered what I could. She made me feel important and wanted. The way I wanted to be to you."

"Jen only looks after herself. She sold you out Friday night—you realise that?"

"Yeah, I do. I was an idiot to think she wouldn't just drop me to save herself. But she was so..."

"Charming? She's good at that. Do yourself a favour, Beka. Find a new job and focus on getting yourself back on track. And if you need a reference, give me a shout."

"Really?"

"Yes. Up until you lost all your senses and decided to break our confidentiality agreement, you were a good assistant. And I think you've learnt your lesson. You just can't continue here."

"Thank you, Callie," Beka said, her tone humble and grateful.

Callie closed the door and walked over to the sofa, sitting

down ungracefully. Closing her eyes again, she thought about how different she felt now to how she woke up this morning.

A smile crept across her lips at the thought of Jackie peppering soft kisses across her bare shoulders as she came round from slumber, her hand drifting down under the covers to caress the skin of her thigh. Her guilt and disappointment at having just fired Beka was quickly soothed by the warm, comforting feeling which always came from being with or even thinking about Jackie. That woman had made her feel safer and more wanted in the past forty-eight hours than anyone had in the past twelve years.

Letting her head drop back, she let the silence of the room wash over her. She was tired, but it wasn't from her activities over the weekend. It was more a tiredness she felt in her bones after a weight has been lifted.

Pulling her thoughts back round to the present, she focussed on the soft hum of the air conditioning unit and the sound of shuffling and mumbling outside the office door as Beka finished packing up her things. She needed to speak to HR and put in a job request for a new secretary. Maybe in the meantime, she could get some help from one of the other assistants. Did she even really need an assistant? The door opening without a knock soon answered that question.

"Just because no one's out there doesn't mean people can just walk in! Knock!" she shouted without looking.

"Oh, sorry. Do you want me to come back later?" Jackie's apologetic tone reached her, and Callie scrambled to sit up.

"No! No, sorry—I thought you were someone else."

"Who?"

"Anyone. Everyone," Callie admitted as she shuffled to the edge of the seat. "I'm sorry. I didn't mean to shout."

"I did wonder why all of a sudden I had to start knocking."

"You"—Callie wiggled her fingers, beckoning Jackie to come closer—"don't ever have to."

Jackie came to sit beside her on the sofa, close but not touching, much to Callie's frustration. Even without the physical contact, though, Callie felt her body relax a little more from just being in her presence. She gave her a small smile, tired but genuine.

"How did it go? I saw Beka leaving a few minutes ago."

"Fine. Easy in some ways. She didn't really argue or defend herself, just took it. Hard in others. Apparently, it all stemmed from you being back in the picture."

"How come?"

"Beka didn't like the fact she didn't feel such an important aspect in my life anymore. Jen played on that, made her feel worthy, and got her information at the same time."

"I still can't believe she was dating Jen."

"I can. Or rather, I can believe that Jen found her out and used her as she did. By the sounds of things, she's already dumped Beka."

"Poor girl. I know I wasn't her biggest fan, but I didn't want this for her."

"Hmm. Anyway, did you need something?"

"No. Just wanted to check in on you. See your face," Jackie said with a sly grin.

"You saw my face this morning. And yesterday. And the day before that..."

"Yes, well, that doesn't mean I don't want to keep seeing it throughout the day."

"You're such a charmer," Callie murmured as she darted her gaze down to Jackie's lips before snapping it back up. "But we have an agreement."

Callie stood up, making her way over to her coffee station and starting up the machine. She cleared her throat.

"Yes, we do, but I was under the impression that that agreement covered...other activities only. Not visits to look at you," Jackie spoke from where Callie had left her, her voice painfully sultry.

"Problem is..." Callie turned around and found Jackie casually reclining on her sofa, her black heels extending her already gorgeous legs which disappeared underneath her grey skirt. She was fairly sure Jackie chose this outfit on purpose this morning. She remembered the look she gave her as she rolled her stockings up. The consequence of which was them both being nearly late for work. "Those looks lead onto the other activities."

"Not my fault you have no self-control."

"I have no self-control?" Callie said, incredulous.

"Okay. Maybe we're both as bad as the other," Jackie admitted, rising from the sofa and stalking toward her in a way which was entirely too alluring for the workplace. Coming to a stop beside her, she turned to Callie as she lifted her coffee cup from the machine. "What are you doing tonight?"

"I'm..." She was about to declare she was free until she realised that the gala had been on Friday night, and as such, family dinner night had been moved. "Shit. Family dinner."

"On a Monday?"

"Well, I was kind of busy on Friday."

"Fair point," Jackie laughed. "Guess I've waited this long. I can wait another evening," she said, tapping her spoon on the side of her cup.

"You sure?" asked Callie.

"Absolutely fucking not!" Jackie confessed as she strutted away and out of Callie's office to the sound of a throaty laugh.

Chapter Sixteen

Jackie: Are you sure I can't tempt you away? x
Callie: God, you know you could. x
Jackie: Come round when you've finished. We'll spend the evening together. x
Callie: You sure? I've been at yours all weekend. x
Jackie: I've got twelve years to make up for, baby. Get over here later. x
Callie: See you soon gorgeous. x

Callie locked her phone and slid it into the pocket of her trousers before sliding herself out of her car. She practically skipped across the driveway, the thought of the past weekend dampening even her usual anxieties about family dinner. All those worries, that uncertainty, she had been feeling over her emotions towards Jackie was for nothing. Any insecurities she had about how Jackie felt towards her had quickly been eradicated within the first few moments of them meeting again, but she never let herself believe she would be lucky enough to have another chance. Now she was able to act on everything she felt—the urge to touch her, to kiss her, all now realities for Callie.

She closed the front door and kicked off her shoes, greeted by her niece hopping down the stairs and jumping into a huge hug. "Hey, Auntie Cal!"

"Hey, kiddo! I didn't know you were coming for dinner tonight!"

Charlotte, or Charlie as she was affectionately known to the family, was the only child of Robbie and his wife, and it was one of the most obvious father-daughter resemblances she'd ever seen. She shared his steely grey eyes, although they had been a little softened by her mother's genetics, and her hair was thick and lucious, natural chocolate brown waves falling down her back. She was soon to be a big sister, and at thirteen years, the age gap was massive but not insurmountable. Callie had no doubt she would be an amazing older sibling. Seeing her at family dinner was usually dependent on whether she had a party or sleepover, Friday being the prime day with no school the day after for teenage fun.

"Yeah, well, I didn't have anything on tonight. It's a school night." She shrugged.

"Oh, thank you for spending your free time with us. We are honoured," Callie replied sarcastically.

"Shut up! Besides, Dad said Uncle Jake might be less of an arse if I'm here."

Callie stopped dead in her tracks, turning on her heel to face her niece. "Your dad said that, huh?"

"Yep."

"You've not told Uncle Jake that, have you?"

"Do I look stupid?"

Callie laughed. "No. You, kiddo, are definitely not stupid."

"What's up with him anyway? Dad wouldn't say, I only overheard him say something to Mum at the weekend."

"I had to tell your Gran and Grandad something about when Uncle Jake worked at the company. And Uncle Jake wasn't very happy about it," Callie replied, somewhat diluting the truth to its bare basics.

"And Uncle Jake's now being an arse about it?"

"Yes...but can we not keep calling Uncle Jake an arse?" Callie felt the need to say. It may be what Robbie felt about him, and coming to think about it, Jackie as well considering her comments recently. But the last thing she needed was Charlie shouting it out at the dinner table.

"But isn't he?"

"That doesn't matter. I mean, if it's what your dad thinks, then that's your dad, but I'm not sure Grandad's going to like it if you say it."

"Yeah, okay then." Charlie started walking again, followed by Callie into the living room. Barrett and Robbie were the only ones in there, deep in conversation, most likely about the weekend's rugby match, a shared passion between them since Robbie was young, judging by the emphatic gestures they were making. Callie and Charlie made their way past with a wave and hello, not wanting to interrupt the detailed match analysis, in an attempt to find Annie. They found her and Jake talking in the kitchen. Jake turned as Charlie ran up to see what her grandmother was cooking, stopping mid conversation when he saw that she had arrived with Callie.

"Hey, Jake," Callie tried, more for the sake of Charlie than anything else.

"Callie," Jake replied coolly. Clearly, he wasn't planning on trying to put on a front for Charlie either. Both of the boys had inherited their father's pig-headedness. Robbie had not been particularly discreet in voicing his dislike of Jake at home, but Callie wasn't going to be responsible for tainting the view a child had of her uncle. Besides, he was still her brother, and whatever had gone on in the business, she hoped that their relationship wasn't completely unsalvageable.

It had never been perfect, not since she had moved in, but

then, Jake had never been told the full details of why Callie stopped living with Darla. At twelve, Barrett and Annie had considered him too young to deal with the full truth, but it seemed as the years went on, the lack of details and a young boy's imagination had resulted in his own version of events.

Suddenly, Callie had somewhat of an epiphany, a memory of something Jackie had said to her. *My imagination filled in all the gaps.* The thought gave her a new respect and vantage point on what Jake had been through.

She looked at Charlie, now talking with him. Jake was the same age Charlie was now when Callie moved into his home. She wondered how Charlie really felt about having a little brother or sister come into her life. She made a mental note to sit down with her niece sometime soon and have a conversation with her about it. Maybe she could do it at the same time she introduced Charlie to Jackie.

Oh, where did that come from? We're not there yet. No, they weren't there yet, but the thought of being there, at a point in their relationship where they merged their families and their relationship became public, wasn't quite as daunting as it should have been. Maybe it was to do with this being the second time around, maybe it was because they were both older and wiser, but whatever it was, the end result was still the same: Callie's future was Jackie, and there was no debating it.

"Callie, darling, can you get me the milk out of the fridge please?" Annie's voice cut her out of her thought pattern.

"Hmm? Sorry?"

"The milk. Can you pass it to me please?" Annie repeated, and Callie opened the fridge and pulled out the bottle, handing it over to her mother. "Everything okay, darling? You seem a little distant."

"Yes. Yes, I'm fine. Sorry, just tired still. From Friday." It wasn't an outright lie, but Callie was definitely keeping the details to herself. She fought the smirk which threatened to break out, instead focussing on whatever was bubbling on the stove.

Taking a second to calm herself, she turned back to where Jake and Charlie were standing, Jake keeping himself busy making drinks for everyone. She guessed that Barrett was still giving him a hard time, and that was why he was hiding out in the kitchen, especially while she was standing there, rather than being in another room. Wandering over to stand next to them, she was, as usual, the first to break their silence.

"How's things, Jake?" She hated how stilted conversations with her brother had become. Granted, the past two years hadn't been brilliant, usually marred by Jake's bitter comments or gloating achievements, but at least there were some good moments. Now, there were just short answers or awkward silences.

"Not bad. Do you want a glass of this as well?" he asked, holding up the bottle of sparkling water he had been pouring.

"Yeah, sure. Is the lime out?"

"Yeah. Charlie, pass us the lime."

Callie watched as Jake poured a healthy measure of the cordial into her glass, smiling as he also dropped a wedge of fresh lime in it too, making it just how she liked it. He slid it in front of her.

"Thanks," she said, flashing him another grin. Her optimism was short lived, though, as he shrugged and walked off with someone else's drinks. Callie deflated, her shoulders slumping, even though Charlie turned around and gave her an overly cheerful thumbs up. She threw back a tired grin, watching as she followed Jake with the last drink. She sensed her mother come up behind her.

"He's getting there, but he needs a bit longer."

"It's been two months, Mama. And quite frankly, I'm getting tired of trying to make peace when it wasn't my fault in the first place."

"I know, but he feels—"

"I kind of don't care how he feels. You know, it was my foolish idea to keep it a secret, and all he's done in return is be spiteful and bitter towards me. I really wish I'd just come clean in the beginning," Callie spat. Her patience was wearing thin with the entire situation, and considering she had put off seeing Jackie for this, she really wasn't in the best headspace to begin with. "I'm sorry, Mama. I just don't know what else I can do."

"I know, my darling," Annie said, cupping Callie's face in her hands. "I love you. All of you. I hate seeing you all fighting."

"I know, Mama. I wish it could be different."

Callie watched as her mother blinked back tears, quickly changing the subject. "Help me with these plates, will you?"

"Sure."

Callie lifted and balanced three plates on her arms expertly before following Annie into the dining room. Between them, they handed out dinner as the family sat down around the table, Barrett at the top of the table as usual with Annie at the opposite end. Callie sat on one side next to Charlie, Robbie and Jake opposite them. Silence descended, the only sound the scratching of knives and forks on plates as everyone ate their dinner in what had become a sad and painful weekly routine.

"How was the gala?" Barrett asked, cutting into his chicken.

"Yeah, fine," sighed Callie. Her good mood was slowly ebbing away, first because Jake's attitude towards her and now with talk of the gala. She should have known, really, that Barrett would ask about it. And truth be told, she probably did know; it was just that she had chosen to ignore it in favour of more pleasant thoughts.

"Just fine? Callie, I know it's not really your thing to schmooze clients, but you really need to do it if you're going to get new people through the door and keep the business thriving," Barrett almost scolded.

"Yeah, I know." Callie pushed a potato around her plate, watching as it moved the sauce around in its path.

"And making a good impression is more important now than ever." Barrett gave a pointed look in Jake's direction. The action earned him an eye roll from Callie, a scoff from Jake, and quiet admonishment from Annie across the table.

"And there were another four senior partners there to do the schmoozing. All of them were better than me at it."

"Did Jackie introduce herself?"

"Yes, Jackie mingled with all sorts of people. You know she's naturally very good at that sort of thing." Callie fought back a smile. The ease at which Jackie could talk to people was something she had always admired, and she thought back to how she watched her across the room. Granted, her attention wasn't on her conservation; it was on the way that dress hugged her hips, the way it accentuated her collarbone, the definition of her shoulder blades... She cleared her throat as she brought herself back into the room.

"Anyone new this year?" Barrett just wouldn't take the hint.

She looked over to where Jake was sitting, shifting uncomfortably in his chair. She knew Barrett was still angry at Jake, but was he doing this on purpose? She really hoped her father wasn't that childish.

Dropping her fork onto the plate, she broke the tense atmosphere which had settled, losing her patience. "Actually, if you must know Dad, yes there was someone new. Jen is now working for McCallister and Jones, and she was there. With my assistant, actually. So after a rather tense conversation with her, I am now down a staff member as of this morning. I apologise if the social function, which I despise anyway, was made even more unbearable with the re-emergence of my ex-wife out of the woodwork and as such, I don't feel particularly eager to discuss the night."

An uneasy silence settled over the room once again. Barrett and Annie shared a look as if to ask *what are we supposed to say*, Jake was visibly stunned at the admission, and Robbie watched everyone else. The uneasy quiet was eventually broken by Charlie.

"What a cow!" she exclaimed.

A beat of silence followed before Callie burst out laughing at the same time Robbie realised what his daughter had said.

"Charlotte!"

"She's got a point, Robbie," Callie defended through bursts of giggling. Callie gave her niece a wink, grateful for her young mind which just spoke as it thought.

"I know…but, if your mother asks, I've told you off. Maybe next time, don't call her a cow."

"Fine. Then what should I call her?"

"A bitch?" Jake chirped in, a sly grin on his face. Callie turned, her heart swelling at the fact her brother was making small talk and joining in the casual, fun conversation.

"Jake!" Annie admonished this time. "Not in front of Charlie!"

"It was Charlie who started it!" he argued, quite correctly, to another round of laughter.

"Are we just going to ignore the fact that we've had someone in the business feeding information to our competitors?" Barrett interrupted, clearly not seeing the funny side of the situation.

"No. No, Dad, of course not," Callie wheezed. "But I have dealt with Beka accordingly. And Jen for that matter."

"What did you say?" Robbie asked, curiosity piqued.

"I just told her I wasn't going to be intimidated by her anymore." Callie took a calming breath, knowing that for most of the table, her time spent with Jen was not a happy memory. "Enough of my life has been spent worrying about what she did, the things she thought and said. And now that's over. For good."

"Well done, sis," Robbie said, pride evident.

"Thanks," she said. She turned her attention back to Barrett. "Dad, I know you're worried about me and the business, but please believe me when I say that everything has been handled and is sorted. The things Beka supposedly knew and told Jen were exaggerated at best and false at worst. No one is concerned that anything confidential was leaked, and the business can carry on as it was with new customers coming through the doors."

Barrett seemed to visibly relax at her reassurance. "Okay. I'm sorry, I just hate that woman being mentioned in this house."

"I know. And after tonight, she will never have to be mentioned again. Okay?" Barrett nodded once, accepting what Callie was saying. "Besides, Jackie was on top of it all."

Yep, she was on top, alright, she thought with a grin.

∽

Jackie heard the knock on her front door and smiled to herself as she stood up from the sofa. She knew it would be Callie, she'd texted twenty minutes ago as she was leaving her parent's house, but she still felt a welcome flutter in her chest at the knowledge that she was at her door. Despite the fact that they had spent all weekend together, it had felt like forever since she had truly spent any time with Callie. She knew it sounded ridiculous but going back to *just* being friendly in the office was harder than she had anticipated. As if now that she had her back, had a taste of what life with Callie back in it felt like, she never wanted to lose her again.

Pulling open the door, her heart burst with the sight of Callie standing on the other side. Her eyes were tired, and her stance weary; she knew these family dinners wore her down lately, but her face lit up as she looked at Jackie, and Jackie suspected she looked the same.

"Hey," she said, holding out her hand and wrapping her fingers around Callie's, pulling her gently into her house. Pushing the door closed behind them, she drew Callie into her, her arm instinctively wrapping around her waist and holding her close. She bumped her nose against Callie's, teasingly brushing against each other, before she closed the gap, capturing Callie's mouth in a slow, sensual kiss. She lingered, pulling back just enough to tease Callie's lips with her tongue before capturing her bottom lip in between her teeth. Her hands brushed around Callie's hips, pinning her back against the door and tugging gently to release her shirt from her trousers, fingers barely brushing the delectable skin she knew lay underneath but enough to send a wave of goosebumps across Callie's body.

The moan which Callie released into Jackie's mouth only served to spur her on, twisting her around. A thud, a rattle, and the distinct blunt pressure of the sideboard into Callie's back, jolted them back into reality. Callie pulled back, slightly breathless in an all too enticing manner, glancing behind her at the vase which wobbled precariously before turning back to Jackie.

"Shit, Jacs," Callie breathed, her fingers ghosting across her kiss-swollen lips.

"Sorry," Jackie replied, equally as affected as Callie. She rested her forehead against Callie's, the sound of their laboured breathing the only sound in the quiet hallway. "I missed you."

"Yeah, I figured." Callie smiled. "I missed you too."

Jackie lifted her head, taken aback by the stormy gaze which she saw looking back at her. Her eyes flickered down to Callie's lips again, the pull of them almost too great to ignore. Catching her bottom lip between her teeth, she exhaled deeply. Winding her fingers through Callie's, she gave a gentle tug further into the house.

"Come on. Let's get a drink before I kiss you again, and we get nowhere," Jackie said, leading Callie through to the kitchen, not yet wanting to let go of her hand.

"Not sure where the problem is," Callie retorted, a playful edge to her tone. Jackie felt her slide up behind her, resting her chin on her shoulder and pressing the full length of her body against her own. She groaned, the feel of Callie against her all too distracting.

"How was family dinner?" Jackie choked out, desperately trying to keep a hold on the situation for a little longer. She felt Callie stand back and reluctantly sever contact with her altogether as she dropped her hand when reaching the fridge.

"Really? Do you have to bring the mood down?" Jackie handed Callie the glass of wine she had just poured, giving her a look she knew Callie would understand. Before anything else happened, Jackie wanted to know Callie was okay. Callie wilted a little. "It was fine."

"Cal..."

Jackie watched Callie turn and walk away from her, dropping down onto the sofa, placing her glass on the coffee table and sighing. She flopped back, and Jackie could sense the exhaustion coming off her in waves. She followed her, perching next to her and reclining so she was propped against the back of the sofa, her face level with Callie's. Callie's eyes were closed, but she looked pale, as though she hadn't eaten or slept. Well, one of those was partially true. A wave of guilt rolled through Jackie at asking Callie to come over tonight.

"If you need to go home and just sleep..."

Callie's eyes shot open, and her head spun to face Jackie. "Do you want me to go?"

"No! No, of course not." Jackie brushed a strand of hair away from Callie's face, her fingers lingering and running across her cheek. "I just don't want you to feel like you *have* to stay."

"What about if I feel like I *have* to be here?"

"Then you are more than welcome." Jackie lent in for another chaste kiss, wanting to convey her seriousness and sincerity. "But I do want you to talk about what happened at dinner if you feel up to it."

"Surprisingly," Callie started with a sigh. "It wasn't Jake tonight."

"Barrett?" Jackie questioned. If Barrett was starting to give Callie a hard time, she'd hit the roof. She had always known his expectations were high, and she knew that Callie struggled with them sometimes, but she was past holding her tongue.

"Yeah. Nothing too big, don't worry," Callie reassured her, clearly sensing Jackie's concerns. "He just wanted to know about the gala, kept going on about how important it was to make new connections, blah, blah."

"You did great. Besides, that's what I'm there for." Jackie continued to trace her fingers across the contours of Callie's face, taking each angle and dip and committing it to memory. She watched as the repetitive motions relaxed Callie's muscles, her eyes fluttering shut.

"Hmm. Well, I told him about Jen and Beka..."

Jackie's movements stopped suddenly, surprised by Callie's admission. "You did?"

"Yeah. Part of me is sick of keeping secrets," she explained, and Jackie blanched, aware that they were the biggest secret there was, "but also, I kind of just wanted to shut him up. Show him I'm not some weak little girl anymore."

"You are most definitely not weak," Jackie affirmed, leaning in and placing a quick kiss on Callie's lips. "And if you need to tell them about us—"

"Nope." Callie shut her down. "This is one secret I want to keep. Just for a bit longer."

"Okay." Jackie was quieted by Callie pressing her lips to her own, her tongue teasing her bottom lip.

She heard herself whimper at the simple action, a wave of arousal crashing through her body at the simplest touch, her nerve endings lighting up once again. Her hand fisted in Callie's hair, holding her closer, as their tongues slipped over one another, teasing each other's mouths, their kiss quickly becoming heated and passionate once again. She felt Callie nudge her hip, and she took the hint, shifting closer and then swinging her leg over and straddling Callie's lap when sure hands grasped onto her hips and began to guide her.

"Fuck, you are stunning," Callie breathed into the room as she peppered her neck with kisses, lingering over her pulse.

"Callie," Jackie moaned when she felt the distinctive, pleasurable sting of Callie's teeth scrape over her skin. Jackie's hips started to rock, the movement involuntary as her arousal took over.

"Tell me what you want, Jacs." Jackie felt herself get wetter at the question posed to her, Callie doing everything right as she handed over the reins, giving herself over to whatever Jackie wanted and desired. She felt Callie's hands on her backside, pulling her closer, so Callie could run her tongue up the exposed skin of her chest. "Tell me what you need."

"You..." she choked out, voice hoarse with desire. "Always you."

Chapter Seventeen

Callie took in her surroundings as Jackie pulled up to the secluded lodge which she had booked for the pair of them. The area itself was beautiful, the last five minutes of the drive being down a country lane that twisted through the woodland until it opened out onto a magnificent vista of the Peak District. Callie loved this part of the country, the tranquillity of being hidden between the hills soothing for her soul. And Jackie, wonderful, beautiful Jackie who had done nothing but make her smile over the past couple of months had remembered. In fact, she had remembered more than she had let on, Callie suspected, with the lodge being not far away from the hike they did last time they were in this area, twelve years ago. Jackie brought the car to a stop and gave Callie a smile which said *go on then*.

Callie quickly jumped out, striding forward to the edge of the small garden which enclosed the driveway. She took a deep lungful of fresh, crisp air, taking in the lush emerald hillsides, the way the colour shifted where mossy grass made way to pine-filled woodland, the shards of glowing golden light where the sun broke through the clouds and illuminated the landscape. Yeah, she loved it here. She could feel her heartbeat slow, and her worries wash away just standing here for these few seconds.

"You want to see inside?" Jackie broke through the silence, but it was a welcome intrusion, her voice only adding to the quiet sense of contentment washing over Callie. She turned, smiling what she thought must have been the biggest grin she had ever displayed.

"Absolutely."

Jackie held out a hand, beckoning Callie closer, and Callie almost skipped forward, slipping her fingers in between Jackie's, who led her to the front door with an equally gleeful smile. Jackie unlocked the door, but before she opened it and let Callie through, Callie felt herself being pulled into Jackie, a warm, safe arm wrapping around her waist. Callie felt Jackie grin into the kiss, and she couldn't help but mirror the action, moaning quietly as she felt Jackie's tongue flick out and lick across her bottom lip.

"I love seeing you so happy," Jackie whispered as she broke the kiss before pushing open the front door and ushering Callie inside.

"Jacs, this place is amazing..." Callie drifted off as she took in the lodge, almost as awed by it as she was by the land outside. The large open-plan ground floor was accented with all-natural materials; the wooden floor, the slate hearth, and the solid oak dining table all brought a sense of nature coming into the house.

"I thought you'd like it," Jackie replied, walking further in and placing the keys on the dining table before waving Callie to join her. "Down here's the kitchen and living space, with a utility and boot room towards the back. Then upstairs there's two bedrooms and a bathroom. And the master bedroom has an ensuite. And then there's this..."

Jackie walked past Callie, taking hold of her hand as she did so and leading her through the kitchen. Callie's breath caught as she saw what Jackie was referring to. The entire back wall was made up of massive folding doors, providing an uninterrupted view of the peaks which they were surrounded by.

"Wow," Callie whispered, awed once again at the view.

Jackie slipped behind her, wrapping her arms around her waist and resting her chin on her shoulder.

"Thought you'd appreciate this," she muttered softly, directly into Callie's ear. The action sent goosebumps down her arms, and she shivered.

"I love it," Callie replied. She twisted her head, finding Jackie's lips instantly and capturing them in a fierce kiss. Jackie turned her in her arms, her hands settling on her hips, pulling her in closer, as Callie raised her hands and threaded them through Jackie's luscious hair. The small moan which rumbled from the back of Jackie's throat as Callie grasped just a little tighter had Callie's arousal spiking. Cool fingers crept under her hoodie, and Callie trembled at the feel of them ghosting along her skin. As they traced the curve of her waist, a spot Jackie knew was ticklish, another wave of arousal pulsed through her. Callie was going to be ruined in a matter of moments if this carried on, already feeling the wetness pooling in her boxers. Jackie pulled back, taking Callie's bottom lip in her teeth and tugging it gently as she did so. Releasing it, she smirked, her tongue darting out to lick her own kiss-swollen lips.

"Fuck..." Callie breathed.

"Hmm, did you think I'd let you get away with pulling my hair like that and not get any payback?"

"N-no...God, you're something else," Callie stammered.

"We should go get the bags in," Jackie said, taking a step back out of Callie's space.

"Yeah. Yeah, good idea." As far as her body was concerned, the only good idea would involve a bed. Or a sofa. Or any horizontal surface with Jackie laid out across it. She shook her head, trying to clear the fog which was clouding her judgement, watching Jackie walk back towards the door.

"Don't worry, though," she threw back over her shoulder. "Once we unpack, I'll dig out my bikini and show you the hot tub."

"Can I ask you a question?" Callie asked into the stillness of the early evening air. After a brief stroll into the town to get their bearings and grab some essentials from the local shop, they spent the rest of the afternoon making good on their earlier flirting in both the lounge, the bedroom, and against the kitchen counter after dinner. Now, after spending the past hour relaxing in the hot tub, Jackie sat sprawled out on the outdoor sofa, her feet resting in Callie's lap as she gently massaged the soles. She watched as Jackie lifted her head up from the back of the sofa, eyes opening in response to her.

"Mmhmm," she sounded as she took a sip of her wine before placing her glass down on the low table in front of them.

"You know what I did between us last time and this time. But what about you?"

"What about me, what?"

"Did you not find anyone? I hate the idea of you being lonely for so long."

"I wasn't lonely, beautiful," Jackie answered with a soft smile.

"Okay, but," Callie focussed on Jackie's toes, the way they looked so delicate with their nails painted a soft shade of pink. She ran her fingers over them before pressing her thumbs into the balls of her feet, earning herself a quiet hum of appreciation from Jackie. "Was there no one who you thought you could be with?"

Jackie sighed. "There were a few relationships, but nothing that really lasted longer than a few months. My longest was two years."

"What was she like?"

Callie felt Jackie poke her with her toe teasingly. "What's this about? Why are you so interested?"

"Because there's like a whole decade of your life I missed out on."

"It was a pretty boring decade, baby."

Callie looked back up at Jackie, her eyes twinkling in the early evening light. Dusk was just about to settle, and she looked beautiful against the soft pink of the sky where the sun was starting to lower.

"It wasn't all miserable, though, was it? It couldn't have been. I just want you to feel like you can talk about what you did, who you saw then, because it's such a big piece of your life. And I want to know what you did in it."

"Okay," Jackie said after a beat, swinging her legs around and shuffling up the sofa so she came to sit beside Callie. Lifting her arm, Jackie tucked herself under it, resting her head on Callie's chest. "I didn't do much but work. Especially for the first year or two. It was the only way I could get through some of the days. Keeping busy meant I wasn't thinking about you as much. I certainly didn't date for the first two years. In fact, I'd just started seeing someone when..."

She trailed off, and Callie knew what she meant. Callie felt Jackie fidget underneath her, and she looked out across the garden, unsure what to say.

"It wasn't going to last anyway," Jackie continued, "but once I got the phone call from Barrett, the way I felt after it, the sheer pain I felt. I knew I still loved you and that I wasn't ready for anything else yet."

Callie wrapped her arm tighter around her shoulder, running her fingers through the ends of the loose ponytail which Jackie had scraped her hair into when they'd got into the hot tub. She pressed a kiss onto her skin, the faint aroma of chlorine mixing with Jackie's perfume.

"About six months later, work forced me to take a holiday. I'd not taken any leave but the bare minimum, and I was close to burning out. I met this woman there. We were both sitting at the bar one night, and we got talking about why we were both on holiday alone. Somehow, telling a stranger what was going on was so much easier than telling anyone who knew me. We..." Callie felt

Jackie tense slightly before swallowing. "We got together. Just for those two weeks. She was on holiday after losing her partner the year before, and we just clicked, briefly, as we shared our stories."

Callie looked down at where Jackie's fingers were anxiously playing with the hem of the thin hoodie she had on. She stilled the action by lacing her own fingers through Jackie's, squeezing tight in a silent communication of *it's okay, I don't blame you*. She felt Jackie squeeze back, an equally heartfelt *thank you* being sent in reply.

"It was after that I sought out help when I got home. I realised rather than dealing with everything, I'd just been pushing it to one side. And my therapist made sure I knew that it was okay that I hadn't moved on, but it was also okay to move on when I was ready. But to be honest," she sighed deeply, "even when I felt up to putting myself back out there, there was no one who really caught my attention. I always found myself focussing on their faults, finding excuses why they weren't right for me. Like I said, my longest was two years, and the only reason that lasted so long was because we never really fully committed ourselves to it. She travelled for work a lot, and we would meet up when she was back in the country, but really...it shouldn't have lasted that long if I'm honest."

A stillness settled over the pair of them as Jackie finished speaking, the only real movement being the rise and fall of their chests in rhythm with their breathing and the gentle repetitive motion of Callie's thumb running over Jackie's knuckles.

"Thank you," Callie mumbled into Jackie's hair. "I know you think that you can't talk about that time because we were apart and of what I was going through, but I want you to know you can. Your feelings, what you went through as well, are important to me."

Callie lent backwards slightly as Jackie pushed up from where she had been resting, the cool air suddenly slipping between them and betraying how late in the evening it was getting. She couldn't help the small smile as Jackie brushed her hair out of her face, her touch gentle. She tried to focus and lock onto her eyes, but Jackie's gaze didn't still, as she felt her study her face. Finally, after a few long seconds of just being watched, Jackie lent forward and captured her lips in a slow, emotion-filled kiss that stole Callie's breath away.

Chapter Eighteen

Jackie rolled over, groaning slightly at the fact she had woken at all, startled when she found the space beside her empty. Judging by the very satisfying ache in her thighs, falling asleep exhausted and sated beside Callie had not been a dream.

Her mind wandered back to the night before. Callie braced over her, three fingers deep and slowly pushing her towards her climax. Her tongue dragging up her neck, surely tasting the salt from the thin sheen of sweat that covered her body from the two previous orgasms they had teased from each other. She felt herself clench and her body tighten with arousal. God, the way Callie had matured, the quiet, inner confidence she now possessed and that Jackie was privileged to see was the sexiest thing she'd ever witnessed. Suddenly Callie's absence from her side was almost painful, and she threw the covers back, jumping out of bed in her quest to find her.

Jackie grabbed her robe and tied it around her waist as she made her way out of the bedroom and down the stairs. The gentle sound of music playing navigated her through to the kitchen, where she happened across the most beautiful sight. She paused for a moment, leaning against the doorframe to commit it to memory; Callie Montgomery, wearing nothing but a pair of thin cotton shorts and a skin-tight white vest, hips swaying subtly to the music. An overwhelming sense of love washed over her as she simultaneously remembered all the times this had happened before and imagined all the times it could happen again. Some god or deity somewhere had granted her a second chance with this remarkable woman, and this time, she wasn't letting go.

At that moment, Callie turned around, saw Jackie, and instantly smiled at her.

"What are you doing standing there, grinning to yourself?"

"Just admiring the view. Thinking about how lucky I am."

The smile on Callie's face widened at Jackie's words, and Jackie couldn't bear the distance between them any longer. Stepping up to her, she wrapped an arm around Callie's waist, pulling her close and capturing her lips. The kiss was gentle and lingering, but Jackie still felt the familiar and welcome surge of arousal that just being in Callie's vicinity created. Breaking their contact, Jackie placed a final quick kiss to Callie's lips before resting their foreheads together.

"Morning," Callie finally greeted softly.

"Morning. I missed you in bed when I woke up." Jackie sighed, goosebumps erupting across her skin where Callie's fingers trailed up and down her arm.

"Sorry. I woke early and was restless. You looked fast asleep, and I didn't want to disturb you."

"You should have woken me."

"No, it's fine. Besides, I made a start on breakfast. Take a seat; I'll bring you a coffee." Callie gave her another kiss.

Jackie pulled herself up onto the stool at the breakfast bar, looking out of the large bi-fold doors which spanned the back wall of the lodge. The view was spectacular, more so than the website had conveyed, the rolling, lush green hills spreading out as far as they could see. The mist had practically cleared, the last few dewy strands clinging to the highest peaks, and the sky was clear, the heat of the late summer sun starting to warm the lodge.

Callie placed a cup of steaming hot coffee in front of her, dropping a kiss on her cheek but leaving her to enjoy the view in her own time. It was just another thing she loved about Callie and their easy dynamic—the way they didn't need words but could just co-exist, knowing instinctively what the other needed.

Wrapping her hands around her cup, she spied something on the breakfast bar in front of her and pulled it forward, spinning it around to see it clearly. She found herself looking at a near-perfect representation of the undulating peaks which lay out in front of her, the contrast of light and shade where the shadows fell or the woodland thickened delicately portrayed in skillful pencil strokes, crisscrossing across the page to give it texture and depth. She had never forgotten just how beautifully Callie could draw; in fact, hidden at the back of her wardrobe was a shoebox full of all the sketches she had left before. But seeing it in front of her, new and fresh, having not long been committed to the page, overwhelmed her somewhat. She looked up, aware that tears were pooling across her eyelashes when she felt Callie watching her.

"You were sketching?" she whispered, voice full of emotion.

"A little. Don't get too excited; it was nothing big," Callie dismissed with a shrug.

"It's beautiful."

"Thank you." Callie cleared her throat. "I just woke up this morning and felt...I don't know."

Jackie rose from her seat, cupping Callie's face in her hands. "I'm so happy you're drawing again."

"The natural beauty in this place inspires me," Callie explained, closing her eyes as Jackie ran her thumbs along her cheekbones. "But I think it's you more than anything."

"Me?"

"You inspire me. You, and the way you raise me up."

"No, I think it's just because you're happier now," Jackie countered, unable to keep Callie's gaze and instead dropping her hands and taking a step back. "You're happiest when you're drawing, so to know you're anywhere near that place—"

"I'm happiest when I'm with you," Callie interrupted. Jackie's mind went blank, whatever she was about to say next slipping out of her grasp. "So if my drawing, my creativity, my *passion* is linked to that, then it's all down to you. It's back—*I'm* back—because of you."

Jackie felt herself surge forward uncontrollably, grasping Callie's face in her hands and kissing her deeply. All she ever wanted was for Callie to be happy, so to hear it, to see it, and know she had played even just a tiny part in that…it was incredible. She could feel her heart hammering in her chest, threatening to burst with the love she felt. *Love.* Was it too early in this rekindled relationship to throw that out there? Maybe not. If she was honest, she'd never really stopped loving Callie. Her residing feelings for her were what had scuppered any relationship she had tried to have over the past twelve years. She either didn't let herself get too close, wasn't invested enough, or just not interested. The few short-term relationships she'd had all ended quickly, friends never really understanding why, when the other woman was a "perfect match." No one knew that she had already found her perfect match and let her run away.

"Wow," Callie gasped, breathless, when Jackie released her from their embrace.

"Sorry," Jackie said, dropping back down onto the stool, her legs weak.

"Beautiful, *never* be sorry for kissing me like that."

Chapter Nineteen

Jackie hummed to herself as she jogged up the stairs, bare feet landing softly on the plush carpet. They'd spent the day exploring a local farmers market which they had found advertised in the village shop, leisurely strolling around and tasting the local produce, buying and bringing far too much back. But Callie had said she would make dinner with what they had got, and so Jackie wasn't overly concerned.

Callie told her when they first met that she enjoyed cooking, and today, she could see just how much as she awed over the vast range of freshly made breads and artisan cheeses. Jackie's stomach grumbled slightly at the thought of whatever Callie was going to create, despite the fact they had had lunch in a little pub in the centre of the town only a few hours ago. Strolling into the bedroom, she was greeted with the sight of a very naked Callie, pulling her boxers up her toned legs. She got lost in the image, the way her skin was slightly tanned from the last few weeks of summer sun, before the sound of a shocked gasp broke her out of her musings, and she looked up to see Callie's horrified face looking back at her.

"Shit! Sorry, Cal...I didn't...I'll just..."

Even though it was their bedroom, she watched as Callie quickly ran back into the ensuite, slamming the door in her haste behind her. She scolded herself. How could she be so thoughtless and just walk into their bedroom without checking that Callie was dressed? If they were at home, she was always so careful, so considerate that Callie was comfortable. But for some reason, she had just walked in, lost in memories that would now most likely be tainted by this cavernous breach of her trust.

Getting her own emotions in check, she walked up to the ensuite door, tapping gently to let Callie know she was outside before speaking through the wood.

"Cal? I'm sorry, baby. I was in a world of my own, and I just...I didn't see them, I promise." She waited, hoping for some response, but nothing came. "Okay, well, I'm going to go back downstairs. I'll see you when you're ready."

Despondent but not entirely defeated, Jackie took a step back and started out of the bedroom, knowing that the best thing she could do was to wait and let Callie come to her when she was ready. But it didn't make it any easier to do. She hated the fact Callie felt this way. She hated that she felt she had to hide around her, that the confidence she exuded in every other aspect of her life didn't continue into her own body. She hated that Jen destroyed the connection that she and Callie had. However, the click of the bathroom door opening caused her to stop and turn back around.

Callie stood there, a towel wrapped around her body, fingers gripping the material tightly. Her eyes glistened with unshed tears, but there was a look Jackie couldn't quite place also residing there.

"Callie," she started as she took a step closer, wary of not spooking her into hiding again. "I'm so sorry."

"No," Callie replied, almost whispering. She walked forward, Jackie watching every step until she came to stop just in front of her. "I want...I need you to..." Clearly unable to finish what she was saying, Callie turned and let her towel drop to the floor.

They were paler now, time having worked its magic and

causing them to blend more with the rest of her skin, but they could still be seen. There was no mistaking what they were, the slightly darker, newer skin clear against the rest. She remembered how Callie told her they were worse than expected because of the infection which had set in after days of not being treated. But by now, years later, they had faded and were no longer as prominent as they once were. However, she knew for Callie, they were as fresh and ugly as the day she had first shown her.

Jackie's stomach turned, the reality hitting her once again. Long seconds passed, before she raised her hand, and she let her fingertips tentatively trace over the faint mark on her shoulder blade. She followed the mark down, then jumped onto the next, tracing a pattern across her back. Callie shivered underneath her touch. Jackie leaned forward and pressed her lips to where Callie's neck met her shoulder.

"I love you," Jackie whispered against her skin.

She felt Callie release the breath she had been holding and prepared for tears that never came.

"I love you, too," Callie muttered, her voice shaking with emotion.

She had known for quite a while that her feelings for Callie had never really subsided, that they still burnt as fiercely and brightly as they had when she last saw her and spoke those words twelve years ago. But saying them out loud, letting Callie know how she felt, filled her heart with joy. And hearing them back? She never thought she would be so lucky as to have that happen again.

"You are beautiful," Jackie spoke into her skin as she marked a path along her shoulder with slow, purposeful kisses.

Jackie wrapped her hands around Callie's waist, pulling her close against her own body, spanning one hand across her stomach, revelling in feeling the soft and supple skin of her slightly toned stomach underneath her palm. Callie let her head fall back, Jackie's lips now by her ear. "Let me show you," Jackie whispered.

Nerves fluttered in her stomach, but they fought with excitement as Callie leaned further back into Jackie's body. The feel of her bare skin underneath her hands was intoxicating, and a wave of arousal rolled through her. Taking a small step back but still holding on around her stomach, she ran her free hand up Callie's spine, kneading gently around her shoulder blades, before running it back down again. Callie's breath hitched as Jackie lent in, bringing her mouth to her ear.

"I love every single part of you," she uttered, and she felt Callie tremble beneath her touch. "Everything about you is amazing. The way you smile, the way you love, your laugh. I love it all."

Callie moaned softly and shook as Jackie's hand inched downwards, teasing across the top of her thigh.

"Jacs..."

Jackie walked them forward, guiding Callie with her until they reached the bed.

"Do you trust me?" she asked, pressing a soft kiss just below her ear.

"Always."

A couple of weeks had passed since Callie had told her about her past, and since her revelation, Jackie had noticed a change in the young woman. She seemed lighter, free around her as if a weight had been lifted. She had never been particularly reserved around her, but it was almost as if sometimes she doubted her actions, but now, that doubt had evaporated. The affection she felt from her was warmer, more freely given, as if she had stopped holding back. And if she was honest, her past, and the changes she had seen since, only served to heighten her affection back.

She heard the padding of bare feet on the soft carpet behind her and smiled at the return of Callie's presence. They had spent the day out in the hills, hiking, just the two of them in the open air, and it had been exhilarating. Once they got back, Callie had gone to freshen up, alone as she always did. But that was only a few minutes ago, definitely not long enough to wash away the aches from a full day of walking.

"Thought you were showering?" Jackie asked, secretly pleased when she felt warm arms wrap around her hips and Callie's body pressed against her back.

"Thought you could join me," Callie replied with a kiss. There was a tremble in her voice, but when Jackie turned around, she instantly got lost in her eyes which had turned a stormy blue.

"Are you sure?"

"Yes." Callie stepped backwards, Jackie instantly missing the feel of her body against her own, but pacified when Callie pulled her into step, walking back towards the bathroom. "I really want you to join me."

Callie led Jackie to the shower, turning away to switch on the water. Jackie watched her body from behind; she could see the nervous tension in her shoulders, the rise and fall as she took a deep breath.

"Callie, if you're not ready..."

"I am. It's just no one's seen them since..."

Jackie took a step up to Callie, mirroring her position from earlier and wrapping her in an embrace from behind. "You're beautiful." She walked around until she was standing in front of Callie and peeled her own t-shirt off. She dropped it to the floor, her bra quickly following. Next, she pulled off her leggings and pants before taking a step back into the walk-in shower. "But I won't look until you tell me it's okay."

Callie nodded. Jackie knew this had to be on Callie's terms, but she also knew that sometimes Callie needed a little show of support and reassurance. She watched as Callie untied the knot of her robe, dropping it to the floor. She was already naked underneath it; Jackie wondered if she'd been looking at herself, studying her scars before she came to find her. But she found it didn't matter. The point was she had come to find her. And she was now offering the most precious thing to Jackie. She couldn't get this wrong. Offering her a hand, she smiled softly as Callie wrapped her fingers around her own, stepping into her space. The spray of the water was warm against her skin as she led them both under the shower.

"You really are beautiful," she repeated. She always told Callie regularly how attractive she found her, but now more than ever, she needed to convey that.

She lathered some soap onto a sponge and started washing Callie, hands drifting teasingly over her wet skin. She watched as Callie's eyes fluttered shut as she feathered the sponge over her breasts, her nipples instantly hardening even with the heat of the shower. She let the sponge, and her hands, travel lower, lovingly washing each and every inch of skin, before placing a finger underneath Callie's chin and tilting her face upwards. Kissing her gently, she asked a silent question. Are you ready? If not, it's okay.

Callie answered without words, slowly turning under the water, holding her breath as she showed herself fully for the first time to Jackie. Jackie's eyes trailed over her back, following the path of pale pink scars which littered her skin, swallowing down the emotions which threatened to overwhelm her. She felt the bile rise in her throat as she saw the distinctive rectangular shape of where a buckle had torn into her skin across her ribs, that scar standing out above the rest. She needed to stay steady, to keep her own feelings in check, so she could give Callie what she needed: reassurance and strength. Lathering up the sponge again, she traced it over Callie's shoulders tentatively; even though she knew they wouldn't still hurt all these years later, she was timid in her touch. Lovingly, she washed Callie's back, urging her backwards under the spray once she had done, quickly washing herself as well, before reaching past her and shutting off the water.

Stepping out of the shower, Jackie grabbed a towel, quickly drying herself before wrapping Callie in a fresh towel and leading her into the bedroom. With all the love she felt in her heart, she began to dry her, taking even greater care where the skin was raised and red, the newer skin glowing from the heat of the shower. Each gentle swipe of the fluffy soft fabric was followed with a kiss, Jackie savouring the fresh, undiluted taste of Callie on her lips.

"Can I take you to bed?" Jackie asked between kisses. "I want to make love to you. Show you just how much you're worth, how beautiful you are to me."

Callie nodded as Jackie ran the towel over her body, dropping to her knees to dry her legs, before pressing a kiss into the soft flesh of the inside of her thigh. Jackie felt her quiver beneath her mouth, and she could smell her arousal already. Sure fingers wound through her hair and gripped gently onto her scalp, holding her in place. She could hear Callie's breath come in soft pants, and she kissed her again, this time moving up her leg a little more.

"Is that what you want, baby? You want me to taste you? Feel my mouth on you?"

"Jacs," Callie moaned, her hips bucking at her words.

"Whatever you want, baby." Jackie smirked as she dragged her tongue along her skin, edging dangerously close to where she knew Callie wanted her. "Tonight's all about you."

Callie groaned as Jackie stood up, pulling herself away from her legs, but within seconds Jackie had guided her back to the bed, urging her to lay down. Bracing herself above Callie, she let her fingers trace the curves and contours of her body; the dip of her clavicle, the rise of her breast, the flat of her stomach with her soft, gentle feminine curves. Her finger teased underneath her breast, thumb brushing over her nipple, causing a gasp from Callie. "You have the most amazing breasts," she muttered, bringing her mouth over one and teasing with the tip of her tongue. Callie moaned, threading her hands through Jackie's hair and encouraging her to continue. As she did, her hand stroked over the smooth skin of her stomach, and she felt the goosebumps break out across her body as she found a ticklish spot. Pulling her mouth reluctantly away, she glanced up at Callie, her breath catching at the sight. Callie's head was thrown back, mouth open and eyes screwed shut in what she hoped was pleasure. "Okay?" she checked in, her voice husky with desire. Callie nodded sharply, a gentle tug on her hair giving her the go ahead to carry on. Jackie happily complied, this time peppering kisses down Callie's torso, pausing to swirl her tongue around her belly button. She could feel Callie start to rock her hips, trying to relieve some of the tension which she no doubt felt. Jackie could feel it, too; every inch of new, uncharted, untouched skin she kissed only increased the want she felt swirling low in her belly.

Shuffling until she was lying on her stomach on the bed, she ran her hands up Callie's legs, urging them upright until the soles of her feet were pressed flat against the mattress. This was not the first time she had pleasured Callie with her mouth, she knew that it was Callie's favourite way to come even though she wouldn't admit it, but this time was different. Everything was different. She pressed a kiss into the flesh of her thigh, taking another moment to look up at Callie, this time to find her looking back at her. Her eyes were impossibly dark, and her lip was caught in between her teeth, hair tousled from their activities.

"Are you sure?" Jackie asked, brushing the back of her hand up the inside of her leg.

"Yes," Callie replied, without hesitation, voice thick with unattended arousal.

Jackie dipped her head, taking a long, slow swipe through Callie's centre, met with the twin sensations of Callie's taste on her tongue and the sound of her intoxicating moans in her ears. Instinct and desire quickly kicked in, her actions fuelled by the sounds which Callie was making. Her tongue swirled around her clit, before teasing at her entrance, and she was rewarded with a sharp tug of her hair, causing her to gasp into Callie. She could feel her own desire pooling between her thighs and the delicious ache which accompanied it. Each flick of her tongue caused a new wave of arousal to flow through Callie, and Jackie revelled in the feel of her against her mouth. After a few minutes of tracing random patterns against her sex with the tip of her tongue, Jackie could feel Callie quiver underneath her, and her own arousal pulsed again. She was painfully turned on, but tonight, this right now, was all about Callie. She could wait. It didn't stop the groan from falling from her lips, though, vibrating through Callie.

"Shit, Jacs," Callie groaned. "I'm going to... I need you here, Jac. I need to see you."

There was a desperation, a pleading in Callie's voice that Jackie couldn't and wouldn't ignore, and she quickly pulled away, only to push herself up Callie's body, kissing her deeply. Callie moaned into her mouth as she tasted herself, and as she did, Jackie slipped two and then three fingers into Callie.

"Oh." Callie groaned, hands fumbling to brace Jackie onto her thigh. The pressure against her aching centre was incredible, but she lifted herself up onto her knees.

"No, this is for you..." she panted, kissing Callie again.

"I want—" She was broken by another guttural moan. "I want you to come with me. Please." She wrapped her fingers in Jackie's hair again, kissing her before they rested their foreheads together. "I need you with me."

Something about Callie's words resonated, a deeper meaning hidden beneath the surface, and Jackie knew what it meant.

"I'm right here, baby."

Jackie lowered herself back down onto Callie's thigh and groaned with the relief it provided, eyes fluttering shut. She rocked with each thrust of her fingers, forehead to forehead with Callie, breathing the same hot, humid air. She could feel Callie's fingers on her hip grasp at her, short nails digging into her skin, and she tightened around Jackie's fingers. When she opened her eyes, all breath left her body at the intense look Callie was giving her. Tears were pooling in her eyes, and as she blinked, they slowly tracked down her cheek. Instantly she stopped, scared she was hurting her in some way.

"Baby?"

"Please," Callie urged almost silently.

Jackie understood then what the tears meant. She wasn't in pain, but Callie was giving herself to Jackie. She kissed her slowly, her fingers curling and flexing inside Callie, watching every flicker of pleasure ripple across her face, feeling her stiffen beneath her.

"Wait, baby, wait for me. I'm so..." She whimpered. "I'm so close."

Callie's eyes opened and locked on hers as she ground harder onto Callie's thigh, letting out a moan as she felt the delightful, perfect pressure against her clit. Her slick fingers kept their pace, never faltering, holding Callie on the edge for a few more moments until their orgasms consumed them both, their mingled screams of pleasure flooding into the room.

Jackie slowed her movements, watching Callie's features intently, studying every line as her muscles slackened and she fell back to the bed. For a few moments, the room was shrouded in silence except for their laboured breathing until Callie broke, letting out a sob as her emotions flooded forward.

"Oh, baby."

Jackie gently withdrew her fingers, lifting herself up on her hands and knees above her, conscious of how much she wanted to wrap her in her arms but not wanting to smother her. Callie's hands came up to cover her face.

"I'm sorry," she sniffled from behind her hands.

"Hey, hey, no. It's okay, come here."

Jackie rolled onto her side and slid an arm underneath Callie's head, urging her closer. Callie rolled over swiftly, burying her face into Jackie's chest. Jackie could feel the warm tears on her skin, her heart aching for each one, but knowing that this was something Callie needed to do. She needed to free herself of this guilt and pain she had been carrying around, and now the dam had burst, she wasn't going to be the one to tell her she needed to stop. Instead, she combed her fingers through her hair, scratching at her scalp, pressing tender kisses onto her forehead, and whispering gentle words of love into the room.

After a while, Jackie had no idea how long, she felt Callie's sobs calm into hiccuped breaths. "Thank you."

"Thank you for trusting me. I know that can't have been easy. How do you feel?"

"Tired," Callie sighed.

"It's a big thing, baby. It's not wrong to feel exhausted by it." A wave of guilt washed over Jackie. "I'm sorry if I was wrong. You know, if we shouldn't have—"

"No! I needed it. I wanted it." Callie pushed up the bed, cupping Jackie's face and kissing her sweetly. "I need you," she whispered.

"You have me, baby. I'm not going anywhere."

As they lay collapsed on the bed, Jackie spent a second revelling at the feel of Callie in her arms. All of her. In that moment, wrapped up in Jackie's embrace, just the two of them with nothing, both figuratively and literally, between them, Jackie felt nothing but love towards Callie and pride in who she was. She pulled her closer, if that was even possible, and buried her face into Callie's hair, taking in a deep breath and inhaling her scent.

"Thank you," Jackie mumbled into Callie's hair, garnering a soft laugh from the woman.

"You're welcome. Thanks back at you."

"Not for that." Jackie laughed back. "Although, I am *very* grateful."

Callie feathered her fingers down Jackie's side, her skin erupting in goosebumps at the gentle touch. Despite her orgasm only just subsiding, the action started a fire inside of her again. Tempering down her arousal before it took control, she tried to focus on what she was thinking, a feat always made slightly harder with a naked Callie next to her. The importance of what she was trying to communicate took precedence, though, keeping her thoughts focussed on what she needed to say.

"I mean, for trusting me again. Today and just with everything recently."

"I love you, Jackie." Jackie felt Callie shift as she pushed herself up off her, her hair falling down around her face. Jackie pushed a strand behind her ear, keeping her hand resting on her cheek, quickly getting lost in the stormy blue eyes which gazed down at her. "I don't think I ever really stopped. I should never have disappeared; I should have had more faith in you."

"Shh. There's no point in wishing we did anything differently back then. But from now on, beautiful, it's me and you, okay? We'll take on everything that comes our way together."

Chapter Twenty

"I'm sorry you can't come this evening," Callie spoke against Jackie's lips. She was meant to have left the house fifteen minutes ago, but they had both been pleasantly distracted by what had turned into a very heated goodbye kiss.

"I'm not..." Jackie mumbled back, thumbs brushing teasingly across the top of Callie's jeans.

Callie pulled back at the comment, frowning in confusion. "I thought you wanted to make it official. *Let's just do it*, you said."

"Yeah, as in, let's just rip this plaster off. It doesn't mean I'm looking forward to it," Jackie muttered, leaning in again to try and steal another kiss. Her advance was quickly rebuked by Callie taking a step back, removing her completely out of her space. "Where are you going?"

"Are you doubting this?" Callie could see the clarity return to Jackie's previously lust-clouded eyes as her face morphed into regretful concern.

"God, no. Of course not, baby." Jackie took a step closer, wrapping her hands around Callie's cheeks, holding her face firmly. Callie tried to look away, but she was caught in Jackie's gaze, and she knew that was her aim all along. She knew that Jackie was about to say something she wanted Callie to understand she meant with all her heart. "I love you, and I want the world to know you're mine. But likewise, I kind of like just you and me in our little bubble. I just don't want it to burst."

"Are you worried about Dad?"

"In as much as I know that it's going to upset you and it won't be easy." Jackie sighed, and Callie watched as she lent into her, her vision filling with Jackie's beautiful face, until she closed her own eyes, feeling Jackie's forehead press against her own. "I just want to protect you from any more hurt."

"God, I love you," Callie murmured, capturing Jackie's lips in a kiss that quickly became passionate once again. Callie lent back into Jackie's body, forcing her to stumble back into the wall, and pinned her there with her hips.

"Fuck, Cal..." Jackie breathed as Callie ghosted her lips over the jumping pulse in her neck. "You better go before I keep you here for good."

"Never thought I'd hear you turning me away..."

"Not turning you away. But maybe I have something for us if you return quickly."

"Oh yeah? Like what?" Callie asked, tongue now soothing the skin where her teeth had just nipped.

"Remember when we went away for my birthday? To that little boutique B&B in Bath?"

"Yeah." Callie chuckled. For a B&B, they'd spent far more time than just bed and breakfast in their room. "Barely left to see the city."

"Remember what we took with us? What we used..." Callie stopped in her tracks, the memories flooding back. A half groaned half whispered *fuck* slipped past her lips at that particular memory. "I may have done some online shopping. Got us something new." Jackie continued when she knew that Callie was on the same page.

"That's not fair," Callie said, voice raspy and hoarse with pent-up frustration.

"Quicker you come back, quicker you can find out what it is that I've bought."

"I hate you," Callie growled.

"No, you don't. Have you got your key?"

"Right here." Callie smiled as she fished her keys out of her pocket and held up the silver token she was gifted earlier in the morning. In fact, her smile hadn't subsided since Jackie nervously slid the key across the dining table, sheepishly announcing that she had got a copy cut for Callie so she could come and go as she pleased.

"Fab. Just let yourself in when you get back."

～

The sound of scratching and fumbling from outside her front door piqued Jackie's attention. It sounded like someone was trying and failing to open the door. She looked at the time on her phone; it was only six-thirty, and she wasn't expecting Callie home for another couple of hours. It was Jake's birthday, and considering it had been barely ninety minutes since Callie left, there was no way they had finished up just yet. The fumbling noise sounded again, followed by the distinctive click of her lock opening, settling her panic slightly.

But then came the sound of heavy footsteps, a crash, and a thud. Jackie shot from the sofa, rushing into the hallway to find a pale and shaking Callie slumped against the bottom of the stairs. It may have been twelve years, but Jackie recognised the signs of her girlfriend in the throes of an anxiety attack straight away.

She dropped to her knees in front of Callie, ensuring she was directly in her eyeline, and hovered her hands over her knees. She so desperately wanted to scoop her up in her arms, but she knew if she startled Callie, she could trigger another wave of panic.

"Callie? Callie, sweetheart, can you hear me?" Jackie asked softly, and she exhaled a breath she didn't know she was holding when Callie's eyes tracked up to her face, nodding ever so slightly. "Okay, sweetheart, I need you to work through your routine, okay? We'll do it together. Tell me five things you can see."

"F-front door," Callie sucked in a shaky breath, voice wavering. "Shoes, picture, you, plant pot...oh. Oh, I'm sorry." Jackie looked beside them where Callie's gaze held, finding the remains of a plant pot, broken ceramic mixed in with soil and leaves in a pile on the floor. That explained the smash, but right now, she wasn't concerned about it.

"It doesn't matter. Look at me again." Jackie waited until Callie's focus returned to her. "I don't care. Four things you can feel."

"The floor, the stairs, my jacket, my keys."

"Good, keep going. What can you hear?"

"The TV, the washing machine, the traffic."

"Two things you can smell..."

"Your perfume." A subtle shift happened in Callie's demeanour as she recognised the scent. Jackie noticed and smiled to herself. "I can only smell your perfume."

"That's fine. And last?"

"I can taste coffee."

"Well done, baby. Now take a deep breath, and when you're ready, we can move. But there's no rush."

Jackie watched as heavy eyelids drooped in front of her, the colour returning slightly to Callie's cheeks, but the rest of her body was clearly exhausted.

"Can I..." Callie coughed, clearing her hoarse throat. "Can I have a hug?"

"Absolutely," Jackie answered, already shifting round to sit beside Callie and scooping her into a bone-crushing, comforting embrace. Callie's head fell to her shoulder, and Jackie's fingers combed through her hair, attempting to soothe Callie even further.

"I'm sorry," Callie mumbled.

"Don't want to hear apologies, sweetheart. You've nothing to be sorry for."

"I smashed your plant."

"It's only a plant. I'm more worried about you. How did you get home?" She suddenly realised she had referred to her house as their home, but now wasn't the time to dissect that slip of the tongue.

"I drove."

"Callie..." Jackie knew how dangerous that was if her anxiety attack had started before she had left her parents, which she was guessing it had.

"I know, but I just wanted to get home. I was fine; I managed to hold it off so it didn't start properly until I got here."

"That's not the point. Why didn't you call me?"

"Because we haven't told them yet..."

"I don't care about that. All I care about is you and the fact you are safe. I'd have come to get you in a flash—screw whether your parents found out or not." Jackie could hear the steel in her voice, but she failed to care. As far as Callie was concerned, she had and would always be fiercely protective. Be damned with the consequences. They could deal with those later as long as Callie was safe and well, she didn't care. She tempered down her annoyance, knowing that it wasn't what Callie needed right now. Besides, she wasn't even sure what she was annoyed at; it felt a lot less like Callie driving home and more directed somewhere else. "You want to go sit on the sofa?"

"In a minute. I still feel a bit fuzzy."

"Okay."

They sat there in silence for a few minutes, Jackie trying to take comfort from the feel of Callie beside her. The feel of her hair running through her fingers, the weight of her head on her shoulder, the way her breathing was slowly calming down to its normal rhythm.

"I had an argument with Jake," Callie said quietly after a while.

Jackie tried hard to hide the way her body stiffened at the mention of his name. He was causing Callie a lot of stress at the moment, and it wasn't sitting well with Jackie.

"What happened?"

"We were looking through some old photos, and there was this one of his twelfth birthday. Robbie joked that I looked miserable. Jake started on his usual rant again, about how it was probably because I was pissed it wasn't all about me. And I said I couldn't even remember it. And I couldn't. But all Jake could go on about was how selfish I was, and I couldn't do anything. I just shut down. Mum pulled me out of it, but it felt so much like…"

Jackie took a deep breath. She knew what Callie was reliving in that moment. "When Darla confronted you."

"Yeah."

"Oh, sweetheart."

"I don't know how I made it out without…I just made an excuse and left."

Jackie sat for a moment longer while Callie worked through whatever was going through her head, breathing deeply to keep herself settled. She smiled when Callie rolled her head sideways and opened her eyes, gazing at Jackie.

"I'm sorry I kind of ruined our plans as well."

"Doesn't matter. All that matters is that you're safe and here with me now. Can I get you anything?"

"Some headache tablets. And then maybe we can just curl up on the sofa under the duvet for the evening?"

"Sounds perfect, baby."

Chapter Twenty-One

Callie glanced at the mobile phone, which was once again vibrating across the coffee table.

"You can't ignore them forever, sweetheart," Jackie said from the kitchen, drawing her out of her reverie.

"Hmm? Yeah, I know," Callie answered, biting the skin down the side of the thumb in a nervous habit. She looked around as she felt the sofa dipping beside her, seeing Jackie having joined her.

"What are you worried about?"

"Oh...everything. Telling them what happened, them fussing over me, the very real probability of telling Jake everything." Her phone screen lit up, indicating another voicemail message had been left and was waiting for her to listen to.

"You know, the longer you ignore them, the more chance that Barrett is going to go round your house, and then he's going to really freak out when you're not there."

"God, I wish I could tell them I'm fine and that I'll ring them when I'm ready, and they leave it at that," Callie mumbled, somewhat churlishly.

"Why can't you?"

"Because they wouldn't let me. Not while they think I'm alone."

"So tell them you're not. Tell them you're with a friend." Callie gave Jackie a look which asked *do you really think that'll work*. "Surely it's better than just ignoring them until they break down your door in a blind panic?"

"Yeah, fine." Callie relented as she lent over to pick up her phone. She softened at the small smile Jackie flashed her way as she got up and headed back to the kitchen.

"Callie!" Annie answered, after barely one ring, clearly relieved at her daughter's contact.

"Hi, Mama."

"We were worried about you. Apart from your text last night, we hadn't heard from you. And whatever you say, we know what Jake said upset you."

"Yeah, it kind of did." Another glance at Jackie, who was now making her way back to the kitchen counter to make them lunch, gave her another boost of bravery. "I kind of had an anxiety attack when I got back."

"Oh, Callie. You should have rung us. We could have come over so you weren't alone."

"I wasn't alone."

"What? Who was with you?"

"Jackie." The sound of her name caused Jackie to turn around, the look of surprise on her face visible from across the room.

"Jackie? Jackie who?"

Callie took a calming breath, settling her nerves. "Jackie Taylor."

"From the office?"

"Yes." She could hear Annie relay the information back to Barrett, who was obviously standing next to the phone listening in on the conversation. "I know Dad's there; you might as well put the phone on speaker to save you having to repeat what I'm saying."

"Callie," Barrett came on the phone, his voice a little distant over the loudspeaker, but the confusion was evident. "Why was Jackie there? I didn't realise you two were that close."

"Actually, I was at her house, Dad. And I still am." Callie caught Jackie's eye, holding her stare. "Because we're together."

There was a muted silence on the other end of the phone as what she'd just said settled and sunk in. As she waited for the reaction from her parents, Jackie made her way back across the room to Callie and clasped Callie's face in her hands, tears glistening in her eyes. *I love you*, she mouthed before pressing a quick, gentle kiss to her lips.

"Callie…"

Jackie pulled back as she heard Barrett's tone down the phone, but Callie was grateful when Jackie's warm hand found her own and squeezed.

"I know this is a shock, Dad. But I think it's time that things were out in the open. And if I'm going to be honest with Jake, then I need to be honest to you as well."

"What do you mean you need to be honest with Jake, darling?" Annie cut in, shushing Barrett when he tried to draw attention back to the revelation about his daughter and former colleague.

"I mean, I can't keep living with his anger and resentment towards me. I'm sick of being blamed for all his mistakes."

"That's his —"

"It may be his problem, Ma, but it comes from not understanding the situation."

"Are you okay telling him? Do you want us to be there?"

"I think we all need to talk," Barrett said plainly, a quiet rage lacing his words.

"I think Dad is right. I can be around this afternoon if you can call Jake. And I think Robbie should be there. That way there are no more secrets between any of us."

"I'll call the boys and let you know what time they can be here."

"Thanks Mama. Dad?"

"We'll talk when you're here." She heard him whisper something to Annie before she guessed he walked away, leaving her mother on the end of the phone.

"Ma?"

"You've just dropped a bit of a bombshell on him, Callie. Give him some time."

"Yeah," said Callie, defeated. She didn't expect everything to be perfect, but she also had been left feeling she was being ignored by her father.

"We love you, my darling. I'll text you when I've spoken to the boys."

"Love you too, Mama."

Callie hung up the phone, closing her eyes. She felt warm arms wrap around her and squeeze her tight, and she melted into the embrace.

"I am so proud of you," Jackie mumbled into her hair.

"It wasn't my intention to tell them. But I needed them to know I wasn't alone. That I was with someone who loves me and is looking after me. It just felt right to tell them then. They need to know someone else is looking out for me now."

"Always, baby." Callie lent into the kiss which Jackie granted her. "Do you want me to come with you?"

"I don't know what would be for the best. I want you there, but I'm not sure that it will go down well." Callie sighed. "Then again, not sure it will ever go down well."

"I'll be there if you ask me to. But I think this first conversation needs to be between you and your family. Only because there's more to discuss than just us."

"I know."

"But that being said, I will be there however you want me to be. In the room, sitting outside in the car, on the end of the phone..."

"I'll be okay. Got to be brave, right?" Callie said, standing up and throwing a thumb over her shoulder. "I'm just going to go get changed."

"Hey." Jackie caught her wrist as she walked past the sofa. "You're the bravest person I know."

Callie twisted her arm, releasing Jackie's grip and linking their fingers together.

"Thank you for making me brave. I wouldn't be able to do this without you."

"You wouldn't have to do this if it wasn't for me." Jackie pointed out.

"I also wouldn't be half as happy as I am now." Callie smiled. "Am I okay to come back here when I'm done?"

"I'll be waiting," Jackie promised with a smile that could temper down the worst of Callie's anxieties.

Chapter Twenty-Two

"Sit down, everyone," Barrett said firmly, shocking everyone into doing as he said. He waited until they had all found somewhere to sit before speaking. "It seems like there's a lot going on in this family that I'm not aware of. And that ends now."

"Dad," Callie dared to interrupt him. She shrunk slightly under his glare but continued to hold his attention. "I know you're angry at me, but this is not why we are here."

"Callie—"

"Barrett." That single word from her mother stopped his rebuke. Everyone turned to look at her. For all her warmth and love, she could be firm when she needed to be. And although she didn't take that tone often, when she did, everyone stopped to listen. Barrett was wise enough not to finish his sentence; he started pacing instead.

Annie turned to address Callie and her brothers. "Jake, your behaviour and attitude towards Callie has got to change. We let it go when you were a teenager, but you're a fully grown adult now, and you should be mature enough to take responsibility for your own life and actions. Not blame them on your sister." Jake rolled his eyes at the conversation he had no doubt heard a thousand times before. "No, Jake! I am serious. Callie has never been here to take anything away from you. It was our fault..." Annie looked at Callie. "Jake was too young at the time, but we should have told him later and not just left it to you. Then maybe he would have understood and behaved differently."

"Told me what?" Jake asked, suddenly intrigued.

"I—"

Annie stopped Callie with a hand up. "Callie moved in here because her mother, Darla, hit her. She beat her and left her for days on her own."

Callie was taken aback by the tears in Annie's eyes. She had never seen either of her parents show any emotion towards the situation except Barrett's rage at Darla. Annie's focus had always been Callie's wellbeing.

Annie turned her attention to Callie, grasping her face in her hands as if she could psychically transfer all her love into her. "We always wanted you here with us, my darling. But the law was different then and always favoured the mother even if she wasn't... And we never knew how bad things were, or we would have tried harder. I love you so much, my darling, just as much as my own boys. You are mine, no matter what."

"I know, Mama," Callie whispered through her own tears.

"She...hit you?" Jake's voice wavered with a previously unseen emotion. Callie swallowed down her tears, turning to her younger brother.

"Yeah," she choked out.

"Why didn't you tell me?" he asked, turning to his parents.

"Jake, I'm sorry we kept this from you for so long. That wasn't our intention. But when Callie came to live with us, we thought you were too young to understand. Then it just got harder to talk about, but really, we should have told you as soon as you were old enough."

"I...I'm sorry, Cal. If I had known..." Jake shook his head.

"You'd what? Not been a complete arse to me for the past twenty years? Yeah, that doesn't really wash with me, Jake. I'm sorry, but I never did anything like what you were making up in your head. I had no desire to take your place or push you out of the family. I stayed out of the way, minded my own business, supported you in everything you did...I even lied to Mum and Dad for you. And all you've ever done is treat me like some intruder in your life."

"Callie, I—"

"I love you, Jake. I will always love you because you are my brother. But if the past few years have taught me anything, it's that I can't and won't have toxic people in my life. And I don't even think you realise how much damage your words do. You've gotten so wrapped up in this little world you created in your head that you can't see reality."

Jake had the good grace to look ashamed. He cast his eyes down to the floor, his neck flushing with embarrassment.

"I'll be better. Please, Callie, don't shut me out." He stood and stepped towards Callie, holding his hands out in a plea of forgiveness. "I know you can't just forgive and forget everything I've said, but will you at least give me a chance to make it up to you?"

"Jake, I'd love that, but—"

"Please, Cal," he begged.

"I need to look after myself. I'm not saying no. I'm just saying it's going to take time. Things aren't just going to be fine because you say sorry, Jake. We're not kids anymore."

"I know. I know. I just want a chance. Maybe we could get together, just me and you, and talk it all through. Please?"

Callie could see that Jake was being sincere. The regret was rolling off him now that he knew the truth and had gotten a dressing down that was twenty years in the making. More than anything, she wanted this whole situation to be over with. But she also knew that Jake needed to know just how much hurt he had caused, and everything couldn't be fixed overnight.

"Yeah, okay," Callie conceded.

Jake smiled at her, genuine happiness and relief flashing in his eyes at Callie's answer. "Suppose it's too soon for a hug?" he chanced, shoving his hands in his pockets and almost looking like that young boy she'd grown up with.

"No." Callie stood and wrapped her brother up in her arms, resting her chin on his shoulder. She couldn't remember the last time they'd embraced like this, and while that saddened her, it also left her hopeful for the future. She wasn't about to forget his transgressions, and there was a lot which they needed to talk about, but for now she could at least meet him in the middle.

"Can I get in on some of this?" Robbie's strong arms wrapped around Callie and Jake's shoulders. Callie released one of her arms from around Jake's neck and hung it around Robbie's back.

"Well, this is all very touching, and I'm glad that you two have cleared the air, but there is one other thing which needs talking about," Barrett's voice cut through the peace, his tone steely and serious.

Callie sighed, the trio breaking off from each other. Jake and Robbie wore matching confusion on their faces before looking at Callie.

"What's going on?" Robbie asked.

"Dad," Callie pleaded. She knew the news would be a shock, but she really didn't think it warranted the anger Barrett was so clearly displaying.

"Where is she anyway? Afraid to show her face? Leaving you to explain this one on your own?" he seethed.

"No." Callie exhaled slowly, trying to keep herself calm. Her anger wasn't going to do anything but exacerbate an already tense situation. "She offered to come, but I told her to stay at home."

"I'm lost..." Jake queried to the room, looking for an answer.

"Me too." Robbie agreed.

"Do you want to tell them? Go on since we're sharing with your siblings."

Callie rolled her eyes. She really wasn't bothered about telling her brothers. She knew of everyone, Robbie definitely wouldn't have anything to say, and judging by Jake's recent apology, neither would he.

"I've been seeing someone." Callie bit her tongue as she heard Barrett scoff from across the room. "Jackie Taylor."

"Jackie Taylor," Jake muttered the name out into the room. "She sounds familiar."

"Should do. It's—" Barrett started.

"Oh! Jackie! From the office!" Jake exclaimed as the penny dropped. Robbie looked at his brother, then at Callie, her face breaking into an uncontrollable grin just at the mere mention of her girlfriend's name. It was a look which confirmed everything for Robbie.

"Hey! Congrats, little sis! About time you found someone." Robbie wrapped her in another one of those big bear hugs he was so free at giving.

"Yeah. She seems nice. I mean, from what you said about her. And a couple of the guys I still speak to from the office have said she's pretty cool. Maybe we could get together sometime?"

Jake smiled at her tentatively. Callie recognised the effort he was putting in after years of firing off snarky remarks by default.

"Yeah, that would be nice."

"Is no one else bothered by this?" Barrett interrupted again.

"Should we be?" Robbie asked, clearly confused as to why his father seemed so upset by the notion.

"She worked at the company—*my* company—while you were children."

"That's an exaggeration, Dad," Callie scoffed.

"She's old enough to be your mother!"

"Is she?" Jake laughed. "She looks good if that's the case!"

"How would you know?" Robbie fired back.

"Some of the guys at the office said —" Their brotherly banter was instantly quieted by a look from their mother which said *now is not the time.*

"She's fifty!"

"She's forty-eight, and there's fifteen years between us, which still does not make her old enough to be my mother. Not really." Callie brought her speech back round to the point. "That's not even the problem, though, is it Dad? The problem is that it's *her.*"

"Of course, that's the problem, Callie! She's my friend. I've known her for nearly twenty years. I trusted her. And she's thrown that back in my face."

"Dad!"

"No, Callie! I used to think anyone, *anyone*, was better than that sorry excuse for a wife you had, but this —"

"She's nothing like Jen!" Callie was mortified that Barrett could even mention Jen and Jackie in the same breath, let alone attempt to compare them.

"She may not be as manipulative as Jen, but she's got just about as many morals to do this."

"Barrett," Annie warned from across the room.

"How can you even begin to think of them in the same way? Jen was cruel and heartless; she saw someone broken and weak who she could control and get her own way with. Jackie is nothing like that. She is loving and caring; she lifts me up and supports me." Callie could feel an ache in her chest at the mere thought that anyone could consider Jackie cruel.

"You might not see it, love," Barrett said, softening his voice and making a move towards Callie, but she took a step back. Her father was serious. And once, she would have been able to understand his hesitations. But with Jackie? How could he think this of his friend?

"Take it back. What you've just insinuated...take it back."

"It's true, Callie. You can't see it, but this isn't right."

"And you?" She turned to her mother, something akin to

disappointment settling in her chest at her father's reaction. "Do you feel this way?"

Annie looked between Barrett and Callie before she settled her focus on Callie. "No."

"Annie —"

"No, Barrett. Yes, it's a shock and something which I don't think either of us imagined happening, but I do know that for the past couple of months, Callie has seemed happier and more relaxed than I can remember her ever being. And if that's down to Jackie, then I can't be mad or angry at the situation or at her." She walked up to Callie, studying her face. "Does she make you happy?"

"Yes, she really does, Mama. She's everything I've ever wanted and needed." Callie could feel herself grin. Yes, Jackie held a power over her, but while Jen's was coercive and controlling, this one was self-empowering and enlightening. It lifted her up and held her strong when she wasn't. This one was love. "I love her, Mama."

"Oh, for fuck's sake!" Barrett shouted. "She's clearly trouble, Callie. Who else would be okay with creating tension like this in a family—"

"No," Callie declared, her voice firm and sure. "You don't get to stand here and bad mouth her. Not in front of me. Have your opinion. Fail to listen to everyone around you. But you do not get to say those sorts of things about her while I am here."

"Can we just calm down?" Annie pleaded.

"No, Ma. If he's going to be like this, we can't. As long as he's got his thick head on, he's not going to listen to anything I have to say."

"Too right I'm not. You're wrong, Callie. She will hurt you."

"The only person being hurtful right now is you!" Callie spat back.

She breathed out a shaky breath, unsure how she was holding herself together while she was this furious. She knew he wouldn't take it well, she even thought he might not speak to her for a while, but this? The accusations and stories he was making up in his head? She couldn't deal with those.

"When I left here last night I was scared and panicked, and the first thing I did was go to Jackie's house. Not to hide on my own, not to shut myself away. To be with the person who I trust most in those moments. And she sat next to me and talked me through every single second. She looked after me. She cares for me. And I'm not letting that go."

Callie turned to leave, stalking towards the door.

"Callie, please stay," Annie begged, grasping onto her wrist as she left.

"I'm sorry, Ma. I'm tired, and I want to go home."

"You mean to her," Barrett grumbled.

Callie rolled her eyes. Even now her father couldn't help but have a say.

"My darling, I know you must be tired, especially if you had an attack yesterday, but—"

"Do you need to see a doctor?" Barrett jumped up, stepping towards the door to be nearer his wife and daughter. "We can find that therapist again if that's what you need."

"Oh my God! You did not just... Dad, having one attack does not mean I need to start therapy again. I am not weak. I asked you to talk; I wanted everything out in the open. But I can't talk to you when you're like this." She shook her head as she looked at their father, disappointment growing. Callie leaned into Annie, pressing a kiss to her cheek. "I'll call you, okay, Ma? Love you."

"Love you too, my darling."

And with a final, unreturned glance at her father, Callie walked out of her parent's house.

Chapter Twenty-Three

Jackie looked up from her computer and through the glass front of her office. From where she had repositioned her desk a couple of weeks after arriving at the company, she could see across the open space and into Callie's office. She hadn't intentionally done it for that reason—it also gave her an uninterrupted view of the rest of the office and made her own office feel more accessible to the rest of the staff. And in her defence, you couldn't see the entirety of Callie's office. It was only when she was working at her drafting table Jackie could see her. If Callie moved to her desk or if she was at her sofa then she was out of view.

Right now, she couldn't see Callie, which meant she was probably working at her desk. Just like she had been for the past two days. She definitely hadn't done any designing since the weekend. In fact, her newly re-found habit of drawing again for pleasure in the evenings had abruptly stopped after her confrontation with Barrett on Saturday. Jackie wasn't surprised, though. Stress had always been Callie's biggest creative block, and if she produced anything during those periods, it was below her usual standard, which only contributed further to the pressure she was feeling.

Jackie was, however, concerned about how much she was avoiding the subject. Callie had given her the pertinent points when she had returned, none of them particularly surprising, but she hadn't said much more about it. Instead, she made her excuses and went for a shower before spending the evening silently seething on the sofa. Jackie thought maybe she just needed some time to process what had been said, but now they were three days on, and nothing more had been said.

She sighed, chewing the end of her pen—a bad habit which only flared whenever she had something on her mind. She really didn't want to push Callie to talk when she wasn't ready, and she was usually pretty good at gauging when that balance shifted. As it stood, it was miles away.

She spotted Callie walking out of her office and across the open space, weaving through the desks of her team and heading straight towards her own door. Even her walk was weary; where it had recently picked up, a small spring to her step, that had disappeared into her feet almost dragging across the carpet. Jackie knew she hadn't slept over the past two nights, feeling her toss and turn beside her and then always up and dressed before Jackie even woke.

"Hey." Callie came to a stop at her doorway, hands shoved deep in her pockets and shoulders slightly slumped.

"Hey," Jackie replied, standing from her desk and moving to greet her. "Everything okay?"

She gestured further into the room, nodding to her sofa before closing the door behind them.

"Yeah," Callie sighed as she dropped down on the sofa, letting her eyes droop for a second. The one thing Jackie was grateful for was that Callie was not hiding just how drained she was when it came to Jackie. Not talking was one thing but hiding her emotions...that was a red flag in Jackie's book.

"What's up?" Jackie asked, sitting down beside Callie and brushing the hair from Callie's face.

"I need to draft an email to the senior partners and HR. Let them know about us."

"Has Barrett said something? Is he trying to cause trouble?" Jackie asked, concerned he could seriously be so put out by their relationship that he would make life difficult for them. Apart from an angry text message she received from him on Saturday night, she hadn't heard anything from him. She knew he could be stubborn, but this would be a new low.

"No. God, no. I've not even heard from him since Saturday," Callie said. It was the first time she had mentioned her father since Saturday, and Jackie counted it as a small victory. "We need to do it anyway. I guess we should have done it before now. I just don't want you or me being pulled up and questioned about it if they hear it from somewhere else. You know what gossip can be like around here."

"Okay, sweetheart." Jackie was touched by Callie's concern for her, even now when she was dealing with so many other issues. "Do you want me to do it?"

"No..." Callie may have answered in the negative, but her body language told another story, her shoulders once again dropping even further.

"How about we do it together?" Jackie suggested, standing up and grabbing her laptop from her desk. "If we do it now, we can get it out of the way, and then we don't have to think about it anymore." Jackie settled back against the sofa next to Callie, dropping a gentle kiss to her temple. Technically it was against their own 'no relationship in the workplace' rule, but that one hadn't always been adhered to, and right now, comforting Callie was more important than following some self-imposed guideline. The action was clearly gratefully received, Callie's mouth turning up into a small, barely recognisable smile. "Okay, tell me if you want me to change anything..."

Jackie opened a fresh email and began to type, narrating so Callie could hear what she was typing.

"For the attention of the senior partner team: I would like to take this opportunity to inform you that myself and Callie Montgomery are engaged in a..." She stopped, creasing her brow. "What do you want to say?"

"Dating? In a relationship? Having wild, rampant sex at every given opportunity?"

"Ha!" Jackie barked, the snarky sarcasm a welcome glimpse of the Callie she wished was more present. "While all of the above are true, I'm not sure I want *that* many details revealed."

"Hmm, you're right," Callie muttered. "If they knew just how hot you were, someone might try to steal you away."

Jackie looked at Callie where she sat, collapsed back on her sofa. Her eyes were closed, dark circles shadowing them, her skin a little pale. She wondered if she had eaten anything other than the very small slice of toast she practically nibbled at for breakfast. She looked exhausted, and Jackie couldn't blame her.

Along with the past two nights of little sleep, she'd also had an anxiety attack on Friday, which was the thing which set off this chain of revelations in the first place. That drained her enough as it was, let alone without being able to properly recover from it. She cupped her face gently in the palm of her hand, turning it to face her as Callie's eyes slowly opened.

"Never, baby," she declared softly. "No one could ever steal me from you. I wouldn't go."

"I love you," Callie replied with a tired grin.

"I love you, too. So how about we finish this up, maybe leave out the bit about the wild sex, and then you can get off home and get some rest."

"Jacs—"

"No arguing. You're exhausted. Go home. You can always get some work done if you really feel like it, but at least you can curl up on the sofa while you do it. Besides, can you honestly say you've got anything done this morning?"

Callie scowled at Jackie, Jackie only quirking an eyebrow as she silently answered back to her.

"Fine," she huffed, "but only if I can go crash on your sofa instead."

"You never have to ask, baby."

∼

Jackie pushed her front door open, leaving the bag she had just picked up at the shop on the floor. She kicked her shoes off and wandered into the living room. The house was entirely quiet, and for a moment, she thought Callie might have actually gone to bed. If it wasn't for her car parked outside, she might have even thought she wasn't here at all.

But as she rounded the sofa, she saw why everything was silent. She might have not made it to bed, but the exhaustion had finally caught up with Callie. Laid out across the length of the sofa, head propped at a slightly awkward angle where she had slipped down, and wrapped snugly in a blanket, Callie was fast asleep. Jackie didn't know how long she had been asleep but was just grateful she was. Drifting closer, she knelt beside Callie's head, brushing the hair from her face and tucking it behind her ear, noting that she was still in her work clothes underneath the blanket. It appeared as though she did literally make it home and just crash.

Jackie must have brushed a ticklish spot as Callie's face twitched in an adorable fashion before her eyes flickered open.

"Hey, babe," she mumbled, her voice still gravelly with sleep.

"Hey, beautiful."

"What time is it?"

"About three," Jackie answered, her fingers still threading through Callie's hair in a repetitive, soothing action.

"You're home early?"

"I've got a couple of hours in the bank from when I stayed

late." Jackie shrugged. "Cashed some in so I could come home and snuggle with you."

"Sounds like a great idea," Callie said, pushing herself up and stretching out her arms. The action made her shirt rise up, exposing a thin strip of soft skin, and Jackie's eyes immediately trailed it. Even now, sleepy and tired, Callie got her blood pumping.

She cleared her throat, dragging her gaze away from Callie's stomach and back up to her face. "I went to the shops on the way back. Thought I'd make that pesto and parmesan gnocchi bake you liked so much last week?"

"Oh my God, that sounds amazing," Callie replied, pulling Jackie down into her lap from where she had stood up. Contentment settled in her chest as Callie's arms encircled her waist. "It might be my new favourite."

"Even more so than your mum's lasagne?" Jackie exclaimed, leaning back slightly in exaggerated shock.

"Even more than Mum's lasagne."

"Well, let's just keep that between us, shall we? Don't want to upset the matriarch any more."

"I think the matriarch probably has other things to worry about."

Jackie knew that Callie had spoken to Annie, the latter calling every evening since Callie had walked out of the family home. And to her credit, and Jackie's relief, the conversation never involved Annie trying to convince Callie of anything, not even speaking to Barrett. She needed to know that Callie was well—that was her main priority. But Jackie could guess that at home, Annie was not giving Barrett such an easy ride. If there was one person who could make Barrett Montgomery shrink back, it was his wife.

"How about I make a start on dinner, and you go grab a shower?" Jackie offered, standing reluctantly from her spot on Callie's lap. As she turned, however, they were both startled by the sound of someone knocking on her door. "I'll get it. You go jump in the shower," she said to Callie as she walked past.

She pulled open the door, expecting someone delivering something for one of her neighbours. Instead, she was shocked to be greeted by an image of Barrett if he was thirty years younger. Yes, the hair was slightly lighter, more mousy than the rich brown of Barrett's, and his face was slightly sharper, but there was no escaping that this was Barrett Montgomery's child.

"Hello," he started, somewhat nervously.

"Hi."

"You don't know me, and I'm sorry to just show up like this, but I'm —"

"Jake?" Jackie hazarded a guess. With a small nod, he got Jackie's defenses up. Despite what she'd heard of his heartfelt apologies, Jackie was still weary of him, the pain and stress he put Callie through not so easily forgotten.

"I'm sorry to just turn up like this but I was wondering if Callie is here?"

"I..." Jackie hesitated. She wasn't sure if Callie wanted any of her family to know where she was, even though it was only Barrett she seemed to have fallen out with.

"I get that you don't know me except from what Callie has told you, and I know that hasn't been great. And I can see that you care for Callie a lot, so I get if you're not willing to let me see her. But if you could just tell her I called by, and if she could send me a message to let me know she's okay? I know she's angry with Dad, we all are, but we just want to make sure she's okay. And let her know that...well, that we want to see her soon."

Jackie softened at the obvious show of concern from Callie's youngest brother. He wasn't the brash young man Callie had described, and maybe what Callie said about Jake being mortified at his behaviour after her revelation was genuine.

"I'll pass on your message, Jake."

"It's fine," Callie spoke from behind Jackie, appearing in the living room doorway.

Jackie turned at the sound of her voice and instantly sensed the tension which had crept back into her body at the arrival of Jake. She leaned against the door frame, arms wrapped around her body in a seemingly disinterested gesture of nonchalance, but Jackie knew better. Jackie could see the defensive walls which Callie had erected. The subtle way her leg bounced, the way her fingers were gripping just a little too tight into her biceps, and the way her eyes wouldn't quite focus on Jake's face were all giveaways.

"Hi, Cal." Jake smiled nervously.

"How did you know where to find me?"

"Oh, I went to the office, but your secretary said you weren't in for the afternoon. And then I saw Jackie leave, and it seemed kind of early, so I followed her in the hope that you were here..." To his credit, Jake looked extremely sheepish at that admission, and he turned his attention to Jackie. "I know that sounds dead weird and is probably not doing anything to endear me to you. I am sorry. I just wanted to make sure Callie was alright."

"Yeah, it's a bit weird Jake," Callie said.

"If it helps, I've been sitting outside since you arrived, wondering how to make it sound less creepy."

"Not really," Jackie broke in, still wary though she could see the concern in his slightly bizarre and misguided actions.

"Yeah, fair point. Anyway, as long as I know you're alright, I'll leave you be."

Jackie watched as Jake took a step back, heading back to his car. She looked over her shoulder, giving Callie a look which she hoped she understood correctly.

"Jake!" Callie shouted as she made her way towards the door, stopping him in his stride.

"Yeah?" he replied, an optimistic look in his eye as he stopped and turned around.

"You fancy maybe staying for a cuppa?"

Chapter Twenty-Four

Callie had never been more nervous sitting in her own family's kitchen than she was right now. After a slightly awkward first conversation with Jake, she'd also spoken to Robbie on the phone, and both had convinced her to meet with Annie while Barrett was out of the way. Annie, it seemed, had been spending the past week trying to talk Barrett into calming down and maybe starting to at least acknowledge the fact Callie and Jackie's relationship was genuine. Barrett, at the very mention of Jackie's name, would either storm out of the room ranting or fall silent. Callie knew which was worse; as much as his temper could be fierce, Barrett not saying anything was far more worrying.

"How are you?" Annie asked as she slid a cup of tea across to her before sitting down opposite. "You look well."

"I'm fine, Mama. And it's only been a week. What did you expect?"

"I know. But I'm so used to seeing you every other day that a week feels like forever these days." She smiled wistfully, and Callie knew what she was thinking. Those three years she was living in

Manchester, being ground down and belittled by Jen until she was nothing but a shell of her true self, didn't involve many trips home.

"Everything's fine, Mama. She's not like Jen." She hated having to reassure people that Jackie was different from her ex-wife. If her parents just gave her a chance to introduce Jackie properly—as her girlfriend—then they would see that they were nothing alike.

"I know she isn't, sweetheart. I may not have seen her for quite a while, but I remember what Jackie was like. I don't think she had a bad bone in her body. She was certainly an ideal business partner for your father; she tempered his pig-headedness perfectly. But she was more than just the good cop to his bad cop. You could tell she was genuine."

"She's a good person, Ma." Callie looked down, gazing into her tea, a soft smile gracing her lips as she thought about her.

"Tell me about her."

Callie looked up, creasing her forehead at the question her mother had just asked.

"You know her..."

"I know Jackie from years ago, and even then, she was someone your father worked with. We spoke when I was in the office or at functions, but I didn't really know her very well. Like, tell me how you met." Annie shook her head. "Obviously, at the office, but how did things..."

"Actually..." Callie took a deep breath, ready to reveal the true extent of their relationship. "we first met twelve years ago. I'd gone to see this singer, and she was there. I kind of freaked out a bit at seeing her, but she wasn't fazed." She couldn't help but smile at the memory. "After that, it was easy. Everything has always been easy with her. But when I walked away from you, I also walked away from her. I believed you would all be better off without me, including Jackie. And then she came back, and everything just fell into place again."

"So this isn't a new thing?" Annie asked, shocked at her daughter's revelation.

"No, not really. I mean, I didn't expect this to happen when she came back, but..." She shrugged. "I think I've realised we were inevitable."

"And she's good to you?"

Callie beamed. "So good, Mama. She can read me so well. Like, she knows what I want or need before I even realise it myself. She knows how to talk me down. Right from the very first moment, she just did it, no questions asked. And remembered it. Like she will ask where I am and what I need. But she sees more than that as well, you know? She always encourages me to be more than I think I can be."

"You really love her, don't you?" Callie looked up from where she had been staring into her tea at Annie's question, something about her tone making her wonder why she felt the need to ask.

"I told you I did..."

"Yes, yes. I know you did. But I don't think I realised just *how* much you meant it. Not until now, watching you talk about her. I've never seen you smile so much or so freely. I've never seen you so," Annie paused, trying to find the right word, "so at peace."

"That's because she makes me feel like that, Mama. She calms me. Like I can physically feel it, all the stress and anxiety leaving my body when she's near."

"Then hold on to it, my darling." Annie lent over and clasped her hands over Callie's, holding them tight. "A love like that, a person who sees your faults and hardships and sticks by your side regardless, loves you in spite of them, because of them, that's a rare thing. So hold onto it tight and don't let it go."

"But Dad..."

"Leave your father to me. He'll come around."

"Oh, will he?" Barrett's tone cut through the room, ruining the warm and emotionally comforting atmosphere the two women had created. Callie spun round on her seat to see Barrett standing by the door, Annie letting go of her hands and tipping her head to regard Barrett with a look that conveyed just how displeased she was with him.

"Dad! How long..."

"Long enough to hear you convince your mother this *relationship*," he almost spat the word as if it felt uncomfortable in his mouth, "is actually a thing worth pursuing."

"Barrett," Annie warned. But Barrett continued, regardless of his wife's cautionary tone.

"No, Annie. I'm sorry but I just..." He turned his attention to Callie. "I've tried these past few days, once I'd calmed down and it sunk in. I've tried to imagine you and her in a relationship."

"You don't have to imagine—" Callie tried to argue, but Barrett cut her short with a hand in the air.

"I've tried, but I'm sorry, Callie. I just don't feel comfortable with it. To know someone who I considered a friend, who I worked with and practically built my business alongside, is..." he breathed out, choosing his words carefully.

Callie knew what he was thinking, or trying not to think, and she wished he didn't. She wished he saw past the physical aspect of it all and saw the emotion that flowed between them. She wished he could see what her mother had said was so obvious. She wished he would just give her a chance to prove him wrong.

"You're my daughter, and I will always love you, but I just don't think I can ever get past this."

"You've not even tried!" Callie cried, her chest aching.

"I have, Callie."

"How? How have you tried?" she shouted, jumping up from her stool. "Because I haven't seen you try to speak to me in a week. I haven't seen you come to the house or to the office. Not a phone call or a message, nothing. So tell me how ignoring me for a week is you trying to understand anything!"

"I've done nothing but think about you all week."

"And you think that's enough? It's not worked, so there must be no other option?"

"I don't know what you expect me to do, Callie. I can't just change how I'm feeling overnight."

"You can't if you don't try! Jesus! Something doesn't go your way, so you give up? Throw your toys out of the pram and give an ultimatum?"

"I've not given you an ultimatum, Callie."

"Not out-right, no. But I can read what you're saying, Dad. You *can't get on board*, as you say, so it'll come down to choosing between you or Jackie."

"Callie, I'm sure your father wasn't implying such a thing," Annie tried to intervene.

"Yeah, he was, Ma. Because that's how he runs things. He can't think in any other terms than business. And it works when he's down to the wire with contractors and clients, but here, in a family, it doesn't wash, Dad. If you think I'm going to walk away from Jackie, you're mistaken."

Callie walked past Barrett, grabbing her coat as she did so, and not bothering to look at him. She wasn't prepared to lose Jackie a second time, and if her father thought that he could bulldoze her into making that decision, he had another thing coming.

Chapter Twenty-Five

Jackie jumped at the sound of someone hammering on her front door. Her train of thought had been tenuous at best, her mind repeatedly straying to Callie and the conversation she was most likely having. She knew that it was only Annie she was meeting, but she couldn't help but be nervous. Annie was calm and collected, and from what Callie had said, she originally had been open to their relationship, but a week had passed, and anything could be happening. She turned off the television, not that she'd been concentrating on it anyway, and pushed up from the sofa. She barely made it into the hallway, however, when the banging was repeated. Swinging the door open with a level of annoyance at the person's impatience, she was greeted by a flustered and somewhat frantic looking Barrett.

"Is she here?"

"Sorry?" She wasn't trying to be obtuse, but the surprise of having Barrett here and the somewhat random question fired at her put her on the backfoot.

"Callie. Is she here?"

"No, she's at yours. She went to see Annie."

Barrett sighed and ran his hand through his hair. "Yes, I know."

"Barrett, what happened?" Jackie quickly understood the situation. Clearly, Barrett had interrupted Callie and Annie's time together, and Callie left. But what had been said, she still wanted to know.

"We had an argument," Barrett disclosed somewhat reluctantly. "But it's fine. I'll find her." He turned away and headed back down the path.

"Oh, will you?" Jackie lent against the doorframe. Barrett's stubbornness was an enviable quality in boardroom discussions, but right now, it was his downfall.

"Yes, I will!" he shouted back.

"And that's why you're here, is it? Because I know for a fact this is the last place you would want to admit she was. So I'm guessing you've already checked her house and the office and rang her phone? And now you have to admit that there's a chance she's here."

"Well, she's not, is she? So if you care for her as much as you claim you do, why don't you shut up and let me find her?"

"Because she doesn't need finding Barrett! Don't you get it? She doesn't want you to find her right now."

"She doesn't get to make that choice!"

"Doesn't she?"

"No!"

"Why not?"

"Because you didn't see her nearly die!"

The statement hung heavy in the air between them, an uncomfortable truth, before Barrett spun on his heels and started back down the path.

"Try down by the rugby club. Far side of the pitch, where the canal towpath runs," Jackie called out. For all she hated Barrett right now for how he had dismissed Callie's feelings and their relationship, she knew that inside, he was terrified.

The disclosure had the desired effect, stopping Barrett in his tracks.

"Why would she be there?" He turned around. "If you're messing with me —"

"Why would I do that, Barrett? Although I'm not worried about her like you are right now, it doesn't mean I'm not concerned. And just because I'm not particularly happy with you doesn't mean I want to mess with you. Try it or not—it's up to you."

She turned to go back in the house, not prepared to argue anymore, and quite frankly more than a little irritated with his attitude.

"Why would she go there?" Barrett called out, stopping her before she could shut the door. She sighed, tired of his angry, dismissive attitude.

"Robbie used to play rugby there. She would sneak down on her weekends when she wasn't with you and watch him play."

"How do you know that?"

"She told me, Barrett. When she was a teenager, she used to hate the weekends she had to spend at Darla's house, so she would spend as much time out as she could. She would go down to the pitches to watch Robbie train, then sit on the bench behind the club and sketch at the canal. When she got older, and Robbie stopped playing, she kept going. It was like her safe place."

"Why hasn't she ever told me this? Why would she tell you?" Barrett asked, disbelief still lacing his words.

"Because when she was fifteen, she wanted somewhere no one would find her. And even though she's older now, she still needs that place some days. Although now I've messed that up, so she'll probably be pissed with me too," she muttered.

"She never tells anyone anything like that."

Jackie scoffed. "You know, Barrett, I've told you where she'd most likely be. If you want to let your own pig-headedness get in the way of actually believing for just one second that she could trust me enough to tell me something so personal, then go ahead and keep looking for her on your own."

"You've known her for five minutes."

"Twelve years, Barrett!" Jackie finally shouted, her patience breaking. "I've loved your daughter for twelve years! And in each and every one of those years, no matter whether we were together or not, I only ever thought about what was best for her. Even when she literally disappeared and left me, I still loved her. Because somewhere, deep inside, I knew that it wasn't her fault."

Jackie could feel the tears welling up in her eyes; she was unable to control them as they started to roll down her cheeks. "And every day, I wished I'd fought harder, looked for her, not let her just walk away. Because if I had, maybe..."

She could feel her knees weaken at the mere thought of that day. That phone call would haunt her for all her days. Even though she now had Callie safe and well in her life, she could never forget the horror of hearing those words from Barrett.

She swallowed down her tears, clearing her throat. "I'm not discussing this here for my neighbours to hear. If you want to talk, you're more than welcome to come in." She stepped back, holding open the door for Barrett. After a beat, Barrett's curiosity clearly got the best of him, and he stepped over the threshold, brushing past Jackie in a way which was clearly meant to let her know how unhappy he was.

She found him standing awkwardly in the living room, suddenly surrounded by the reality of Jackie and Callie's life together. Callie's laptop set up on the dining table opposite her own where they'd been working earlier in the week. The sketch book and pencils which Jackie had bought her laying on the coffee table, page open to the latest image she was creating. Her jacket, draped over a chair where it had been left after a day at the office. The framed photograph on her mantelpiece of the pair of them—on one side from a hike they took twelve years ago, on the other, the recreation of the shot when they revisited the same place on their recent weekend.

"Does she even stay at her house anymore?"

"Sometimes we stay there, but most of the time we're here. I think she likes the garden," Jackie replied as she leaned against the door.

"When did it start?"

"Which time?"

"The first time," Barrett spat back, obviously still angry at the revelation that this was not just the recent fling he thought it was.

"She'd not long been back from university, and I bumped into her on a night out. She had an anxiety attack, and I made sure she was okay." Jackie smiled wistfully as she remembered their first meeting and the feeling it evoked. "I remember thinking how fragile she must be, yet there she sat, in a toilet cubicle, talking me through her routine...and I realised that she was anything but fragile. She was strong and courageous, and that was so beautiful."

"You stayed with her?" Barrett looked around, shock painting his features.

"Of course I did. I wasn't going to leave her. Couldn't ever leave her after that night." She smiled at the thought of her life now she had Callie back in it. "It didn't happen straight away; I wasn't even sure if she felt anything more than friendship towards me, and I didn't want to push it. But once it did, once I let myself fall, I fell quickly. And I'm sorry Barrett, but I didn't care if she was your daughter. And I still don't. I would have walked away if it was too much for her, but as far as I was concerned, she was the one I wanted to be with and I would have done anything for her. That's still true."

"So where were you? How come she ended up with that absolute bitch of a wife, miles away, rather than here with you?"

Jackie scoffed. "Trust me, that was entirely out of my control. She left me a letter one day, telling me that she couldn't be with me anymore, that she needed to be alone." She walked over and sat down on the sofa, exhausted by their conversation already. Resting her elbows on her knees, she rubbed her face, trying to prepare herself for what was to come. "I didn't understand why at the time, but I couldn't get hold of her when I tried to ring her to talk. She'd blocked my number and left. It was only a few weeks later when I spoke to you that I found out she was in Manchester. It was why I left, if I'm honest. I couldn't stay around here anymore. Everything reminded me of her."

"I thought you'd just got another job."

"I had, but I was unhappy here."

Barrett looked away again, then gave in and slumped into the armchair by the window. "I rang you," he said quietly after a minute.

"Hmm?" Jackie was finding herself tiring and also wanted to know where Callie was. Despite knowing she was okay and more than likely just allowing herself some space to clear her head, it didn't mean Jackie was happy at being here with Barrett rather than with Callie.

"I rang you. When Callie was in hospital, I rang you."

Jackie sighed. "I'm sorry. I'm not meaning to take anything away from you and Annie; I know it was hardest on you as a family. And I know you didn't know. But when you phoned..." She paused, taking a moment to breathe, trying and failing to control the emotion in her voice. "That was the hardest thing I've ever had to hear. And I couldn't react, couldn't show the way I was feeling, because no one knew how I felt about her."

"I'm sorry, Jackie. I can't imagine how hard that must have been." Jackie appreciated how difficult it was for Barrett to admit that. The shock must have shown on her face. "I'm not devoid of all emotion, Jackie."

"I know...I'm just surprised. It's the first time you've acknowledged that my feelings for Callie are genuine."

"I never knew about the fact you two had...that this wasn't the first time. She never told us."

"When was she meant to have done that exactly? I can't imagine you exactly gave her a chance, Barrett."

"I just...I was shocked. I still am. You're one of my oldest friends, and then to find out that you and my daughter..."

"Are in love."

Barrett looked over at her.

"We are, Barrett. I love her, more than anyone I have ever met. I've never stopped over the past twelve years. And I will keep loving her, keep trying to make her happy, for as long as I can."

"I just want her to be happy."

"She is. *We* are. But at the moment, the thing causing her the most worry is everything going on with you and the family. First Jake, and now this. She doesn't always say it, but I see it. I see the tension in her in the run-up to every family dinner and the sadness when she comes home. And she was hoping that getting everything out in the open would be the beginning of the end of it all. But instead, it just caused more arguments. We are so happy in this part of our lives, and we want to be able to be like that everywhere, not just inside these four walls."

"You helped her. With the Jake situation?"

"I helped her put together the numbers so when she told you, she could have some cold hard facts to help soften the blow. I know that's how you deal with things, that you need to see a good year versus a bad year."

"And last week when she had an attack? She came here?"

"It's not the first time, Barrett. And while I hate seeing it, at least if she's here, having one in front of me, she's not at home alone or in her car somewhere. She told me what to do that first time we met, and I've never forgotten. Why would I when it's so important to her?"

"I'm sorry," Barrett conceded. "I was so caught up in it being you that I didn't give her the chance to tell me these things."

"She doesn't expect you to just be fine with this. She knows that it is going to be strange for a while, but she just wanted you to at least say you'd give it some time. That you'd give us a chance."

"I've made a right mess of this, haven't I?" Barrett fell back into the chair.

"It's fixable, Barrett. Just listen to what she's telling you."

Chapter Twenty-Six

Callie looked out across the canal, the early evening summer sun pleasantly warming the back of her neck. She was surprisingly calm and had been since she arrived a couple of hours ago. She felt relieved, like a weight she'd been carrying around for years had been lifted. She looked at her watch; she would give her father another ten minutes, then head back to Jackie's.

Jackie had rang her not so long ago, pre-warning her rather apologetically that she had told Barrett where she was. To Callie, there was nothing to forgive. Her father had gone to Jackie's to find her, and by what Jackie had said, he was coming to her with a slightly different mindset and version of events than he arrived with. And Jackie only ever did anything in Callie's best interests.

She heard the crunch of pebbles behind her before the steps stopped.

"Callie?" Her father sounded more unsure than she had ever heard him, and it was unsettling hearing a voice that was so intrinsically linked with authority sound so nervous.

"You took your time. Jackie rang twenty minutes ago to say you'd left."

"Trying to gather my thoughts. Work out what I wanted to say to you."

"Didn't realise 'sorry' was so difficult to figure out," Callie threw back.

"Yeah...I deserve that."

"Bloody hell." Callie finally looked over her shoulder at Barrett. "Never thought I'd hear you admit you were wrong."

"Yeah, well, I'm not a complete idiot," Barrett admitted, groaning as he sat down on the grass beside Callie. The silence settled between them for a few moments before Barrett continued, "I'm sorry, Callie. I tried to run my family like I run my business, and that's not the way to do things. My brain's not wired to deal with ifs and maybes and grey areas. I focus on the things I know I can fix, and those which I know I can't, I ignore. It's why your mother and I work so well together; she softens all my hard edges."

"You're not hard, Dad. It's not that you're a bad parent. You'd do anything for any one of us. And we all know that."

"Even Jake?" Barrett scoffed.

"Yes. Even Jake. But sometimes, our lives pan out differently than expected, and that's what you struggle with. Sometimes it's like, if we tell you something that wasn't in your imagined plan for us, you don't know how to factor that change in. So you'd rather just ignore it. Or get angry at it. Like Jake. He tried so hard for so many years to make you happy. Rather than admit to you that he didn't know what he wanted to do, he just kept working around things, bending the rules to try and get the results he thought you wanted to see. So he could prove to you he was a success."

"Can I ask you a question?" Barrett said quietly, continuing when Callie nodded. "Do you want to even be part of the business? Or did I push you into that as well?"

Callie took a deep breath, formulating her response. "It's not that I don't want to be part of it. Sometimes I wish I didn't have to deal with the bureaucracy and bartering of it all, though. Ironically, for a job where I draw, the more stressed I get with the business, the less I'm able to. My creativity vanishes, and that's because I'm too busy worrying about revenue than just designing."

"I'm sorry, Callie. I never knew you felt that way."

"I know you probably don't want to hear it, but Jackie being there helps. She knows just how much I don't like the business side of it and sees the effect it has. She takes care of that side of things so I don't have to worry about it. And, before you say it, I know it's her job, but she goes beyond that, you know? She re-frames things so I know what I need to know, separates out the important bits from the rest of it so my focus is clear."

"Like with the situation with Jake?"

"How did you know she helped with that?" Callie asked, surprise painted across her features.

"She told me. She was telling me about how you were struggling when she first came back."

Callie hated being described as struggling. It took her back to a time when she really was struggling, and it instinctively made her feel weak.

"I'm not weak, Dad. Once, maybe. But not now," she said, her voice low.

"I don't think of you as weak. I never have. You went through the most horrific ordeal I can imagine at such a young age, and you came out on the other side. Yes, there may have been difficulties along the way, you may have got lost and thought that there was no way out...but the way I see it, the fact you are still here, sitting in front of me and talking sense into me..." He bumped shoulders with his daughter. "That's the sign of one of the strongest people I know. Because not only did you survive, but you came out a better person. And you were pretty great to start with."

Callie looked up at her father, tears welling in her eyes. "I love her, Dad."

"I know you do, sweetheart. And I can say without a shadow of a doubt that she loves you too. No one has ever had the balls to call me pig-headed. But Jackie Taylor did. And she did it for you."

Callie laughed, the sound wavering with unshed tears. "And it may take some getting used to, but I will get there. Anyone who makes you as happy as you are now deserves at least that chance."

"Thank you, Dad."

"Plus, I've heard she wanted to knock Jen's head off at the charity gala, and that's a win in my book any day."

Callie couldn't help but let out a bark of joyous laughter, which in turn made Barrett laugh. As it subsided, he hooked his arm around her shoulder, pulling his only daughter into his body. "I love you, Callie. You'll always be my little girl, and I'm sorry that I haven't always dealt with things well. But one thing I do know is I am proud to say you're my daughter. And I always will be."

"Love you too, Dad."

They sat there, letting the cooling breeze blow past them for a few minutes while the intensity of their conversation settled in and the peaceful atmosphere of the canal did its work. They watched as a swan effortlessly glided across in front of them, the gold of the setting sun glistening off the water's smooth surface.

"I can see why you like it down here, Callie."

"Yeah. It's nice. Tranquil. And you know that charcoal sketch I did for you and Ma that hangs in the hallway?"

"Yeah?"

"It's from just down the towpath. About a mile, that way." She pointed round the bend of the canal. "There's a little viewing point which looks out over the nature reserve. Nice little spot for a romantic picnic, if you get the urge." She nudged her father with a wink.

"Hmm, I might remember that. But in the meantime, I'm getting too old to be sitting on the grass. Help your old man up, will you?"

Callie jumped up, brushing her jeans down before standing in front of Barrett and holding her hands out. Between them and with a grunt, Callie helped him off the ground.

"Christ, Dad, I think you need to lay off the lunches."

"Oi!" Barrett exclaimed, only partially offended by the insinuation.

"Seriously, I think I need to have a word with Ma. Little less steak and chips and a few more salads..."

"If you dare! Come on. I'll give you a lift to Jackie's."

Chapter Twenty-Seven

Callie glanced at her watch for the third time in ten minutes, tapping her foot impatiently against the tiles of the kitchen floor, taking a sip of her lukewarm, nearly empty coffee. She wasn't entirely sure what was taking Jackie so long to get ready; she didn't take this long to get dressed on office days, and that involved a beautifully pressed pantsuit, a full face of that gorgeous but subtle make-up, and her hair styled in any number of ways. But today, when they were just going for lunch, she seemed to be taking twice as long. Pushing off from the counter, she walked out to the bottom of the stairs.

"Babe, are you nearly ready?"

She was greeted with a huff and the distinct yet muffled sound of Jackie grumbling from her bedroom. Unsure what was going on and why she wasn't getting a coherent answer, Callie jogged up the stairs. She was met with an unknown thud and more grumbling. Finally making it into the room, the source of the mysterious thudding became clear as Jackie flung what Callie assumed to be the second shoe of a pair into her wardrobe. Knelt down on the floor in front of it, another three pairs of shoes were out on the carpet, and the bed was covered with at least six or seven different items of clothing, and that's what Callie could make out from her position in the doorway. She smiled to herself, suddenly very aware of what the issue was.

"Hey, babe. You okay there?" she asked, leaning on the doorframe.

Jackie turned, clearly surprised by Callie's appearance. Shock soon turned to frustration again, though, as she turned back to the shoes in front of her pulling another box out from the wardrobe.

"I can't decide what shoes to wear."

"What are the options?"

"My black knee-high boots, or my brown ankle boots."

"The leather ones or the suede ones?"

"The leather. Oh," she sat back again on her heels. "Maybe I should go for the suede ones?"

Leaning forward, she began to crawl towards the wardrobe, clearly in search of the newly suggested brown suede boots. Callie pushed off from the doorway, gently resting her hands on Jackie's shoulders and stopping her going any further.

"Okay, babe. Step away from the shoe closet."

"But—" Jackie started.

"But nothing, babe. Just leave the shoes and sit a minute," Callie said, guiding her back to sit against the bed behind them. Once Jackie was seated, she shuffled around and sat next to her, kicking her legs out in front of them. "Want to tell me what's up?"

"Nothing. I was just getting ready. Just need to grab some shoes, and we can get going."

"Yeah. Sure you do. That's why you've got,"—Callie looked around, doing a quick tally of the amount of footwear around them—"eight pairs out."

Jackie shrugged. "I have a lot of shoes."

"Yes, you do, babe. But I'm not trying to talk about your shoe obsession right now. I'm talking about why it's taken you"—Callie looked at her watch; she couldn't help but smile as she did so, it being a gift from Jackie just a few days earlier—"thirty-five minutes to choose a pair."

"It hasn't!" Jackie exclaimed incredulously. Callie pushed her arm in front of Jackie, urging her to take a look at the time. "Oh. Are we late?"

"No, we left ourselves plenty of time. But it doesn't matter anyway. I'm more concerned about why you're so worried about lunch in the first place."

Callie watched as Jackie released a resigned sigh, leaning back fully against the foot of the bed. She took in her features; she really did look beautiful today. Informal Jackie was her favourite iteration of her girlfriend, and while she wasn't in full casual mode, she also wasn't in full business mode. Each had its own perks if she was being honest, and today, Jackie had hit a perfect balance between them. Her black skinny jeans clung to her hips and accentuated her long slender legs, the loose, oversized t-shirt hanging perfectly off one shoulder showing just enough skin to not draw attention but more than enough for Callie to want to explore further. Her hair was up in a perfectly-styled-to-look-unintentional messy bun, and she'd foregone wearing her contact lenses, meaning her eyes were perfectly framed by her glasses. Yeah, today, her girlfriend looked stunning.

"I guess"—Jackie startled Callie slightly; she'd almost forgotten she had asked a question in the first place— "that I'm just worried about what's going to happen at lunch. What if Barrett changes his mind? What if he sees us together, and it's too much for him?"

"So?" Callie shrugged. "If he does, the outcome would be the same as it was going to be last week. We walk away until he is okay with it. Just because it's a few days later doesn't mean I'm just going to change my mind. My loyalties still lay with you."

"I know," Jackie sighed.

"Do you? Because you don't sound so sure." A cold dread washed over Callie. "Y-you're not having second thoughts, are you? You're not thinking this is too much like hard—"

A sudden, firm kiss to her lips silenced Callie mid-sentence, and after the initial shock, she settled into the embrace, her shoulders relaxing and dropping, and she hummed at the feel of Jackie's lips. Exhaling slowly in an attempt to calm her now racing heart, Callie inconspicuously licked her lips as Jackie pulled away and rested against her forehead.

"Nothing to do with you could ever be considered too difficult or hard. It will always be worth the effort," Jackie affirmed quietly.

"So, what's wrong then?" Callie stayed pressed forehead to forehead with Jackie, relishing the physical contact with her. There was something visceral about touching Jackie, something soulful and life-altering she couldn't describe but she needed on a daily basis, just as the oxygen she breathed.

"I don't know. I guess I just never thought we'd actually get here. Not with everything that we've been through to get to this point. I spent so long either hiding with you or fighting for you that I never let myself think about what it would really be like openly being with you."

"You didn't imagine us together?"

"I did," Jackie smiled, that warm, secret smile she only ever gave Callie and which made Callie's insides melt. "But mainly, it was just us in the picture. Going on holiday, or out for day trips. Going to the theatre or dinner. Even just evenings curled up on the sofa together, wrapped up ignoring the world..."

"They're my favourite times," Callie admitted, stealing another kiss. She pushed herself closer to Jackie, the urge to do exactly as Jackie had described taking over.

"Mine too. But I'm about to do the whole meet the parents thing, which is nerve-wracking at any age. And your dad is Barrett Montgomery."

"And you, my love, are Jackie Taylor. The only woman apart from my mother, brave enough to call out Dad in his stubborn, thick-headed ways and come out the other side," Callie said, leaning in closer, lowering her voice. "Which, by the way, was really fucking hot."

Callie watched as that familiar smirk crept across Jackie's face.

"Yeah?" she asked, pushing their faces closer together, nudging her nose against Callie's as Callie teasingly moved her mouth just out of reach. "I'll remember that."

"Come on, we can't sit here all day. Grab any of these shoes and let's get this over with," Callie said, jumping up and offering Jackie her hand. Pulling her up from the floor, their bodies collided as Jackie got to her feet. The sensation of her nudging into Callie set her nerve endings on fire, and she wrapped an arm around Jackie's waist and held her close. Taking her lip in between her teeth she studied Jackie for a second, smiling as they locked eyes with one another.

"Thank you," she uttered quietly.

"For what, beautiful?"

"Coming back. Giving me a second chance." Jackie brushed the hair from Callie's eyes and rested her palm on her cheek. Callie instinctively lent into her hand, loving the way it perfectly formed around her cheek. "Just being so amazing with everything these past few months."

"Anytime, beautiful. It wasn't even a decision I needed to think about. Looking after you, *being* with you, has always been second nature from the moment I met you. And I wouldn't want it any other way."

"I don't think I realised how much I needed you to put me together again," Callie whispered, nuzzling into Jackie's hand.

"You don't get it, do you?"

Callie opened her eyes where they had fluttered shut, her face scrunched into a confused frown.

"Get what?"

"For every time you say I fixed you, each time you credit me for holding you together, I feel the same way about you ten times over. I was broken for so many years, Cal, and I'm not saying that to make you feel guilty, but to let you know just how much you mean to me. And as much as I worked to get back to something even resembling the old me, there was always a piece missing. A piece you held and put back the day you kissed me again for the first time."

Callie swallowed back the tears at Jackie's heartfelt confession. She never knew Jackie felt quite as strongly as she clearly did in returning to Callie.

"Hey, don't cry, baby."

"No, no, they're not sad tears. Not really. They're just...it's..." She fisted her hand on Jackie's t-shirt, pulling her impossibly closer. "God, I love you."

"I love you too. Now, let's get this over with."

Chapter Twenty-Eight

Jackie straightened the knife on the table in front of her for the fifth time in as many minutes, dropping her hand into her lap once she had done so. She paused for a breath, before her hand came up again, doing the same with the fork. A warm hand settled over hers before she could take it away, and she looked up to see soft eyes regarding her.

"Sorry," she offered to Callie. "I'm just a bit nervous still."

"Yeah, I can tell." Callie lent further into Jackie's space. "I don't think I've ever seen you so unsettled. Where's all that sexy boardroom confidence I love so much?"

"It disappeared the moment I stepped into this restaurant." Despite her and Callie's talk before they left, Jackie's fears and concerns had been playing on her mind throughout the journey to the restaurant where they were meeting Barrett and Annie. They had grew tenfold since they sat down.

"Everything will be okay, babe. In it together, right?" Callie lent into her, kissing her slowly. Jackie got lost in the feel of Callie's lips, the soft, luxurious sensation of her tongue brushing teasingly across Jackie's bottom lip and sending a wave of heat rushing through her body. A sharp cough brought her crashing back into the room, arousal quickly making way for embarrassment. She heard the snigger from Callie beside her, and shot her a glare as they stood to greet Barrett and Annie.

"Hi, Dad," Callie greeted Barrett. Jackie watched as the two shared a hug, aware she'd never really seen this side of their relationship. Yes, she'd spent many evenings at their house when she was at the company before, but Callie had either been at university or was already at home, so there was no greeting necessary. And since she had been back, it was rare that Jackie had been in the company of both of them together. She wondered if that was by Callie's design. When they were together before, she knew that Callie tried to avoid all three being in the same vicinity at the same time for her own comfort more than anything. So now, Jackie got to watch as the pride and love that each shared for the other individually came together and it was like the final gap had been bridged. Something warmed inside her at seeing father and daughter together.

"Hello, Jackie." Annie broke her out of her musings, both leaning in to greet each other. "It's lovely to see you again."

"Yes. You too." Jackie breathed out. She then turned to Barrett who had ended his embrace with Callie. "Barrett."

"Jackie. Well, this is…"

Jackie didn't think she could recall a time when Barrett looked so unsure as to what to say or do with himself.

Annie leaned over to her husband's ear. "Sit down, Barrett."

Everyone sat, and Jackie exhaled a deep breath, relaxing slightly when she felt Callie's hand come to rest on her knee and give it a reassuring squeeze. She turned, giving her a small smile in thanks, but she knew the gesture was timid and full of nerves. And she wasn't the only one, judging by the atmosphere which hung over the table.

"This place looks lovely. I've been wanting to come for ages, but your dad never takes me anywhere these days," Annie started, clearly trying to find a neutral ground. "Have either of you been before?"

"Umm, yes," Jackie answered, "I've had a couple of lunch meetings here. But I've always been watching the clock so I'm looking forward to enjoying it without having to rush off." *Depending on how this goes*, she thought to herself.

"Callie tells us the business is doing brilliantly now you're back, Jackie."

"Oh..." She felt herself wilt under the compliment slightly. "It's not just me. Barrett left a great team behind, and Callie is amazing at what she does. It's her who keeps the customers happy with her designs." Jackie flashed Callie a smile, pride radiating off her.

"I think we make a pretty awesome team," Callie replied, giving her look which was so full of love it made Jackie melt.

"Yeah, we do."

"Well," continued Annie, breaking the pair out of their gaze, "I think that's pretty plain to see. And we're really happy for you both. Aren't we Barrett?"

Jackie turned to face Barrett, expecting to see his signature glare from across the table. Instead, she was greeted with a look she couldn't quite place. If she didn't know Barrett Montgomery better she would say it was...contentment? Happiness? Pride? Whatever it was, it was tinged with a hint of humility Jackie had never really seen before from him.

"I owe you two an apology."

"Dad..."

"No Callie," he cut her off with a hand in the air before placing it on the table. "I know I've said it to you both separately, but I want to say it to you here while you're together. I reacted badly. It was a shock to hear that my only daughter and one of my oldest friends are"—he cleared his throat— "in a relationship. But

Jackie, when I spoke to you, once I stopped being so fixated on being angry and actually listened to what you were saying, I could see how much you care for her. Callie's notorious for hiding what she's really feeling."

Jackie looked from Barrett to Callie, who dipped her head coyly with a breathy chuckle.

"But hearing how she confided in you, that you knew things none of us did…it really made me realise just how much trust must be between you two. She's never had that with anyone, and I can't begrudge that for her just because it makes me a little awkward."

"I know this is going to take some getting used to, Barrett," Jackie offered. "We never expected you to just accept it, but you have to believe me when I say I only want the best for Callie." She turned her attention onto Callie, needing her and her parents to understand the sincerity of her words. "I love her. I have for twelve years, and I'll do everything I can in my power to make her happy. And if the time comes when I'm not enough to do that anymore, then I'll let her find whatever it is that does."

"Babe," Callie said, a waver in her voice, "that's never going to happen."

"I hope it doesn't. But I need you *and* your parents to know that I'll never hold you back from being happy. It would be devastating, but it would be worth it if it meant you're happy." The thought of ever being without Callie in her life was too painful to even contemplate, a dull ache already settling in her chest at even uttering the words. But she meant every word.

"Well," Annie said, clearing her throat, and bringing the atmosphere back down to somewhere less intense, "I think we can both say that we can see the positive effect you have on Callie. And the love you two have for each other is beautiful to see."

"It's not just one-sided. She does so much for me, and I don't even think she realises." Jackie's gaze floated back to Callie, unable to keep her eyes from her for a more than a few seconds.

The waiter coming over broke Barrett and Annie's attention

from the pair, allowing them a moment of respite from the conversation and the weight of the emotions which had been laid open in the last few minutes. Callie took the opportunity to lean in, Jackie shivering as she felt her breath against her ear.

"I love you so much."

Chapter Twenty-Nine

Jackie turned the water off and stepped out of the shower, quickly drying herself off before wrapping the towel around herself as she cleared the mirror of steam with a swipe of her hand. She studied her own face, taking in the slight wrinkles which were starting to show around her eyes and how the silver flash through her hair was slowly spreading further. Callie had made her feel younger and freer than she had in years, not since they were together the first time, but the effects of time couldn't be completely erased just from being happy. She rolled her neck, hearing the bones crack. The last few weeks had taken their toll, but now everything seemed to be back on track. And with this afternoon's lunch out of the way without any recriminations, they could actually start to live their life as they'd always wanted. Callie was more relaxed than she had ever seen her, and it was evident in everything she did.

Wandering into the bedroom, she spied the boots which had caused her so much stress earlier. Smiling at the memory of her minor meltdown, she boxed the boots up, sliding them into their place in her perfectly organised shoe closet. That was Callie's doing as well. Fed up with falling over the long line of shoes that edged around her bedroom, she arrived one day having ordered a brand-new wardrobe, fully equipped with enough shoe boxes and shelves so Jackie could organise and display her ever-growing collection of shoes. Moving onto the next wardrobe, she grabbed a hoodie, smiling even further as she eyed Callie's clothes hanging next to her own, the number of items growing on a day-to-day basis. They spent more time here than anywhere else, they certainly didn't spend any nights apart anymore, and if things fell into place...she cleared her throat, trying to not get too far ahead of herself.

Walking over to the chest of drawers, she pulled out a pair of loose-fitting yoga pants and a t-shirt. Throwing them onto the bed, she turned to the dressing table and started to apply her moisturiser, closing her eyes as she rhythmically massaged it into her skin.

She heard the sound of Callie's footsteps, taking the stairs two at a time before they suddenly stopped. Confused, she turned to find her girlfriend looking at her. No, it was more than just looking. It was...she could see her eyes track up her body, slowly dragging up her naked legs, the towel wrapped around her barely covered body, lingering over her chest, until they settled on her face, her mouth slightly ajar.

"I..." Callie croaked, the rest of the sentence trailing off into a strangled silence. Jackie chuckled, amused by how she had been rendered mute by something so simple as her in a towel, a low throaty sound which did nothing to help Callie, judging by the way she saw her swallow thickly. When Callie gazed at her like that, when she devoured her with just one look, the lines and wrinkles all faded into submission. Boosted by the confidence that a dumbfounded Callie gave her, she sauntered over and wrapped her arms around her girlfriend's waist, loving the fact that she had the ability to reduce the confident, determined young woman she saw in the office every day into a stuttering mess.

"Everything okay?" she asked Callie with a quirk of her eyebrow. It was a cruel trick; she knew Callie found the action unbelievably sexy, especially when she threw it in a discussion in the boardroom. In fact, it was during a business meeting the kink had made itself known, Jackie reducing both the client and Callie to nothing but a quivering mess with the look, but for very different reasons. She sighed as she felt Callie's cool nose nudge against her neck; it was getting late, and the autumn chill was starting to settle as the evening drew in.

"Mmm, I am now," she mumbled, placing a kiss against the skin over her pulse.

"Today was nice, wasn't it?"

"Hmm," Callie sounded, not really giving an answer, but Jackie could forgive her. They'd already discussed on the car journey home how each of them felt that the lunch had gone. There was no need to dissect it all again, not when Callie was peppering gentle butterfly kisses up her neck. The sensation was sending flashes of goosebumps down her bare arms.

"Mmm, that feels good," she whispered, losing herself in the attention Callie was lavishing on her.

She felt Callie wrap her arm tighter around her waist, pulling her in closer to her own body, before spinning her around and walking her backwards. Her back connected to the wall, and she gasped with the soft impact. Her head fell backwards as Callie dipped down, her mouth never leaving the skin of her chest, her hand finding the edge of the towel and dragging it up. Callie's fingertips felt electrifying as they slid up the still damp skin of her thigh, and she shivered as they edged closer to where she definitely needed them. Callie's tongue traced lazy, random patterns across the top of her breast, and she wound her hand through her hair, holding her close. She could feel herself getting wetter with each passing second of teasing, even just her towel too restrictive against her quickly heating body.

She felt Callie push up against her. She loved feeling the weight of Callie against her, something about the way it cocooned and surrounded her made her feel both safe and excited simultaneously.

Suddenly a memory flashed into her head, a conversation they had had, a promise, a *teaser*, which Jackie had dropped before everything had blown up over this past week or so. And right now, with Callie pressed against her in every conceivable way, her hips holding her in place, her mouth trailing its way across her skin, she really wanted that final part of the puzzle.

"Cal..." she rasped out.

"Yes, babe?" Callie muttered as she unhooked Jackie's towel, allowing it to drop to the floor.

"Maybe we could—oh God, that feels good." Jackie lost her train of thought as Callie dropped to her knees, placing openmouthed kisses across the jut of her pelvis. Forcing herself to think a little clearer, she finished what she was trying to say. "You remember the gift I bought us? We never got to try it out."

Suddenly the kissing stopped, and Jackie looked down to see deep, impossibly stormy eyes staring back up at her.

"Oh. You want me to..."

"I mean, only if you want to, obviously," Jackie was quick to reassure. As much as she needed to feel Callie inside of her soon, she would only ever do anything if they were both comfortable and onboard.

She was answered by Callie pushing up onto her feet, her lips crashing down on hers, taking her breath away with a kiss that overflowed with desire. Almost instantly, Callie's tongue sought entrance to Jackie's mouth, and she happily obliged, her hips rocking up into her involuntarily as Callie ground down her own to meet her.

"Where is it?" Callie panted as she broke away, trailing her lips down her neck instead in sloppy kisses.

"T-top drawer of the dresser."

Callie stepped sideways and opened the drawer rummaging around, while Jackie took the opportunity to sit down on the end of the bed. She let her eyes roam over her girlfriend's body; even fully clothed, she was still the most beautiful woman she had laid eyes on. Her jeans clung to her hips and legs, accentuating every feminine curve, and her strong and loving arms, toned and on show in the loose sleeveless vest she was wearing. An image formed in her mind, those toned arms straining as Callie held herself above Jackie...a quiet cough brought her attention back as Callie stood in front of her, clasping the silicone toy in one hand, the straps hanging down. Even that sight sent Jackie's want skyrocketing, desire making her eyes almost black.

Jackie beckoned for Callie to stand between her legs, unbuttoning her jeans and pulling them down. Callie quickly kicked them off before repeating the action with her boxers. She couldn't help but smirk and give Callie a look when she noticed just how wet they already were. Teasingly, she let her fingers dip in between Callie's legs, brushing her lips and causing Callie to groan low in her throat. But not wanting to give her too much too soon, her fingers were gone as quickly as they appeared, instead wrapping around the soft silicone toy and taking it from Callie's hands.

"I loved it when you took me like this last time. Feeling you inside me, yet your arms surrounding me." She pressed a kiss onto Callie's stomach and felt Callie's hand instantly come up to hold her there, fingers threading through her hair. "It made me feel so sexy and loved and protected all at once."

Jackie pulled back out of Callie's loose hold, guiding her to step into the harness and sliding the straps up her legs before adjusting the toy, the shorter end sliding through Callie's slick folds. "I meant it when I said this one was for *us*." She shifted the toy a little bit further, delighting in the way that Callie gasped and gripped her shoulder as it slid effortlessly inside her.

"Oh..." Callie breathed, legs trembling under Jackie's hands.

"And," Jackie said, tightening the straps, "I also love it when you come with me."

Callie's eyes snapped open, and within a second, she pushed forward, forcing Jackie down on her back on the bed. Jackie shuffled backwards until Callie was braced over her on her hands and knees.

"You are so fucking sexy," Callie murmured, eyes raking over her body.

Callie's tongue traced a path up Jackie's neck, and Jackie wrapped her arms around her back, pulling her close. Their lips met in a slow, sensual, passionate kiss, and Jackie moaned into Callie's mouth when, after a moment, she gently rolled her hips, the toy between them brushing against her sex. The sound spurred Callie on to repeat the action, her fingers moving across her chest, mapping the expanse of skin beneath her.

"Cal..." Jackie breathed. She knew that Callie was taking her time, making sure she was ready, but she could also tell she was struggling to hold back. She could only imagine how worked up she must be feeling, judging by her own desperate level of arousal and the fact that every roll of her hips also had the toy stroking inside Callie. "Cal...please."

Sure fingers swiped through her, and she moaned at the feeling, her hips bucking up of their own accord.

"Fuck, you're so wet," Callie muttered as she replaced her fingers with the head of the toy. A few long, teasing strokes had Jackie's hips canting upwards, but it wasn't enough. Jackie needed Callie inside of her, needed to feel the push of her hips against her own, the weight of her body on top of her.

"Please, Callie. No more teasing."

"Not teasing, babe," Callie said with a kiss, "just making sure you're ready."

"I am. I'm *so* ready for you."

Callie carefully lined up the toy and guided it into place, confidently pushing her hips forward. The first feel of it released a guttural, almost feral moan to be released from Jackie, who dug her nails into Callie's shoulders. Callie paused, looking into Jackie's eyes, giving her a moment to adjust.

"Okay?"

"Yes," Jackie breathed. Just having Callie this close, inside her but not even moving, was overwhelming, but her body was already craving more. She lifted her head up to kiss her, grateful for her consideration.

Jackie didn't take her eyes off Callie's as Callie pulled her hips back slowly, and she prepared herself for the slow slide of the toy back into her. But then, without warning, Callie snapped her hips forward, and Jackie's eyes rolled back into her head with pleasure.

"Oh fuck!" Jackie screamed, her hand coming to cover her eyes as Callie started up a relentless pace, somehow knowing just what Jackie craved without Jackie even realising it herself. At this rate, she would be done within seconds, each grind filling her perfectly. A hand slid down her leg, tickling the smooth skin behind her knee, before pulling it up and holding it there, allowing Callie to reach even deeper. Jackie could feel herself getting tighter with each thrust, and she knew she was rapidly reaching her peak. Opening her eyes, her vision was filled with Callie above her, pupils blown wide, her skin glistening with a thin sheen of sweat, lip caught between her teeth as she focussed solely on Jackie and her pleasure. Leaning up, she grasped her face in her hands, tugging her towards her and kissing her deeply. Breaking off when oxygen became an issue, they panted harshly into each other's mouths. "Fuck, you feel so good," Jackie breathed. Suddenly Callie's hips stuttered, her rhythm breaking somewhat, and she groaned low in her chest.

"Fuck, Jacs..."

"Are you close?" Jackie asked, knowing the answer from the way that Callie's forehead screwed up, and she had switched it up to short, sharp strokes, changing the angle so it still kept pushing Jackie to her release but also herself, Jackie imagined.

"Yes..."

"Me too, baby...fuck..."

A final thrust and Jackie came; her eyes slammed shut as lights flashed behind her eyelids. She felt herself pulse around the toy and heard Callie groan, her own orgasm following right behind. Long, slow, glorious seconds passed before she felt Callie delicately lower her leg and then herself, safe arms bracketing around her, before the heavy, comforting weight of Callie's head resting on her chest. Jackie wrapped her arms around her back, squeezing her close.

"Oh fuck...that has to be the best gift I've ever bought," Jackie mumbled into Callie's hair, garnering a chuckle from the woman on top of her. The gentle movement jostled the toy which was still inside her, eliciting a small groan of oversensitivity.

"Hang on, babe," Callie murmured, slowly and carefully slipping out of Jackie before removing the toy and the harness from herself. She dropped it down on the floor before rolling back over on top of Jackie with a contented hum.

"That was incredible." Jackie kissed Callie's forehead as she nestled into her

"You're fucking incredible," Callie mumbled into the warm skin of Jackie's chest, pressing a kiss over her sternum. "You okay? It wasn't too much?"

"Mmm, no, baby. It was amazing." Jackie ran her fingers through Callie's hair, scratching lightly along her scalp as she knew she liked. She was met with an appreciative hum. "What about you? How were things on the other end?"

Callie sniggered. "Things on my end were very satisfying. It was just that you were too blissed out to notice."

"I had good reason to be," Jackie said, running her fingers down Callie's side, relishing in the ticklish squirm it produced in the other woman. "You were amazing."

Callie pushed herself up off Jackie and looked down at her with a look that could only be described as adoring. In that moment, Jackie didn't think she'd seen anything as beautiful as Callie as she was now, hair mussed, skin glowing, radiating love and beauty.

"Are you happy?" Jackie asked, suddenly needing to know that Callie was pleased with how their life was progressing. She would never take for granted having or creating Callie's happiness again. How could she ensure that she had everything she needed to live her life without any more stress or upset if she didn't ask? How could she ensure she was enough for her if she didn't put it out there? The potential of hearing an answer she didn't want to hear was nothing compared to the possibility of Callie being so desperately miserable again.

"So unbelievably happy, babe," Callie answered, the sincerity rolling off her in waves, giving Jackie nothing but reassurance that she was telling the truth and everything she was witnessing was honest. "You, this life, it's all I've ever dreamed of. Twelve years ago, now, every moment in between. There were times when I thought I'd missed my chance to have it." She leaned into Jackie's palm when she stroked across her cheek, "But now, I'm not taking it for granted. This is everything. I love you—if anything, I love you more now than I did back then. And if I'm honest, I think I love you more each day that passes. There's always something new I notice, something that surprises me or takes my breath away. You, Jackie Taylor, are everything."

And that was more than Jackie ever needed, or wanted, to hear.

Epilogue

"Can I open them yet?" Callie asked, feeling the car slow before, she thought, turning a corner.

"No," Jackie chuckled. "You're really not very good at this, are you?"

"What, being blindfolded and bundled into a car? Surprisingly no."

"You don't usually complain about the blindfold."

Callie could tell Jackie was smirking from the tone of her voice. "I really hope we're alone right now," she muttered, feeling her cheeks blush.

The car came to a stop, and she sensed Jackie lean into her, confirmed by the soft tickle of her breath on her cheek. "Completely alone," Jackie murmured, straight into her ear. "And later, if you're lucky, I'll get this blindfold out again. But for now," her tone changed, bright and playful, "we're here!"

"Jacs!" Callie groaned. It still amazed her how Jackie could turn her on so much with something as small as a sentence. And just that one had the arousal shooting through her. She shuffled in her seat, conscious of the wetness which was pooling in her boxers. "Jacs?" she questioned when she didn't get an answer.

The car door opened, and she turned her head in that direction.

"Give me your hands," Jackie instructed.

"Seriously?" Callie couldn't believe she was still being subjected to this torture. Whatever it was Jackie was trying to keep a secret had better be worth it.

"Just a moment more, then you can take it off, I promise," Jackie reassured, her voice softening and soothing Callie's aggravation.

Callie swung her legs around, clasping Jackie's hands which found her own, before stepping out of the car. She felt gravel crunch under her feet and a cool breeze blow through her hair. She'd let it grow out a little recently, and it seemed to be a hit with Jackie as well. The chill in the air made her shiver a little, and she shuffled her feet on the spot. Autumn was well into gear, and although she was missing the longer days and warmer nights, the thought of winter evenings curled up with Jackie filled her with a sense of love and warmth.

"Okay." She could feel Jackie behind her, and the tickle of her voice on the shell of her ear made goosebumps rise across her body. She felt the scarf around her eyes slacken but not be removed completely. "You can look."

Jackie dropped the scarf, and with it, Callie's face scrunched in confusion.

They were standing in the gravel driveway of a Georgian house, which was big enough for two cars. To her right was a front garden, consisting of a lawn and some shrubbery, clearly once loved and designed with a purpose but now slightly neglected and overgrown. The front door was a British racing green in colour, again a little faded, and was bordered on either side by bay windows. A large oak tree shadowed over them, leaves starting to thin thanks to the change of season.

"What do you think?"

"About what?"

Broken

"The house! I know you love this area." The excitement was clear in Jackie's voice, but Callie was unsure what she was excited about.

It was true, though. Callie had driven through this area plenty; it was en route to her parents' house. It was quiet and very suburban, but the houses were beautiful with lots of period features. She'd once been to an open viewing of a similar house a few streets over and was in awe of the original architraves and rails, the tiled fireplaces in the front rooms, and the small stained-glass window in the front door. Out the back, she knew there was a decent-sized garden, and if the front garden was anything to go by, she imagined it was beautifully planted and sculpted to show off the best of the space.

"I think it's gorgeous. But I don't know why we're here," she admitted.

Jackie moved around to stand in front of her, taking hold of her hands.

"I have an estate agent friend. She's been looking out for property for me to buy since I moved back, but everything she showed me just didn't feel right. Until a couple of months ago, I asked her to change what she was looking for. To this." She pointed behind her. "I think the reason I didn't pick any of the houses she showed me before is because the next house I want to live in is *our* house. Our home." Callie felt herself grin at the admission. She couldn't deny it was something which she had also thought about, especially considering they didn't really spend any time apart. Jackie continued. "She called me a few weeks ago. The gentleman who lives here is moving in with his son. She'd been asked to value the house, and then she rang me. As soon as I heard where it was, I knew you'd love it. And when I saw it, I knew it had to be ours. So I put in an offer."

"You bought this house?" Callie asked, gobsmacked.

"Yeah."

"This is your house?" Callie was wide-eyed and a little taken aback. This was not the news she had expected to hear this afternoon.

"No. This is *our* house." Jackie turned back around Callie, so she was behind her and rested her chin on her shoulder, her arms wrapped around her waist. "I've had to do it under my name to keep it quiet from you, but my solicitor has drawn up the papers to put you on the deeds and mortgage. What do you think? It needs a bit of work, but most of it is just redecorating and modernising to what we want."

"What we want..." Callie repeated softly before turning in Jackie's arms. "I love it. And I love you."

"Yeah?"

"Yeah. I love these houses; you know I do."

"I know. But it's a big ask, moving in. And especially when I've already bought the house."

"You think it's a big move?"

"Not for me." Jackie shrugged. "For me, it feels like where I've wanted to be for months. From the first time you stayed at mine, back when I'd had my accident and I found you sleeping on the sofa. I didn't want you to leave then, and I don't want to have somewhere which is either mine or yours. I just wanted ours."

"I want that too," Callie whispered, leaning her forehead on Jackie's. "And it doesn't feel big or monumental; it just feels like where I should be."

"Is that a yes?"

"You never actually asked me a question. But yeah, it's a yes." Callie chuckled.

Jackie captured Callie's lips in a slow, sensual kiss that stole her breath away. "Want to see our new home?" Jackie asked, jingling a set of keys in front of Callie. "Start planning what to do?"

Callie smiled as Jackie pulled her up the drive towards the front door with a matching grin. "Can't wait."

SIGN UP

SIGN UP to my mailing list to be the first to hear about new releases, and to be in with a chance of winning books!

About the Author

Ami Spencer has always been writing in some way or another, but it wasn't until long, lonely night feeds with her second baby that she started to take it seriously. Originally from Norfolk, she now lives just outside Halifax, with her wife, two children, dog, cat and fish. The dog and cat can regularly be seen on her Twitter feed, impeding her in some way from writing. She spends her time (when not working and writing) usually trying to wrangle said two children into doing something. When that fails, she gives up, instead choosing to read, and letting them run riot until they need feeding.

You can find her on her social media;
Twitter: @aspencerwriter
Facebook: www.facebook.com/amispencerwriter
Instagram: @aspencerwriter

Printed in Great Britain
by Amazon